Born in Lancashire, Freda Lightfoot has been a teacher and a bookseller, and in a mad moment even tried her hand at the 'good life'. A prolific and much-loved saga writer, Freda's work is inspired by memories of her Lancashire childhood and her passion for history. For more information about Freda, visit her website: www.fredalightfoot.co.uk

THE *SUNDAY TIMES* BESTSELLING AUTHOR

Freda Lightfoot

Always in My Heart

ONE PLACE. MANY STORIES

HQ
An imprint of HarperCollinsPublishers Ltd.
1 London Bridge Street
London SE1 9GF
This paperback edition 2016

First Published in Great Britain 2016
By Harlequin Mira, an imprint of HarperCollinsPublishers
1 London Bridge Street, London, SE1 9GF

ISBN: 978-1-848-45437-8

58-1116

Printed and bound by
CPI Group (UK) Ltd, Croydon, CR0 4YY

Also by Freda Lightfoot:

Historical Sagas
Lakeland Lily
The Bobbin Girls
The Favourite Child
Kitty Little
For All Our Tomorrows
Home is Where the Heart Is
Gracie's Sin
Daisy's Secret
Ruby McBride
Dancing on Deansgate
Watch for the Talleyman
Polly's Pride
Polly's War
House of Angels
Angels at War
The Promise
My Lady Deceiver

The Luckpenny Series
Luckypenny Land
Wishing Water
Larkrigg Fell

Poorhouse Lane Series
The Girl from Poorhouse Lane
The Woman from Heartbreak House

Champion Street Market Series
Putting on the Style
Fools Fall in Love
That'll Be the Day
Candy Kisses
Who's Sorry Now
Lonely Teardrops

Women's Contemporary Fiction
Trapped

Historical Romances
Madeiran Legacy
Whispering Shadows
Rhapsody Creek
Proud Alliance
Outrageous Fortune

Biographical Historical
Hostage Queen
Reluctant Queen
The Queen and the Courtesan
The Duchess of Drury Lane
Lady of Passion

One

1944

Rain pounded upon the windows as the small bus wound its way along narrow lanes. The sound of its grinding gears as it lurched around a bend and began to climb steeply upwards stirred Brenda from a deep sleep. Blinking herself awake, she gazed out at the scramble of sharp peaks, jutting rocks and smooth green-humped hills, disappointed they were not lit by the warmth of September sunshine. Yet she felt some relief to have at last reached the Pennines. The journey had been long and difficult. She still shivered at the memory of being halted and searched by a German guard at the foot of the Pyrenees in Spain. A terrifying moment! Now, after years of danger she was at last safe; in a bus driving mile upon mile over beautiful open moors cloaked in purple heather.

Eventually the vehicle stopped and the driver called out, 'Trowbridge Hall.' Hitching her heavy bag high on to her shoulder, Brenda climbed out of the warmth of the bus into the chill damp of the valley. When first she'd set off from France she'd felt dizzy with anticipation, filled with hope.

But much as she had longed to reach her destination, now a nervous tension was setting in. She could remember all too well the scowls, furious arguments and strong tone of disapproval on the day she'd been thrown out of the manor house all those years ago.

Today it felt strangely silent as Brenda walked down the rutted track, the only sound that of her boots squelching in the mud, a clogging mist swirling about her. Thankfully it had at last stopped raining. Turning a corner, she paused to gaze up at the tall chimneys, mullioned windows and grey stone walls of this grand house. For a moment her nervousness faded even if the mist did not. When at a low ebb during her recent troubles she would often bring to mind the majesty of these rolling hills, and the autumn glory of the scabious, goldenrod and blue harebells that clustered the verges. The memory of this place had at times helped to keep her sane.

Her heartbeat quickened as she recalled coming to work here back in the spring of 1939. That was the day she and Jack had first met, and despite her being no more than a mere scullery maid and he the son of a wealthy land owner, they'd fallen in love almost at first sight. At just seventeen she'd been young and eager for a new life, utterly captivated by his good looks, his gentle kindness, and the way his blue-grey eyes smiled at her. Whenever her day's work ended and she'd take a walk for a breath of fresh air, Jack would be sitting on a wall or leaning against a tree waiting for her.

'I thought I'd show you around,' he'd said with a

twinkling smile the first time she'd found him there. The thought had thrilled her.

'Oh, that would be lovely.' She'd felt herself blushing even as her insides tingled with excitement.

They'd stepped out along the path into the wood, the dog at his heels as Jack explained how he didn't want her to get lost. 'It's not a good idea to venture too far on your own as it's all too easy to lose your way in these woods,' he'd warned.

'I confess I am more accustomed to the busy streets of Manchester,' Brenda had admitted, gazing in wonder at the bluebells in bloom. It was May and she could hear the rippling chatter of fieldfares celebrating the coming of warmer weather. 'Or at least the Castlefield part of the city. I'm more used to walking along canal towpaths than in woodlands. Never really been out much in the countryside before, but it is so beautiful here I'd love to explore it.'

'Then take care if you set out for a walk to always leave markers, such as a small pile of stones at every turn in the path to mark your way. We call them cairns. Then you can retrace your steps by following them on your return.'

'What a wonderful idea. Thank you, I'll remember that.'

'And if you should ever get lost, follow a stream down-hill towards the river, then walk north along the riverbank back to the house. You can judge the direction by checking the green moss that grows on the northern side of the trees. It certainly does here in the Pennines. But it would be safer and much more fun, don't you think, if we were to walk out together? And Kit does love a good walk,' he'd said, introducing her to the farm collie.

Meeting his gaze, she knew in that moment they were meant for each other, and his desire for them to walk out together had little to do with the dog. The expression in his eyes was utterly captivating, reaching to the heart of her.

After that, it seemed perfectly natural for them to meet up every single evening. And when he eventually stole a kiss she'd responded with eagerness, loving it when he almost lifted her off her feet to gather her in his arms. Explosions of pleasure had shot through her, almost as if she'd been waiting her entire life for this moment.

Fond as Brenda was of the city of Manchester where she'd been raised in an orphanage by nuns and still had many friends, she instantly fell in love with the beauty of Saddleworth, and the dramatic and rugged Pennine hills and moorland. She soon came to think of herself as a country girl, if working class and a bit plain and plump with fluffy brown hair. Jack, however, always regarded her as gorgeously curvaceous, and adored the twinkle in her downward-sloping brown eyes. It was certainly true that she was rather well endowed, but liked to think that her round face generally appeared cheerful, even if there was sometimes a flutter of nerves behind her eyes. How she'd loved it when he'd whispered such compliments as he kissed her. She smiled now at the memory.

They'd naturally tried to keep their feelings and meetings secret, only too aware that his family would not approve. They'd carefully avoided visiting the local villages of

Trowbridge, Uppermill and Greenfield together in case people Jack knew spotted them. Much safer to remain high in the hills where few people roamed.

But then one afternoon Jack's father, Sir Randolph, caught them together locked in the kind of clinch that clearly revealed their love for each other. Sadly, he was an ice-cold, aloof sort of man. Perhaps living as he did in this fine house with a large estate and money to answer his every need, caused him to be bossy and self-opinionated.

'Girl, return to the kitchen where you belong,' he'd roared. She'd spun on her heels to scurry away as fast as she could, tripping over tree roots and stones in her anxiety to escape his fury. Jack had stoutly remained where he was, clearly preparing himself for a lecture.

Brenda had found herself instantly dismissed. Jack was ordered to go to France to stay with his French mother, who'd returned to Paris some months previously on a visit to her family. She showed no sign of returning any time soon, which did not surprise Brenda, bearing in mind she had such a controlling husband. Brenda had been sorry to see her go, as it was this lovely lady who had offered her the job in the first place. Lady Stuart had been a regular visitor to the orphanage and very friendly with the nuns who'd brought Brenda up.

Jack made no protest to this plan, as he adored his mother, but instead of leaving Brenda behind he'd suggested she go with him. Brenda had been unable to speak a word of French at the time, yet loving him as she did, how could she resist the temptation?

Her time in France had felt like a real adventure to her. Memories she would nurture forever in her heart. She'd worked hard to learn the language, and happily helped Jack to care for his dear mother who was not at all well.

When war broke out they'd quickly married and enjoyed such a happy time together, until the dreadful effects of bombs and fighting took their toll, robbing her of the love of her life. Brenda's heart still bled at the pain of her loss.

Now she was quite alone, and the events that had followed his death were a period in her life she desperately strived to block out. Returning to her late husband's home had been a difficult decision to make, but so important. It was vital that she find her son and prayed this would provide the answers she needed. After all her efforts to resolve the issue had failed, this seemed like the only solution left.

There was no one around to welcome her, all doors closed and curtains drawn. Perhaps dear old Kit, no doubt too old now to be out working with the flock, might offer a welcome, unless he too had forgotten her. As Brenda hitched up her bag and set off again along the track, he must have recognised the sound of her footsteps for he was suddenly scampering towards her, his wittering greeting a positive warble of doggy ecstasy.

'Hello, old boy. So you do remember me, even after all this time. How wonderful.' Brenda went down on one knee to rub the collie's ears, chuckling at the way his whole body seemed to wag with joy, his tongue caressing every inch of her face. Fighting back tears she smiled as she stroked him. Then hearing the crunch of gravel and the sound of heavy boots approaching, her smile quickly evaporated. Rising slowly to her feet, Brenda strengthened her resolve, as she had learned to do throughout the years of war. Surely her father-in-law could do no worse to her than what she'd already been forced to endure.

'Good lord, so it's you, girl.'

With relief Brenda saw that it was Jack's brother, if sounding every bit as cold and arrogant as his father. Stiffening her spine, she took a breath. 'Good to see you again, Hugh.'

'What the hell are you doing here?'

Brenda faced him with a shot of her well-tuned courage. 'I believe as Jack's wife, or rather his widow, I do have that right.'

He gave a snort of disbelief. 'You're claiming to have *married* him?'

She blinked, stunned by this response. 'You surely knew that we married late in 1939?' Perhaps Jack had never mentioned their marriage because he was fearful of being cut off from his family completely, in view of his estrangement from his father. Camille was constantly cautioning her son about Sir Randolph's temper and possible reaction.

Hugh glowered at her. 'Jack never wrote to tell us about any damn wedding, so why would I believe you?'

'Why would you not?'

'Because you're a feisty little madam. Always were.'

'Please, we need to talk.'

Lifting his head to glare up at the grey sky as rain again began to fall, he marched to a side door and flung it open.

'Very well, you can stay tonight, and explain exactly what did happen to my brother.'

Stifling a sigh, Brenda went to pick up her heavy bag then followed him into the house along the passage towards the kitchen, which was no doubt where he thought she belonged. Every step she'd taken in recent years seemed to have led to yet more trauma. Making decisions had never been easy in the terrifying world following Jack's death, and despite believing she'd made the right ones, it had all gone terribly wrong.

Two

France, 1940

Brenda stood washing dishes at the sink in the kitchen of her mother-in-law's elegant apartment, quite close to the Jardin des Tuileries. Surrounded by gilt mirrors, chandeliers, glorious armoires and huge arched windows, she spent every day cleaning, washing and cooking, rarely setting foot outside except to buy food at a local market. Ever since Jack's death a strange sense of detachment had enveloped her, leaving her largely oblivious to whatever was happening in the world. It felt as if she was living in some kind of frozen bubble, so devastated at losing him that she could barely think, let alone eat or sleep. Camille, his dear mother, was equally distraught and had largely confined herself to her room. Brenda continued to care for her, not only out of love for her husband, but felt she could never neglect this lovely lady who'd become almost like a mother to her too.

'I thought you might like an egg custard with your afternoon tea,' Brenda said to her now as she set a tray on the small coffee table by her chair.

'Oh, what a lovely girl you are.' Camille's pale face creased with a smile in a valiant attempt to disguise the bleakness of grief. 'I wouldn't have the first idea how to make one of those tarts, even though it was a favourite treat of Jack's.'

'Mine too,' Brenda said, with a slight tremor to her voice. 'Let's sit and enjoy it together, then I'll run a bath for you before dinner. I've managed to find us some fish, if only a small piece of cod. But we can liven it up with some rice and tomatoes.' There was a serious shortage of food these days, although the smartly uniformed German military were able to fully indulge their own appetites for fine meals, beer, women and dancing, no doubt viewed as a reward for their victory.

'You are so amazingly resilient,' Camille said as Brenda switched on the small gas fire to warm up the cool bedroom. 'But you mustn't work too hard, my dear. You and that little one you are carrying need rest, so do take an afternoon nap each day.'

Sleep was not something Brenda felt in need of right now. Whenever she closed her eyes, her mind would vividly replay all she'd learned about the manner of his death. Reliving how he must have run for cover when he'd heard guns going off all around him. Was his memory of her his last thought on this earth? Brenda would prefer to think he died instantly, not lying on the ground in pain and anguish, waiting for the end to close in upon him. Terrified of such nightmares, she found that keeping busy was the only solution. Retiring to her bed only when exhaustion overwhelmed her, Brenda could manage to sleep more deeply and avoid them. It also gave her a reason to go on with life.

'Exercise is good for me,' she smilingly replied, settling herself in the armchair opposite. In addition, she was doing her utmost to persuade Camille to eat more, as she was increasingly thin, a sad fragility about her. She'd never been particularly robust. Despite only being in her early fifties she'd aged considerably since her son's death, her golden blonde hair turning silver grey almost overnight.

'Did you hear any news while you were out shopping today?' Camille politely enquired, her tone of voice flat as she sliced up the tart.

'When I bought our bread this morning the *boulanger* told me that although the southern part of France around the spa town of Vichy is seen as a *zone libre*, Marshal Pétain, who is in control, still insists upon cooperating with Hitler. He apparently believes the state has greater rights than the people. So the area may not be as free as he claims it to be.'

Camille's pale-blue eyes narrowed as she considered this. 'That may well be the case. The man does have strong fascist sympathies.'

'The *boulanger* also said I should take care, as there's a growing resentment among some French that the British haven't done enough to help prevent the German invasion.'

'An attitude which will make them anti-British as well as anti-Nazi. Perhaps you should go back to England while you can, dear girl, to be safe.'

'Would you come with me?'

The older woman's eyes frosted over as she avoided meeting Brenda's gaze. 'As you know, I have no wish to return to my over-controlling husband. I was born and brought up here in France. This is my home.'

They both fell silent following this familiar response, concentrating on enjoying an unexpected treat, the eggs made available thanks to a neighbour who kept chickens. Were it not for her fondness for this dear lady, and the fact she was expecting Jack's child, Brenda knew she would have returned to Manchester long since. She missed it badly, and her many dear friends, particularly Cathie whom she'd known for most of her life, as well as Jack's sister Prue. There were times when she ached to hear a northern voice cracking jokes with their deliciously dry sense of humour. But here she was, stuck in France.

Thousands of Parisians had already fled the city. Just days before the invasion, at Camille's insistence she and Jack had tried to leave. They'd found the Gare de Lyon packed out. There were hundreds of people carrying mountains of luggage, desperate to get on a train and escape the threat of occupation. There were women wheeling babies in prams, young men barging about, and children and dogs running everywhere. Then a station porter had called out, '*Il n'y a pas de trains.*' As there were no trains, with a resigned sigh she and Jack had drifted back to the apartment.

As summer progressed Brenda noticed many neighbours who had escaped returned home, having suffered from starvation, bombing raids and severe losses to their families or belongings out on the open roads. Some were ordered back by the Germans, yet other people were still desperately striving to get away. And who could blame them? France was in complete turmoil: shops and restaurants closed, clothes, shoes and even furniture littering the streets. Chaos reigned as the Germans now occupied and ruled most of the country.

Brenda's mind flipped back to the day in June when the enemy had first entered the city. It was a moment in history that would never be forgotten. Jack had held her close, his arm tight about her shoulders as they stood together watching the rumble of tanks, guns and thousands of soldiers stream along the streets, the crowds mingling around them eerily silent.

'We can't allow them to get away with this,' he'd murmured through gritted teeth. 'We need to drive them out.'

'How can we possibly do that?' she'd asked. 'These German soldiers look extremely tough and determined, and very strictly disciplined.'

'We should make life as difficult as possible for them. If they request information or assistance for any reason we could pretend not to understand, send them in a different direction, or tell them the wrong train time.' He gave a wry smile. 'Believe me when I say there will be huge objections and resistance to their attempt to control the French.'

That night they'd made love with more passion than ever before, feeling the need to overcome fear and depression by putting some happiness back into their lives. It was a time Brenda would always remember, the moon shining upon them as if to glorify their love.

Jack spent all of the next day out with friends. The phoney war was over and their lives had changed forever. A Resistance movement did indeed spring up, intended to provide the Allies with intelligence, attack the Germans at every opportunity, as well as assist any Allied soldiers or airmen in need of escape. Many such groups emerged across all occupied territory.

Having a French mother, Jack showed far more compassion for the French than he did for the Nazis, and gladly joined the group in Paris. How brave he was. He used the code-name Randall, a slight variation on his father's name, and quickly became involved in many dangerous projects. He did a great deal of good for the cause. Fearful though she'd been for his safety, Brenda had felt enormous admiration for his courage. He was a man of honour, so not for a moment would she have attempted to stop him. She would spend a largely sleepless night awaiting his safe return. Then, tragically, one morning she was visited by a colleague who sadly informed her that while engaged in a valiant attempt by the local Resistance group to blow up a tank, he'd been shot dead by the enemy. She'd been utterly devastated.

As always, pain tightened her throat at the thought, her mouth feeling dry and rancid now that he was gone forever from her life. She was quite alone, locked in her own private world. If only…

'I've had a letter from my cousin Adèle,' Camille said, thankfully interrupting these distressing memories. 'She asks if she can come on a visit, as she's quite alone now that she's a widow. Her poor husband died of a heart attack around the same time we lost Jack. I shall write and say that she would be most welcome, don't you think?'

'Of course. What a splendid idea.'

Camille's cousin arrived just a few days later. Smartly dressed in a green coat with padded shoulders and a big fur collar, a wide-brimmed velvet hat and matching gloves, she looked very much an aristocrat. She was small and neat in stature but big of heart, with a pert mouth, chestnut-brown bobbed hair, and caring dark eyes that gleamed out at the world from behind gold-rimmed spectacles. Brenda saw her arrival as a good thing. The cousins had long been close friends and were clearly both in need of company to help cope with their grief.

Perhaps the poor lady also felt a certain fear in living alone, as did everyone these days.

If Adèle decided to stay on, Brenda thought she might try once more to return home to England, although she really had no idea how that could come about. In the meantime she must concentrate upon keeping in good health. Her pregnancy seemed endless, and due to the shortage of food, not at all easy. But she could not wait to hold Jack's child in her arms.

*

The situation worsened considerably in the months following Jack's death. Paris became a different place. Coupons were needed for bread, meat, groceries, clothes, coal, everything. And they became increasingly hungry and cold. Each day Brenda would join other local Parisians in the public squares to search for any scraps of wood she could find to burn. Since the apartment had no open fire or chimney and they'd run out of gas, she made a brazier from an old tin that provided a small amount of heat, the smoke dispensed through a pipe that ran out of a nearby window.

Every street, including the beautiful Plâce de Concorde, the Eiffel tower and all public buildings, bristled with swastika flags. There were posters depicting John Bull as a killer, among many other anti-British images. Signs that gave directions in German with barely a word in French visible. And the sound of goose-stepping boots was everywhere.

On visiting the British Embassy, Brenda found that it was indeed closed. Even the skeleton staff present at the start of the occupation had departed south. According to reports the borders into Spain were also kept largely barricaded. Trains to England were still not available. Sending a letter to England was also a problem as they were generally blocked. It was very evident that finding a way out of France would be almost impossible.

She felt trapped.

Many other women were too: dancers, singers, nurses and governesses, rich ladies who loved to spend their time travelling around Europe. Even French widows who had married Englishmen were likewise looked upon as outcasts. The German hatred of the British was all too evident. People without the right documentation or who were Jewish tended to hide away, desperate to avoid being imprisoned or shipped to Germany. Some would be arrested simply for listening to the BBC. A dreadful prospect.

Brenda gave birth to a son on 27 November, less than a month from her own birthday, which helped to ease the dark pit of anguish devouring her. The two ladies took good care of her and all went well. How fortunate she was. She would sit and gaze in wonder at his tiny fingers and toes, the soft pale baby-blue eyes, and the way his sweet lips pursed or smacked together whenever he was hungry. He was utterly adorable. She spent every moment of every day bathing, feeding and nursing him, and tucking the little fellow into his crib cuddled up with the silver-grey fluffy monkey she'd bought for him just before his birth.

Now it was Adèle doing all the cooking, cleaning and shopping, running up and down stairs, fetching and carrying, without a word of complaint. Even Camille did what she could to help, despite her rich, aristocratic heritage and fragility.

'I do appreciate the care you've both given me. Being illegitimate, I was born in a home for unmarried mothers,' Brenda said, giving a wry smile. 'So I have no family of my own.'

'Goodness, I didn't know that,' Adèle said, looking slightly surprised by this news.

'The nuns were extremely good to her. Did you ever find out who your mother was?' Camille asked.

Brenda shook her head. 'I don't even know her name. I was given the surname Noel by the nuns because I was born just five days before Christmas.' She really had no wish to find her mother, and still nursed a deep resentment at having been abandoned at birth. It was a most cruel and unfeeling thing for any mother to do. Brenda certainly had no intention of ever abandoning her own child. He was already the joy of her life.

'Never mind, darling, you have a family now,' Camille said, giving her a hug.

'You do indeed,' Adèle agreed. 'We love you and this little baby. What are you going to call him?'

'I can't decide. Should it be Jack? Certainly not Randall, or that would remind us forever of this dratted war. What was your father called?' she asked Camille.

She smiled. 'Unlike my mother, he was English, and called Thomas.'

'Oh, I like that. Thomas it is, then. Although I shall probably call him Tommy.'

Three

1944

It felt strange to be back in England, her nervous tension still very evident, churning her stomach. At least Brenda no longer needed to speak French, and according to the latest news, France was now in the process of being liberated. De Gaulle had led a procession of the Free French down the Champs-Élysées. The Allies were also starting to arrive, including the British, the American and the Canadians. The war at last seemed to be drawing to an end. Would that help her to resolve her own problem?

The warmth of the big farm kitchen offered a small degree of comfort. The familiarity of the stove, the clutter of old chairs, Tiddles the cat rubbing against her leg, and the chink of the old flowered tea pot and mugs they'd used when she was but a girl were all still in evidence. As was Mrs Harding, the housekeeper, who pretty well ran this house. Busy rolling out pastry, she glanced up as Brenda entered, her eyes widening in surprise. 'By heck, it looks like a bag o' muck has just walked in.'

Brenda chuckled, accepting this comment as typical

evidence of the cook-housekeeper's Lancashire sense of humour. She had always been good to work for. 'I dare say I do after such a long journey in this dreadful weather.'

Mrs Harding's faded old eyes softened. 'Eeh, and you're soaked to the skin, chuck.'

'I'm afraid so.'

'Would you like a cup of tea?'

'Oh, that would be lovely, thank you,' Brenda warmly responded. She could remember enjoying the cook's home-made biscuits kept in a jar on the dresser, a treat she would also welcome right now, judging by the ache in her belly. Brenda moved to seat herself at the big pine table but Hugh stepped quickly forward to block her way.

'Take off your filthy boots, then come upstairs with me,' he ordered in brisk, no-nonsense tones. 'You said we needed to talk.'

Brenda made no attempt to argue but did as she was told. Setting her boots on the mat by the back door, she dutifully followed him in her stockinged feet. But, expecting to be led into the drawing room, she was startled to be shown instead into Sir Randolph's study. Parking himself in the large chair behind the desk, he turned to glower at her with narrowed eyes, arms firmly folded across his broad chest. He looked very like his elder brother, save for the sour expression on his handsome face, which Brenda found most disconcerting.

'What were you hoping to achieve by coming here?' he snarled, not even offering her a seat. 'Considering you are illegitimate, you were most fortunate to be given a job, thanks to the kindness of my mother. You then lured my brother into your bed and ran off with him. Had you not behaved so stupidly, he would still have been alive. So why on earth would I allow you to stay, in view of how you completely destroyed his life?'

Brenda stood rigid before him, still clutching her heavy bag, her wet hair dripping down the neck of her blouse. A shiver ran down her spine as she struggled to keep her temper in check. 'We fell in love. What is so wrong with that? Your father found us kissing out in the woods, not in bed together. It was his decision to banish us from the house, and Jack's that I go with him to France. Since I loved him, why would I not agree? We were very happy together, and I still do love him with all my heart. Losing him has been utterly devastating.'

Losing her darling child had been equally dreadful, but she was reluctant to speak of that right now. This did not seem quite the moment to explain all that had happened to her over these past years, and why exactly she had returned. If Hugh didn't believe in her marriage or her devotion to his brother, why would he trust in anything she told him? And asking him questions while he was in such a foul mood wouldn't work either, even though she desperately needed answers.

'Jack would still be with us if he hadn't joined the Resistance movement. What on earth possessed him to be so damned stupid?'

Brenda drew in a breath to calm the flare of irritation lit by this dreadful remark, holding fast to her courage. 'In case it has missed your attention, France was taken over by the Germans back in June 1940. Being half French, as are you, why would he not join the Resistance? Jack was extremely brave and honourable, doing what was right for his mother, her friends and family, and the country.' Lifting her chin, she met his furious glare with pride in her eyes.

He was silent for some seconds as he met her gaze, then grumpily remarked, 'Jack should have left France long before the Nazis arrived.'

'His mother wanted him to return home too, but he was reluctant to abandon her as she wasn't too well. She's a lovely lady, so why would he do that when she needed our care?'

'She could have come with you. My father wrote to her countless times pressing her to do so.'

'We also tried on numerous occasions to persuade her, but she declined. Camille is very much a daughter of France, and that is where she feels she belongs. Once the Germans occupied the country, it was not easy getting out. And as Jack's widow, I cared for her after his death.'

'Sadly, both my parents have now departed this life, so if you see this place as a future home you are very much mistaken.'

Horror unfolded within her. 'Are you saying your mother is dead? Oh no, that's dreadful.' Wasn't finding Camille the very reason she'd come? Striving to remain calm, Brenda struggled to decide how much she should tell him. Before she managed to reach a decision, a knock sounded at the door and the butler entered carrying a tray of tea, cakes and biscuits. Her stomach churned. She couldn't remember the last time she'd eaten, whether it was one day or two. Maybe even longer.

'Thank you so much,' she said, taking the cup and saucer with a hand that trembled slightly.

Relieving Brenda of her bag, he brought up a chair. 'Mrs Harding says to tell you that she is warming some soup, which you can have when you're ready.'

'Oh, do thank her for me,' Brenda said, giving him a grateful smile.

'That will be all, Carter,' Hugh snapped.

'Sir.' Giving a slight bow, the butler tactfully withdrew.

Brenda took a very welcome sip of tea and a quick nibble of one of Mrs Harding's delicious ginger biscuits, striving to keep her nerves in check and hold on tight to her fading courage.

There was silence for some moments, then he gave a snort of derision. 'So where's the proof of this alleged wedding?'

'If you mean by way of a marriage certificate, all papers were taken from me, being British.'

Slamming his fists on the desk, Hugh leaned closer, his jaw tight as his teeth ground together. 'I do not believe a word you say. Had my brother truly married you he would have told me so, despite our father's disapproval. As I say, Papa is no longer with us either, but *I* still need proof.'

'You have my deepest sympathy for your loss,' Brenda told him with some depth of emotion. 'I fully understand how you must feel. It has taken me years to come to terms with my own grief, and it was the same for Camille. When did each of them die?'

'Papa died of a heart attack less than a month ago, Mama some time in 1941, or so I believe.'

'Do you know where she was living at the time?' Brenda instantly asked, her heart thudding.

'I assume she was still resident in Paris.'

'No, she'd left by then. Her cousin Adèle had come to join her and the pair of them proved to be a great support for each other. But when the situation grew more danger-ous in Paris they decided to move to her cousin's home somewhere in the Loire Valley. Do you have her address?' Now Brenda awaited his answer with a tremor in her heart. Wasn't this the reason she'd returned to Trowbridge Hall, hoping her precious son would already be here waiting for her? But if not, she could at least find out where Adèle lived.

'Never heard of the woman. But then I know little about the French side of my mother's family. That's enough talk for now,' he said, and opening the study door, Hugh flicked his hand to order her back downstairs. 'You can stay in your old room for tonight. We'll speak again tomorrow.'

Brenda's heart sank to her soaking-wet feet, and keeping her head down so that he could not see the tears in her eyes, she walked out of the study.

*

Taking himself off to the drawing room, Hugh felt an odd stir of guilt within him. His brother was indeed a brave man, and they'd been quite close. Was his reluctance to accept this girl's possible marriage with Jack really because of her illegitimacy and low status, or because he'd lost all hope of a marriage for himself? Their father hadn't listened to Hugh's desire to join the army, insisting he become a farmer, as that was a reserve occupation. Even Susanna, his darling fiancée, had been against him joining the forces, quite happy with him being a farmer too, as it was much safer. An attitude which made it all the more tragic that while visiting her parents back in London, she'd died along with them when their home had been hit by a V-1 flying bomb just a few weeks ago. A lovely and perfectly innocent lady who wouldn't hurt a soul was now gone from his life. How cruel and heartless war was.

But there were other problems.

He shook out the *Manchester Evening News* and scowled over yet another report depicting misery and gloom, the entire country complaining about rationing and poverty. This war was costing a fortune, both in men's lives and coin of the realm. His own finances were suffering along with everyone else's. There'd been a time when whatever the Stuart family touched had turned to gold, or brass at least, and plenty of it. Now, the biscuit factory was rapidly going downhill thanks to food shortages, and the best workers having joined up. Not to mention his father's stubborn determination to remain in the Victorian age and never update anything.

Bearing in mind the state of austerity the country was in, it was astonishing they were also facing a huge inheritance tax payment, following his father's death. Sir Randolph should have thought things through more carefully and prepared for this possibility. Sadly, he'd been entirely selfish, spending money on gambling, horse racing and grand cars, as if there was no tomorrow. An obsessive, and utterly controlling aristocrat.

How would they even survive as a consequence not only of war issues, but this huge amount of death duty?

And having lost everyone who mattered to him, Hugh's appetite to acquire the necessary interest and energy to run the family estate and business had entirely disappeared, let alone the driving ambition he'd once possessed. He'd once been bursting with ideas and the desire to expand. But even increasing the low flour quota allowed due to rationing, could only happen if they acquired further outlets, which he really had no interest in doing, his mind now obsessed with debts.

Admittedly, they were probably much better off than this girl, but she really had no right to pretend to be his brother's widow, simply to get her hands on family money. She was just a greedy little madam. Jack would surely have told him if he had married her? Yet he did probably love her.

He rang the bell for Carter. The butler quickly entered, again giving a slight bow. 'Are you requiring a glass of whisky, sir, before you retire?'

'That would be excellent. Oh, and tell that young girl she can stay for a few days, until she has made the necessary arrangements for her new future back in Manchester, although she'll need to make herself useful in return for the free accommodation offered.'

Carter's face tightened a little as he politely responded. 'Very good, sir, I will inform her of that fact. I'm sure she will be most helpful, as she always was.'

*

Desolation still threatened to overwhelm her. But maintaining her courage, a skill she'd acquired over the years of war, Brenda savoured with gratitude a simple but delicious dish of home-made soup and a bread roll for supper, before climbing up to the attic room where she'd resided years ago.

It appeared that Hugh was in charge now. Not an encouraging prospect. But why had the conversation between them been so angry and difficult, his tone sharp with prejudice against her, not least because she was illegitimate? He was arrogantly treating her as if she was a greedy little scullery maid. The advice she'd received from her late mother-in-law had been to take care not to inflame her husband's temper. His son appeared to be very much a chip off the old block, and vehemently defending herself wasn't proving to be easy. Brenda did not want a penny off him, but she had to consider her own son's future, once she'd found him safe and well and brought him home.

But it seemed that yet again all her efforts had been to no avail.

One moment she'd felt she had all the riches in the world: the love of her life and a child on the way. Now all of that happiness had gone and the pain in her heart made her feel weak with agony. Dropping into bed with exhaustion, she fell asleep within minutes. It was then that the nightmares once again surfaced.

Four

France, 1941

In theory, as an enemy alien, Brenda was required to go to the *Mairie* every day to sign in. But the thought of presenting her British passport to the German officers now in control of the city hall filled her with fear. She really had no wish to reveal her identity, or to be searched by anybody. Thanks to Jack, her French was now reasonably proficient, and Brenda did her utmost to give the impression she was of native origin, even making sure she never wore any of the clothes she'd brought with her from England.

However, she was all too aware that as an English woman she presented something of a danger to Camille and her cousin. Anyone found harbouring British nationals would be liable to arrest, or worse.

'I wish I could find some form of employment to justify being stuck here,' she said to her mother-in-law one evening. It was over a month now since baby Tommy had been born and she felt quite fit and capable of working. Being January, winter was upon them and the cost of food and fuel was increasing daily, assuming they were able to find any.

'Your job is to care for your child,' Camille smilingly told her as she rocked her grandchild in her arms before handing him over for his nightly bath.

Determined to at least pay her way, Brenda looked for work day after day, enquiring about jobs in hospitals, canteens and various factories. Unfortunately, none seemed impressed by her lack of skills. 'I may not be a nurse but I can cook and clean,' she insisted after yet another refusal.

'We'll let you know,' the stern-faced manager told her, holding open the door to show her out. As always, there were several people milling around, or sitting in the waiting room, probably equally desperate for employment. Reaching the street outside the hospital, she suddenly found a man at her elbow.

'Are you looking for a job?' he asked, speaking in fairly rapid French.

'I am, yes.'

He nodded. 'I might be able to help.'

'Really? That would be wonderful.'

His full lips widened into an appealing smile. 'You can call me Étienne, or Monsieur Bresson if you prefer. I can offer you good money and accommodation too, if necessary.'

'What kind of work do you have to offer, and what skills would I need?' Brenda prepared herself for the usual string of questions, but his response stunned her. 'You speak French quite well for an English girl.'

'What makes you think that I am?' she asked, keeping

her tone light, even as her voice trembled and a chill settled within her.

'I heard you speaking to the manager, and your accent does have a slight British twang to it,' he said, his dark eyes sparkling with humour.

So despite her best efforts, she was still obviously British, which was no doubt the real reason she couldn't find employment. Making no comment, Brenda gave a little shrug and began to walk away, only to find him again at her side.

'I'm aware that finding a job if you are British is not easy, but I can help. I provide work for many ladies with foreign passports. Come, I'll introduce you to them. Very few skills are needed, as they will teach you everything you need to know.'

Unable to resist the offer since he seemed so helpful, and obviously held no prejudice against her nationality, Brenda dutifully followed. He led her along the street then down an alley to a tall, four-storey building tucked into a courtyard.

'Ah, is this a hotel?' she asked, mentally preparing herself for yet another interview. 'If so, then it would indeed suit my skills, as I can certainly cook and clean.'

Giving a little chuckle, he opened the door to show her into a shabby hall. 'It could be considered as such, yes, although those are not necessarily the skills I am seeking.'

Glancing around at the wallpaper peeling from the walls and an array of scruffy doors in bad need of a lick of paint, Brenda politely smiled. 'Well, I could start with this entrance hall, and give it a good scrub and polish.'

Alarm bells suddenly began to ring in her head as she saw a German officer in uniform standing by one of the inner doors. Was she about to be arrested? Reminding herself this was a hotel and not the city hall or a military head quarters, she gave a little nod in his direction. 'I take it you accept Germans as guests?'

'Of course, they are regular clients. This man is a member of the *Wehrmacht*, the German defence force, and acts as a protector for the women who work here. Come with me,' he said, ushering her through the door the man was guarding into a small parlour. It was lined with chairs and sofas, occupied by young girls dressed in floaty gowns or bathrobes, giggling and chatting happily to each other as they smoked cigarettes or sipped wine.

'What is this place?' Brenda asked, suspicion beginning to form somewhere in the pit of her stomach. Young she may be, but not stupid. Why would these women be sitting around half-dressed on this chilly winter's day, even if there was a blazing fire in the grate? As her fears began to escalate, another German soldier appeared out of nowhere. Seeing her standing by the fireplace, he came quickly over, an expression of curiosity lighting his face as his gaze roamed over her from head to toe.

'You must be new. Take off your coat, then I can see you better.'

'Sorry, I don't understand.'

'Do as the gentleman asks,' her escort instructed.

'Why would I do that?' she snapped, giving a little frown.

'Because he is an important client, and has the right to inspect a possible candidate.'

'Candidate for what? You haven't yet informed me what kind of work you are offering, Monsieur Bresson.'

'I assume that, in view of your nationality, you'd be agreeable to do anything in order to avoid arrest. You're a very pretty lady, and I know of many young soldiers who would be only too glad to pay for the pleasure of your company. I can also offer you safe accommodation. The Germans visit this brothel regularly and don't care about a girl's nationality, so long as she is good-looking and amenable. Weekly visits are considered mandatory for all young soldiers to prevent them indulging in sexual excesses with all and sundry, thereby spreading venereal diseases. The girls employed here make good money and are given regular scheduled medical check-ups to keep them safe from such problems, so there's nothing for you to worry about on that score.'

Brenda stared at him in stunned horror. 'What on earth are you suggesting? How dare you! I'm a widow, not a prostitute.'

Glowering at her, he turned to speak in rapid German to the client who, laughing loudly, tugged open Brenda's coat and began to grope her breasts with his large hands. 'Hm, quite full and promising,' the officer said, in perfect English. 'Yes, she's ideal, I'll take this one.'

Gasping with a mix of fury and terror, Brenda slapped his hands away, spun on her heels and stalked off at a rapid pace across the hall and through the outer door, holding her head high. The moment she reached the courtyard, she took to her heels and ran as if the devil was on her tail, because in a way he was.

Respectable jobs, it seemed, were as hard to come by now as transport.

*

Her heart was pounding with fear and exhaustion by the time Brenda reached Camille's apartment. She'd taken great care that she wasn't being followed, and felt hardly able to breathe as alarm reverberated through her. How stupid to trust an absolute stranger and follow him, without even knowing what he had to offer. She'd put herself in serious danger as a consequence of such naivety, and must never do such a thing again. She dreaded to think what he might have done to her.

'What is wrong, dear girl?' Camille asked, watching in dismay as Brenda collapsed on to the velvet sofa in tears.

'You wouldn't believe what's just happened.' The two ladies came to sit beside her, Camille dabbing at the tears dripping down her cheeks with a lace handkerchief.

'Do tell us what has upset you. Are you all right, dear?'

'Fortunately, yes. I thought I'd at last found employment.' Quickly explaining her terrifying story, tears again filled her eyes at the sight of their shocked expressions. 'Once I realised that it was a brothel and not a hotel, I ran hell for leather, as we say in England. How dare that German officer grope me, the bastard! Nothing on earth would persuade me to give myself to any man.'

'What a dreadful world we are living in now,' Adèle said with a sad sigh as she wrapped her arms about Brenda to give her a comforting hug. 'I've heard that Polish and other foreign girls, some as young as fifteen, have found themselves kidnapped and taken to a brothel to be sexually exploited. Thank goodness you managed to escape, darling.'

'You are perfectly safe here with us, but I think you should stay indoors for a while, just in case they come looking for you, dear,' Camille suggested.

Brenda nodded in agreement, feeling bleak and even more trapped. Perhaps it was not a good idea for a British girl to seek work in this occupied city. She really had no wish to ever again be approached by such rogues. Picking up her child, together with his little toy monkey, Brenda gave him a kiss and a cuddle. How she adored him. Bathing, nursing and feeding him in the days following helped to ease her anxiety as the sweet baby scent of her son brought joy to her heart.

Five

1944

Puffs of white cloud danced over humps of hills the next morning as Brenda stared bleakly out of the window, having suffered another fairly sleepless night. Could all these traumas be the reason her confidence was leaking rapidly away? She felt filled with anguish, as if she was falling into that dark pit yet again, quite unable to block out the pain. Yet she'd learned over the years to fight these feelings of extreme anxiety by rebuilding her strength, something she really must work upon.

Mrs Harding, even plumper than she'd been when Brenda had first come to work with her, was still a jolly and cheerful woman and most welcoming as Brenda settled herself at the table in the kitchen for breakfast. For a moment it felt almost as if she'd never been away. Brenda remembered how she used to scrub this big pine table and the slate floors, black-lead the stove and spend hours peeling and chopping vegetables, washing and ironing. Long hard days full of endless tasks.

The housekeeper gently patted her hand. 'Tha looks like tha's been through hell, chuck.'

'You could say that.'

'As have many others in this dratted war, but you're safe home now.'

'It will surely end soon. Even France is on the road to freedom.'

'Aye, as we all will be before too long. And don't fret about Master Hugh being a bit sniffy. It's no fault of yours. As well as losing his parents, his fiancée was recently killed in an air raid. He attended her funeral in London only a week or two ago.'

'Oh, that's dreadful! He never said a word about that.' Was this the reason for his foul temper? 'I was so upset to hear that Lady Stuart had died. She was such a lovely lady, and so kind to me. Do you know where she was living at the time, or where her cousin Adèle Rouanet, with whom she was sharing a home, lives?'

With a puzzled frown Mrs Harding shook her head. 'I only know what Miss Melissa told us, that her beloved Mama died of cancer. Nowt more was said on the subject. We all knew she'd left her husband, but 'twas none of our business why or where she'd gone.'

Brenda let out a heavy sigh, finding herself sinking into silent depression once more.

'So how are you, chuck?' the housekeeper asked, propping her legs up on a stool to give them a rest, since she was generally on her feet all day long.

'I'm in a bit of a quandary right now, Mrs Harding. The

fact is…' Brenda paused, finding herself unable to speak of the anguish she was suffering at having lost her son. She'd lived in hope that those two dear ladies who had cared for them both so well, would have returned to England at some point, bringing Tommy with them. No doubt because of Camille's tragic death, that hadn't happened. At worst she'd expected a member of the family to at least have Adèle's address, but Hugh claimed he didn't even know her. 'I'm fine,' she said at last, giving a brave smile.

In truth, Brenda felt as if her entire life lay in ruins, and could not decide how best to deal with this dilemma. The memory of dear Tommy brought to mind that his birthday would be coming up soon when he would turn four, and she hadn't seen him since he was but a few weeks old. She had nothing left: no husband, no son, not even a job or any income, although she fully intended to find one. She could well need money to help search for him. Once this war was finally over, and she'd retrieved him from wherever Adèle was keeping him safe, Brenda fully intended to build a new life for them both.

Putting on a brave face as she nibbled her toast, Brenda praised Mrs Harding for her delicious home-made jam. 'I used to make this for Camille, exactly as you taught me,' she told her. She'd learned a great deal working with the housekeeper all those years ago, and had enjoyed every moment of it, despite the hard work.

'Thee allus were a good little worker, chuck.'

'Hugh agreed to let me stay for only one night, so I'll be leaving later today. But that's fine by me. I need to find a job, and the best place to do that is in my home town of Castlefield, so the sooner I go the better.'

Mrs Harding scowled. 'Nay, tha doesn't have to go yet, lass. I know he created a bit of a rumpus for thee, but Carter says Master Hugh has changed his mind and agreed you can stay for a few days until you get theeself sorted. No doubt he realises you're in sore need of a rest, or else feels a bit guilty over the way he spoke to thee. Mind, he expects you to help wi' the chores,' she said, giving a droll little smile.

'Oh, I've no problem with that. That would be wonderful. I'm so grateful.' Perhaps he was not quite so unfeeling as he'd sounded?

'It's not been an easy time for any of the family, particularly Master Hugh, despite him being in a reserved occupation as a farmer and businessman. I suspect bankruptcy is also threatening. Finding the necessary ingredients to bake enough biscuits and make a decent profit has not been easy. The company used to produce such a good selection of biscuits, including bourbons, rich tea, homewheat, chocolate, fruit shortcake, ginger nuts and many more. Not possible now, with shortages being what they are.

'Nor did Sir Randolph approve of his son being involved in the everyday work of the factory, instructing him to concentrate upon running the estate. Such a decision did not help Master Hugh to acquire much knowledge on how to run the factory. But then, he and his pernickety father never did get on too well. Now Sir Randolph has departed this life, bless his soul, leaving his son in charge. We can but hope things will improve.'

'I'm sure they will once this war is over,' Brenda agreed, fascinated by Hugh's story.

'Don't rush into making any decisions until tha feels more yerself, chuck. And let me know if tha feels the need to talk. I can tell there's summat on yer mind.'

'Thank you, Mrs Harding. I do appreciate your help. Does Prue still live here?' Brenda asked, as she helped the housekeeper to clear away the dishes, exactly as she'd done in the days when she was employed as a scullery maid.

'Oh, aye! Miss Prudence has her problems too, having also been widowed by this dratted war, which she'll no doubt tell you all about. You'll find her in the dairy, or the vegetable garden, as usual. The good lady manages to keep us well fed.'

Brenda got on with the washing up, feeling very much like a servant again, but at least talking to Mrs Harding had helped to restore her courage and confidence. Once all chores were completed, she'd fully expected to be called to the study for yet another lecture. But receiving no such order, she collected Kit the collie and went off in search of her friend.

*

Hugh was standing by his Bentley when he saw the girl come round the side of the house from the kitchen, the dog bouncing beside her. He remembered all too well the family rows that had taken place when she and Jack had got together. Their father had been appalled by the idea of Jack pairing up with a servant girl. Hugh felt a certain sympathy with that, as Sir Randolph clearly wanted the best for his eldest son. Yet as he watched her spin round to toss the stick for Kit, her face aglow with laughter, brown hair flying in the breeze, he again felt something stir within him. Was it another nudge of guilt because he hadn't defended his brother's decision, or something more?

Noticing him standing watching her, she stopped dead. 'Oh, sorry, didn't see you there. Were you wishing to speak to me again?'

'No, I have work to do. We can speak later.'

Walking over to him, she nodded. 'It can't be easy being left to run everything alone. I can remember how Jack used to say how much he missed the business. He said he really enjoyed working at the factory and told me so much about it. May I come and visit it some time?' she asked with a smile, her round cheeks flushed a pretty pink, her velvet-brown eyes lit by the sun, warm with kindness.

His throat tightened and his senses skittered. She was quite attractive and clearly resilient and strong willed, but he must not allow himself to be seduced by her charm. What did the family business have to do with her? No doubt because she wished to get her greedy little hands upon it. Pulling open the car door, he flung himself into the driving seat. 'Certainly not. The factory is no place for a young woman.'

'Really? Not even when the men are at war and women are fully occupied doing their jobs. Such was the case in

France. The same must be happening here in England too, from what I understand.'

Glaring into her eyes, which now seemed to be twinkling with amusement, he felt a fury escalate within him. Why did this feisty little madam keep attacking him with such caustic remarks, and making constant demands? She was almost as bad as Melissa, if not half so grand. 'Some other time,' he growled, and drove off at speed.

*

Seeing that he was rampant with temper yet again, Brenda felt a sudden need to remember Jack, and explore all the favourite places they'd once enjoyed together. Turning on her heel, she headed towards the woodlands. The mountain rowan were flush with crimson berries, this part of the Pennines also cloaked with beech, oak, ash, Scots pine, birch, hazel, and even wild cherry, although not currently in bloom. How she loved this place. It took her back to the days when she and Jack would walk for miles over the hills, needing to enjoy some time together. Kit the dog would wander along beside them sniffing for rabbits, just as he was doing now. She even found one or two cairns they'd built to mark the way, and added an extra stone to each in memory of their time together. How her heart still ached for him.

Eventually feeling the need of a rest, Brenda settled herself beneath a chestnut tree, remembering how they would sit here to kiss and cuddle, the sweetness of his caresses flowing through her like fire. Brenda well recalled the day he'd proposed to her, following his father's discovery of their relationship.

'I'm so relieved that you've agreed to come with me to France,' he'd told her as he smoothed his mouth gently over hers. 'I can't bear the thought of losing you. You are the love of my life, darling.'

'And you mine.'

'I've been to France many times with Mama, and love it. I hope you will too.'

'I'm sure I will. I would be happy with you anywhere, my darling.'

'It's a wonderful country, and it will be so good to see Mama again. I've missed her dreadfully in recent months since she went back home. I'm sure she'll welcome us with open arms. And no matter what Papa might demand from me, I so look forward to us at last being free. We will be together always.'

'Oh, yes please!'

It had never crossed their minds to consider that the threat of war might hamper this dream. Hadn't the Prime Minister, Neville Chamberlain, assured the nation that he had achieved 'Peace for our time', so why would they worry about such things?

'I'll be leaving by train from Uppermill on Friday morning.'

'I've been ordered to leave first thing tomorrow. I'll be staying with my friend, Cathie, in Castlefield.'

'So you could meet me at Manchester Victoria? I should arrive by eleven at the latest.'

'Of course,' she'd said, kissing him again. 'But we must make sure Sir Randolph doesn't discover our plans. Were he to find out you intend to take me with you, he could change his mind and prevent you from going.'

'We won't tell a living soul,' he'd whispered, cradling her in his arms. Then, with a little smile on his face, he'd shifted on to one knee and grasped her hand. 'As soon as we're settled in France and we've saved up enough cash from my much-reduced allowance, would you do me the honour of becoming my wife?'

'Oh, Jack, I can't think of anything I'd like more. I love you with all my heart.'

That had been the moment when Brenda would have been happy to give herself to him, her heart beating wildly. But even as passion had flared between them, both trembling with need, he'd gently released her. 'Let's not take any more risks, not until we're safely away from this place. I suppose we're taking a risk being here together now. If Papa realises we're missing he could walk through these woods at any moment and find us, which would ruin everything.'

With great reluctance they'd parted, softly repeating their promises to each other. Brenda had spent the rest of the day saying sad farewells to Mrs Harding, Carter, Prue and even Kit the collie. Then she'd packed her small brown suitcase, and around dawn the next morning old Joe had driven her down the long winding hill to the station. She could remember watching the sun rise, lighting the sloping green hills with gold and pink, and thinking how she would miss this beautiful land. Yet she'd also felt an excitement burning inside her at the prospect of a new adventure in France.

When Friday came she'd stood by the clock at Victoria Station by ten in the morning, just in case Jack arrived early. Eleven o'clock came and went and just when she was nearly in tears of disappointment, he'd suddenly come walking towards her through the steam and smoke of the engine.

'Sorry, the train was delayed, but here I am, my darling. Now we can be together forever,' he'd said, lifting her into his arms and swinging her round, making her squeal with joy.

Fortunately, their journey to France had passed without incident, arriving just as Germany declared war. At first it hadn't seemed real, as there were no major battles for some months, everyone calling it a 'phoney war'. But German Jewish refugees were attempting to escape to America or England, synagogues were being burned, and realising things were about to get worse in France too, Jack and Brenda stopped bothering about saving up and quickly married in November that year.

It had been a wonderful wedding. Her gown of tiered cream silk, lent to her by Camille, was the most beautiful garment she'd ever worn in her life. Brenda had felt herself so fortunate, rich with love and happiness. And they had indeed possessed a marriage certificate. Sadly, she'd left it behind at Camille's apartment and now it was gone, along with her son and darling mother-in-law. How would she survive without anyone she loved?

Getting to her feet with a sigh, Brenda called Kit to her, and set off back to find her old friend Prue.

Six

Prue had been astonished to discover how much she loved gardening. It was far more interesting than parading herself at some fancy social function organised by Melissa, her supremely glamorous sister currently living in London, a city she considered far more appropriate for her. But then relations with her siblings, save for dear Jack, had always been thorny. Prue felt as if her family now were the serried rows of vegetables that lined the kitchen gardens, her pride and joy the tomatoes and cucumbers growing in the glass-house against the south-facing wall, or the new autumn variety of raspberries she'd cultivated.

It amazed her to see how quickly a precious plant could grow to full maturity, or just as easily die if it fell into neglect. Gardening was all about life and death, preserving and reproducing. Prue still felt a bit nervous of making mistakes, of pulling up a prize plant thinking it was a weed, of watering too much, pruning too fiercely or not pruning at all. But she was learning all the time. She loved the hens and sheep too. Were it not for the war Prue would have chosen to attend horticultural college, but at least she'd learned a great deal from the land girls who'd helped on the farm. They were now gone, and in their place the farm had been allotted a Prisoner of War.

His arrival had changed her life completely.

There had been times in the past when Prue would ask herself if she truly was content to live here in the Pennines, largely alone, and devote her entire life to tending the garden. What about her future? Didn't she yearn, like every other young woman or war widow, to preserve and reproduce herself as well as the plants and animals? Didn't she long to love and to be loved? Was that the reason she'd rushed into that stupid marriage, her father and siblings seeming most uncaring? Now she would sit in the small cottage she occupied on the edge of the estate, the ache in her heart not for her dead husband, but an entirely different young man.

This morning Prue was happily pruning raspberry canes, working hard as usual, when she spotted him approaching and her heart skipped a beat. He was at her side in seconds but before he could steal a kiss, a flippant breeze whipped her hair across her mouth, robbing him of its sweetness. She laughed out loud at the look of disappointment on his face.

'I love the softness of your skin,' he said, trailing his lips over the curve of her throat, sending a quiver of fierce passion through her as he found the sensitive hollows beneath her ears. 'And you always smell so wonderful: of strawberries or flowers.'

'And sometimes cow muck,' she giggled. 'Oh, Dino, am I allowed to tell you again how much I love you?'

'The more often you say that, the greater my heart explodes with happiness. *Ti amo troppo la mia cara*, and I will always love you. How fortunate I was to be sent here. It is as if I have been waiting for you all my life.'

'You must have suffered so much, being held in that prisoner-of-war camp,' she said, stroking the crisp tufts of his dark hair, which had a slight curl to it. He was tall and fit, with powerful shoulders, long lean legs, and the gentlest brown eyes she'd ever seen.

'More of an internment camp. At least now they are allowing me to get out and work, even though I'm taken back to a camp in Gorton, Manchester, each night. I love working here,' he said with a grin.

'And we love having you.'

'At least *you* do. Not so sure about your brother. I've lived in Ancoats since I was a toddler and, unlike my parents, I hardly speak a word of Italian, apart from being able to say how much I love you. It didn't seem right for me to be arrested. I feel British to the core, even if I might look foreign.'

'You look wonderful to me,' Prue said, kissing him, and he softly laughed.

'You do appreciate that, however much we might feel as if we belong together, it is not going to be easy. Before being transported to the Isle of Man, I was taken to a reception centre in Liverpool. I vividly remember hundreds of us being made to walk to the docks, the roads lined with soldiers armed with fixed bayonets. Crowds filled the streets to jeer at us, hurling insults, all because Mussolini had decided to link up with Hitler's Germany, perhaps in the belief that it was only a matter of time before Britain surrendered. I heard someone shout: 'Hang the buggers.'

'Oh, how scary!'

'I just kept my head down and did not say a word. There are people who now welcome PoWs into their homes, especially at Christmas. But sadly, much of the nation still holds us in contempt. When the war is finally over, waiting for our release could well take time.'

'I'll be happy to wait for you, darling, however long it takes. I will, of course, make every effort to help get you freed as soon as possible. I'm an optimist, so I have every faith we can achieve that, then we can be together forever. Although, I admit, my family may well create problems. I'd like to think Hugh might come round to accepting you. I'll speak to him.'

'That would be very brave of you, *cara mia*,' he said, giving her such a dazzling smile that Prue melted into his arms yet again. It was then that she heard a door bang and quickly pulled away.

'Look out, someone's coming.'

'*Ciao*!' And placing a kiss on her small turned-up nose, Dino grabbed a spade and marched away with it propped upon his shoulder, an expression of tranquil happiness on his face. Giggling, Prue ran to the dairy.

*

Brenda found Prue happily humming 'Don't Fence Me In' as she washed the floor in the dairy. Standing at the door Brenda watched and listened with a smile on her face. Prue was a small lithe young woman with strongly muscled arms and golden blonde hair, and being Jack's much-loved younger sister had always been a good friend. Glancing up, her lids widened to gaze upon Brenda in stunned disbelief. Dropping the hosepipe, she ran over to her, which caused water to spray everywhere, soaking Prue to the skin in seconds. Laughing, she dashed to the tap to turn it off, before flying back to hug her friend. 'Brenda, I can't believe it. How wonderful to see you again. Why didn't you tell me you were coming?'

'I wanted it to be a surprise.'

'It's most certainly that. I thought you were still in France. Oh, I'm so glad to see you.' Prue's soft grey eyes slid over her, narrowing a little in concern. 'Are you all right? You're looking a bit skinny and tired. I dare say you're still grieving for our lovely Jack?'

'I'm afraid that will always be the case. He was a wonderful husband.'

'Ah, so you did marry?'

'Indeed we did, although I haven't yet convinced Hugh of that fact.'

'He is in the depths of despair himself right now, as we all are.'

'I fully understand and offer you my sympathies, darling, as I did to Hugh. Although that failed to calm his temper.'

Prue gave an amused little smile. 'He probably hasn't forgiven you for robbing him of his best pal. They were almost like twins, those two, there being only a year between them. I hope he made you feel welcome. And is he prepared to let you stay? He never even told me you were here.'

'I arrived only yesterday evening, but I'll be staying only a day or two at most.' Were it not for the fact that he was Prue's brother, she might well have explained how Hugh had accused her of seducing and running off with darling Jack. Very sensibly, she remained silent on the subject. 'But that's fine, as I must return to Castlefield, hopefully to find myself a job.'

'Oh, I do wish you could stay longer, but I'm sure you'll succeed in finding one; you're a hard worker. And the city centre is not too far away—an easy train ride—so you can always pop over for the odd weekend. I would love to see more of you, lovey, as I've missed you so much,' Prue said. Tucking her arm through Brenda's, she led her out along the garden path while tossing sticks for the dog. 'So did the members of our staff, although I wouldn't say that was a feeling generally shared by my father or siblings,' she added with a rueful grin.

'I'm fully aware of that fact. I missed you too, and am just glad to be here,' Brenda said, recalling how Prue's married sister, Melissa, had always been distinctly unfriendly and disapproving. Despite her anxious need to find her beloved son, Brenda had returned with some degree of reluctance to the family fold. She'd had few expectations of welcome, having been thrown out simply for falling madly in love with a wonderful young man. Would Jack's grand sister still hold that against her?

Today, however, having found her dear old friend, she was feeling much more optimistic. The sun was shining, a beautiful bright day, which made Brenda feel much better. She'd long believed these hills possessed personalities of their own. Sometimes they appeared sullen and brooding, at others alight with promise. Now they were aglow with purple heather, which was so good to enjoy before the snows of winter blanketed them. She'd suffered enough from freezing snow to last a lifetime.

'Did you enjoy staying with darling Mama?' Prue asked. 'I badly missed her when she left to return to France, but I'm so glad she helped you.'

'It was thanks to your mother that I got this job in the first place. She was always so kind and generous. I came to love her dearly while caring for her in France. When did you last hear from her?' Brenda asked, striving to curb the fear in her tone of voice.

Giving a slight frown, Prue shook her head. 'I can't remember. We received very few letters from her, probably because of the German occupation. But then Melissa received a telegram from a hospital telling us of her death. It was so heartbreaking I had no wish to even read it. It was a difficult time for me. My husband had been killed too, at El Alamein,' Prue told her, then pulled her face. 'We married in something of a rush because of the war, and spent one week together before he was sent overseas. I never saw him again.'

'Oh, how dreadful. I'm so sorry to hear that.'

Prue gave a little shrug. 'I'm not sure marrying him was

the right thing to do. We hardly knew each other. I just fancied him, I suppose. Or else, deep in some secret part of me, I felt the need to rebel against my father for constantly ordering me to marry someone rich. And you know how impulsive I can be. I'm sorry he died, poor man. But even the week we spent together wasn't exactly a happy one. If it wasn't so tragic, it would almost seem like the plot of a Victorian melodrama.'

Brenda giggled. 'Your family does seem to live in the past, and it must be quite lonely at times for you in this remote countryside.'

Hugging her arm closer, Prue whispered in her ear, 'Actually, I do have a new friend. Earlier this year a PoW was placed with us. He was so pleased to be allowed out to work on the land, being originally interned at the Palace camp in Douglas, among other places in the Isle of Man, simply for being Italian.'

'Oh, my goodness! I too was held in an internment camp, simply for being British,' Brenda admitted.

Prue stopped walking to stare at her friend in horror. 'Was that part of the traumas you've had to face? Please tell me more. What kind of a life did you and Mama live in Paris, and how on earth did you cope when the Germans arrived? Oh, do tell me everything, I need to hear all your news.'

Brenda brushed aside these questions with a sad little smile. 'Maybe later. It's a long story and not a pleasant one, thanks to the war. But Camille was very happy to be back in her home country. Sadly, in 1941 she had to leave her beloved apartment to live somewhere in the Loire Valley with her cousin, as I've explained to your brother. But I don't know where.'

'Why would she do that?'

'Because of the dangers involved in staying in Paris. It was a complete nightmare.'

Prue's eyes darkened as they met her friend's gaze with deep sympathy. 'This dratted war has ruined the lives of entire families.'

'Indeed it has, including yours and mine.' How could she be sure that her little Tommy was safe? The chill within Brenda worsened as images and memories she preferred to block out returned yet again to haunt her. 'I like to think that all the traumas I've had to deal with have made me so much stronger. I'm sure the same is true of you too.' Putting her arms about her friend, she gave her a warm hug. 'So what is he called, this PoW?'

'Dino, and we're becoming quite close friends,' Prue said, her cheeks turning slightly pink. 'He's a lovely man.'

'Sounds as if it might grow into something more than friendship,' Brenda commented with a smile.

'It already has, not that I've revealed this fact to Melissa or Hugh. I know they would never approve. If they believed for one moment that I was falling for one of the enemy, I'm quite sure they'd send Dino straight back to the prison camp. And were it not for the fact that I'm their sister, they'd toss me out too, just as they did with you. So please don't say a word to them on the subject, not till I've explained to Hugh how we feel about each other.'

'Don't worry, your secret is safe with me.' Brenda chuckled. 'I firmly believe that we women should be free to make our own decisions in life, particularly when there's a war on. So go for it, girl. Do what is right for you, as I did by marrying your lovely brother. At least we had some happy months together, if not the lifetime we'd hoped for. But the war will soon be over and we must then look to the future.'

'We certainly will, and must help each other as much as we can. I can feel an anguish in you, sweetie, and I believe the only way to deal with such pain is for you to talk about it. I'm happy to listen.'

Looking into her dear friend's eyes, Brenda realised she might well be right. She'd struggled so many times to do that in the past, sadly with little success. It was hard to find the right words to express her emotions. Some elements of the various traumas she'd suffered were now lost to her, shut out forever, perhaps because the stress and strain of remembering was far too painful. She really had no wish to dig down too deep and open that locked box again. But perhaps she could tell a little, if only in the hope that it might help her to sleep better and bring her back into the real world.

Sitting on a bench beneath an old oak tree, Brenda began to speak of what had happened to her following Jack's death. But she resolutely made no mention of the birth of her son. There would come a time when she must reveal more facts, but not right now. She simply couldn't cope with everything at once.

Seven

France, 1941

Brenda kept her head down in the Paris apartment for a couple of weeks. By the end of that time she was beginning to feel quite claustrophobic and anxious to get back to her normal routine. Surely she'd be reasonably safe, or at no greater risk than anyone else? Resistance was increasing. They were bombing railway lines and derailing trains in order to block the lines and make things as difficult as possible for the occupiers of their land, just as Jack had insisted they should. But the Germans always retaliated brutally. As did the British. There were frequent air raids upon the city, and they lived in fear of the apartment being bombed.

It was late one afternoon when she was coming home loaded with shopping, after venturing out to one of the many local markets in the city, that the bridge over the railway line she was about to cross suddenly exploded in front of her. Brenda found herself flung off her feet and knocked to the ground. One moment lights had flashed all around her, then darkness descended.

She came round to find rubble, dust, stones and scraps of burning metal scattered all over her. Terror erupted within her, and gently moving her limbs, she felt deeply relieved to find they were still working, if rather cut, bruised and stinging from the burns. Brenda felt fortunate to still be alive. Had she arrived at the bridge a few moments earlier, it could have been an entirely different story. Staggering to her feet, she gathered up the remnants of her shopping and slowly made her way back to the apartment.

Yet again Camille was shocked to the core at the sorry state of her when Brenda came limping into the drawing room. 'Oh, my dear girl, what has happened this time? Not more trouble?' she cried.

'Don't panic, I've no serious injuries. Just feel a bit shell-shocked,' Brenda assured her, gathering her strength. Then quickly telling them about the bombed bridge, she glanced across at the baby fast asleep in his crib and sent up a silent prayer of thanks that her precious child had not been with her. Keeping Tommy safe was becoming a serious concern.

Adèle at once rushed to fetch hot water, bandages and iodine to tend to the injuries on Brenda's arms and legs.

In the days following, Brenda suffered yet more sleep-less nights, nightmares and constant flashbacks, as if locked back in time and experiencing the incident over and over again in her head. At other times she felt entirely discon-nected from the world, as if she'd dropped back into that black pit she'd fallen into following Jack's death. She would feel entirely unable to concentrate or remember anything, riddled with an intense fear, a sense of helplessness and horror-sensations she valiantly fought to block out.

Camille strived to help her deal with her distress by feeding and comforting her, as well as encouraging her to speak of how she felt, which Brenda found almost impossible to do.

'You should return to England, dear girl,' Camille suggested, as she had a dozen or more times. 'You need to take Tommy home to the house and estate he will one day inherit, and where he will be safe. That is what Jack wished, as it is where his son belongs.'

Remembering the will Jack had written to protect their future family, Brenda fully intended to ensure his wishes were carried out. She looked forward to showing Tommy the farm and land that would one day be his; the great stone barns filled with the sweet scent of hay, the milking parlour and sheep-folds, the lush green intake land close to the house where the flock was wintered. There was so much she'd loved about living and working there. Yet when that could happen was beyond imagining.

'Sorry, Camille, but is this the right moment? Trying to find a safe way out of France will present enormous difficulties.'

Her mother-in-law let out a heavy sigh. 'We could make a few enquiries, quietly among friends.'

Later, sitting drinking a mug of hot chocolate, Brenda met the anxious expressions of these lovely ladies with a suggestion that had been gnawing at her for some time. 'I wonder if we should all leave Paris and find somewhere safer to live outside of the city.'

'Oh, that's an excellent idea,' Adèle said, clapping her hands. 'I've said as much to Camille more than once. We could go and live in my house in the Loire Valley. We'd be much safer there, far away from any bombing, let alone the presence of those dreadful brothels.'

'Why not?' Camille said with a nod. 'At least until we find a way to get Brenda and Tommy safely back to England.'

And so it was agreed.

Wasting no time, they were in the midst of packing clothes and other essentials the following morning when there came a loud hammering on the door. The next moment it was flung open and a bunch of German guards marched in. 'We need to see your papers,' they demanded.

Fear invaded her heart once more as Brenda obediently handed over her passport, realising what was about to happen. She was at once ordered to pack a small bag, which she quickly did, helped by Camille, while Adèle carefully kept the baby safely out of sight. This was what Brenda had dreaded for so long. And what bad luck that it should happen now, just when she'd finally persuaded Camille to leave Paris. Then she remembered that rogue, Étienne Bresson, who'd lured her into his brothel. Had he taken revenge for her refusal to accept his offer by reporting her to the Gestapo?

As Brenda bravely attempted to remain calm, she slipped off her wedding ring and secretly pushed it into Camille's hand. She had no wish for these Nazis to steal this precious item from her. Receiving a little hand-squeeze by way of response, she interpreted this as a promise that her mother-in-law would take good care of it.

Glancing back over her shoulder as she was marched out into the street, Brenda gave her a desperate pleading glance, silently begging her to take good care of her son too, who was far more important. With tears in her eyes and a hand clasped tightly over her trembling mouth, dear Camille gave a little nod by way of assurance.

Tommy at least would remain safe with his grand-mamma, Brenda thought with relief as she was hustled into a black police van and driven away into the unknown.

*

She was taken across Paris to the Gare de l'Est, together with dozens of other women: dancers from the Folies Bergére, governesses, nannies and even prostitutes, despite that rogue's assurance that such a job would keep a woman safe. They were all bundled on to a train. More arrived in the hours following as they waited in the cold and the dark, with no light or heating on board. Like everyone else, Brenda was suffering badly from anxiety about where they would be taken. Germany, perhaps? The only comfort she could find to stem the flood of emotional trauma pulsating through her was that at least her child was safe. If she was to be interned in a prison camp, the last thing she would have wanted was for Tommy to suffer that too.

'Why are they doing this to us?' she couldn't help but ask the woman sitting next to her, as anger ricocheted through her.

'It's in revenge for the British government interning supposed enemy aliens, including Germans and Italians.'

'So we women are putty in their hands, despite being entirely innocent?' Brenda snapped.

'We are indeed, as are many of those interned in England.' She was a most elegant lady clad in a fur coat with a small turban wrapped around her fair hair. 'I'm Emma. Happy to make your acquaintance, particularly in these circumstances,' she said, holding out a hand sparkling with rings. 'We were here in France because my husband is involved in the silk industry. He's also been arrested for having a British passport. I pray to God he will be safe.'

'I'm Brenda.' They shook hands and soon became good friends as they shared their agonies of war.

The journey took days, the train constantly shunted into a siding where it would stand for hours on end. In a way they welcomed this, as with no toilets on board it allowed them to go outside and relieve themselves—if, sadly, in front of the guards. When there were no stops for hours on end the very young and old found it hard to hold on to their bladder, and the stink in the carriages was horrendous. Brenda would use a spare bag, then empty it out of the train window, curling her nose in disgust as she did so. Many women spent much of the journey weeping, children screaming, having tantrums or being sick.

Sometimes they'd stop at a station to queue for food and water, as there was none of that on the train either. It would generally be soup, or bread and sausage provided by the Red Cross or German nurses.

Eventually they arrived in Besançon, an internment camp that looked very like a fortress situated quite close to Switzerland in the foothills of the Jura Mountains.

'At least we've not been sent to Germany,' Brenda said on a sigh of relief.

'Which would be far worse,' Emma agreed. 'And we can now finally leave this foul-smelling train.'

The town appeared ancient but rather beautiful, encircled by a river with woods stretching for miles all around. 'I'd love to explore it,' Brenda said. 'Although I doubt they'll ever allow that to happen, as we are about to be interned.' Camille and Adèle would presumably be on their way to the Loire Valley by now. How she envied them. It occurred to Brenda in that dreadful moment as they climbed out of the train on to a platform slippery with ice, that she had no idea of the address. Bugger! Why hadn't she thought to ask? Sadly, there'd been no time to check such details, as she'd been hustled off under arrest in such a rush. She would simply have to be thankful that at least Tommy was safe.

The women were met at the station by German soldiers barking orders furiously at them. Exhaustion and the freezing cold made her feel so numb, Brenda could barely take in a word they were saying. Not that she understood a word of German. Packed into lorries, the women were taken to the camp, then lined up in the courtyard while the luggage was brought from the train. The cast-iron gates were finally closed and locked behind them.

So here they were, trapped in hell.

Eight

'By heck, you're a good little baker, chuck,' the house-keeper said, reaching for another slice of the blackberry shortbread Brenda had spent the afternoon making. 'Where did tha learn this?'

Brenda laughed. 'As you know, the nuns taught us all how to cook, clean, wash and iron. They considered such skills necessary for every woman. And, of course, I learned a lot from you when I worked here, Mrs Harding. Then while in France with Camille, I was in charge of all the cooking.'

'Well, tha's improved a great deal, I'd say that for thee,' Mrs Harding said as she happily chewed the biscuit. 'The sweet taste of these blackberries makes up wonderfully for the lack of sugar, since rationing puts it in short supply. What are thee making now?' she asked, seeing Brenda start to grate a Bramley apple.

'Bread-and-apple pudding,' Brenda told her. 'Can't use up too much of your flour, but we do at least have some butter from the farm cows, and there's some bread in the bin that's a bit past its best. I thought I'd add apple and a few currants, if we have any to spare.'

'Eeh, I'm sure Master Hugh would love that. I take it you'll be joining the family for dinner tonight? I believe Miss Melissa is expected too, coming up by train today from London, where she now lives.'

Brenda bit on her lower lip as she looked up at the housekeeper in dismay. 'Hadn't thought of that. Not sure they'd welcome me, particularly Miss Melissa.'

Carter the butler gave her shoulder a gentle pat. 'I'm sure they will. Miss Prudence certainly would. And you really shouldn't be working in the kitchen with us. You're no longer a servant, remember.'

'Hugh might disagree with you on that.'

Giving a little chuckle, he said, 'I could ask if you will be expected to attend?'

'Don't bother, I'm really not eager to intrude.' Then with a slight frown, she instantly changed her mind. 'Although perhaps I should, as before I head off to Manchester tomorrow in search of a job I need to know the name and address of the family solicitor. That's where Jack sent a copy of his will. I've no idea what's in it but really should find out, as his mother instructed.'

Carter gave a sad nod of his head, then quickly disappeared up the back stairs.

Brenda pondered this decision as she returned to the kitchen table. A lawyer might also be able to help her find Tommy, for which she'd no doubt need a considerable sum of money to pay him. But she was willing to work her socks off to achieve that. Determined to keep her mind off her worries by remaining busy she thinly sliced the bread, added a drop of lemon juice, lined a basin, then sprinkled on raisins, grated apple and a touch of cinnamon. Topping the pudding off with a second layer of bread, she added a drop of milk to moisten it before putting it in the oven.

Just as she started the washing up, Mrs Harding having nodded off in her chair, the butler returned. He wore a grim expression upon his usually cheerful face as he burst through the kitchen door, his round cheeks flushed scarlet, clearly as much from anger as the heat and steam from the baking.

Woken from her sleep by the bang of the door, Mrs Harding cried, 'Dear lord, what's going on?'

'I'm afraid the answer is no to both questions,' Carter sourly remarked. 'Master Hugh made it very clear that he has no wish for you to join them for dinner. And absolutely refused to provide the address of the family solicitor.'

'Oh, my word.' Mrs Harding looked horrified. 'Does this young lady not have the right to see her late husband's will?'

'Good question. I did ask him that, but since she cannot prove that they truly were married, he says no, she has no right at all.'

Brenda sighed with frustration. 'He clearly has no notion of how difficult life was in France for us British. I'll perhaps have a quiet word with him, and try again to convince him.'

'No need,' Carter said. 'I can provide you with the

necessary information. I'm fully aware of the name of the family solicitor, and where his office is situated in Manchester.'

'That would not be a safe thing for you to do, Mister Carter. Were Hugh to realise you'd revealed it to me, he could very well dismiss you, as his father did me. I will not allow you to take that risk. I think perhaps I *will* go in to dinner with the family. Surely I have that right as his sister-in-law?'

'And you did bake the pudding,' chuckled Mrs Harding.

*

Rummaging through the few clothes she'd managed to bring with her, Brenda found little fit to wear, settling for a very plain brown skirt and a white blouse she'd bought at a market in Spain. They were at least clean, as dear Mrs Harding had washed everything for her. Walking down the grand staircase and across the slate-tiled hall took her back to the days when she'd been a humble servant here. She felt as if she should be setting the table, preparing and serving food, as she'd done back then. No wonder Hugh could not get his head around the fact that she was now a member of his family.

Melissa was in the dining room when Brenda entered; standing alone smoking a cigarette, glass in hand by the grand marble fireplace. 'Good gracious, so you are that whip of a girl who ran off with my brother? You've absolutely no right to come back here.'

Gazing upon her gloriously grand sister-in-law wearing

a cocktail dress of blue silk organza with a tiered skirt and low neckline, Brenda felt like a piece of scum caught on the heel of a boot. Melissa was a classic beauty with an enchanting oval face, grey-green eyes and a haze of soft, silver-blonde curls; the kind of looks that would turn any man's head. And Mrs Harding had surely been wrong about the threat of bankruptcy. It was quite obvious this young woman was not short of money. Facing her with the courage she'd acquired over the years, Brenda managed a polite smile.

'As you know, Jack and I left under orders from his father, and were so in love that we married. However, I am fully aware of your brother's doubts on the status of our relationship.'

'I'm not at all surprised,' Melissa curtly responded as she walked over to the sideboard to pour more gin into her glass. 'If you imagine you can stay for dinner, you couldn't be more wrong. You were definitely not invited.'

'That is perfectly all right. The kitchen staff are most friendly, so I would have no objection to sharing a meal with them.'

'Which is where you truly belong.'

'They would not agree with you on that point, not now that I'm Jack's widow,' Brenda firmly contested. The pomposity of this woman was irritating her enormously. Her sister-in-law clearly believed that being rich and able to parade herself in a grand dining room decked out with glorious chandeliers, velvet curtains, elegant Chinese cabinets and a table long enough to host twenty people, gave her the right to be dismissive of an ordinary working-class lass. Had she no manners? 'There is a reason I am here. With war having broken out, Jack did make a will, to ensure that I was properly provided for. But in order to prove that we truly were man and wife, I need the details of the family solicitor. He could hopefully retrieve the necessary paperwork from France.'

Tossing her half-smoked cigarette into the fire, Melissa snorted with laughter, making her firm aquiline nose puff out. 'Don't be ridiculous! Why would he waste time and money on such a pointless task?'

Brenda quietly ground her teeth while keeping a bland smile fixed upon her face. Now was surely the moment to reveal reality. 'It's not pointless at all. Jack told me that he'd sent a copy of his will to the family solicitor, and as I must consider our son's future, I need to see it.'

The silence following this statement was slightly unnerving, making Brenda almost regret having revealed the truth. The last thing she wished to talk about was the fear she felt for her lost child. A deep voice from behind broke the silence with a snarl of harsh fury.

'What the hell are you talking about? You've made no mention of any son.'

Hugh had chosen that moment to walk in. Turning to face him, her heart pounding, Brenda met his gaze full on. 'You never asked. Thomas, or Tommy, as we call him, was, sadly, not born until after his father's death. Yet Jack was fully aware I was expecting, and looking forward to the birth of his child. As I have attempted to explain, he did make the necessary provision for his family's future security.'

'Where is this alleged son?' Melissa scornfully asked, eyes narrowing as she sipped her gin. 'We've no proof that he even exists.'

'Ah, that is the problem,' Brenda confessed. Her voice dropped as she briefly explained how she'd left him with Camille when she was arrested, believing him to be safe. And had then failed to find him once she'd escaped years later.

'Arrested? Escaped? Are you claiming to be a spy, or do you just like making up yet more stupid stories?' Hugh accused her.

Brenda firmly lifted her chin. 'I'm telling you exactly what happened.'

'Utter nonsense,' Melissa scoffed.

Battling to remain calm, Brenda had never felt more furious. What on earth had possessed her to imagine the Stuart family would believe anything she said? Jack had been the kindest, sweetest man on earth, so why wasn't his brother, who looked so like him, equally kind? Dressed for dinner in a smart black suit with bow tie and white shirt, he appeared most handsome, yet his manner was rude, arrogant and completely unfriendly, even if she did find herself enthralled by the sparkle in his grey eyes. 'It is not a subject I find easy to talk about in any detail, as it's quite painful to remember those years in an internment camp. But if you feel it necessary, I will do my best to describe how it was.' She'd most certainly never admit to all that had happened there. Wouldn't that give them the excuse they sought to claim that Tommy was not Jack's son?

Hugh gave a snort of derision. 'I've heard enough of your lies. Why would I believe this child to be my brother's son when you cannot even prove you were married?'

'What's going on? What are you accusing Brenda of?' Prue had walked in and glared at her sour-faced brother, a puzzled frown on her face.

'This chit is telling even more lies in order to get her hands on our family's money,' Melissa stated in an imperious tone. 'She's claiming to have had a son by Jack, but there's absolutely no evidence of that fact.'

Prue gasped, and with a happy smile on her face clutched Brenda's hands. 'You have a *son*? Why didn't you tell me?'

Brenda nodded, tears filling her eyes. 'Because I find it so hard to talk about. He's lost, as is Camille's cousin, who was helping to look after him. I've spent years searching for him, and came back in the hope he might be here with his grandmother. But with Camille gone, I can't understand why Adèle hasn't been in touch. Where is she? And how on earth am I going to find my son if no one has her address?'

'So you're attempting to put the blame upon other people when it was you who abandoned your child,' Hugh retorted. 'Even when you know from personal experience how wrong that is. If you were planning to move him out of Paris, you would surely know where he was going?'

Hating his tone of voice, Brenda stuck firmly to her courage. 'I was arrested, quite out of the blue, simply for being British. There was no time to organise or check anything.'

'Why would we believe a word you say?' Melissa pompously stated. 'This is a tale you've invented in order to get your greedy hands on Jack's money. I have four children and will not for one moment allow you to rob them of their rightful inheritance.'

Prue put her arm about her friend. 'I do not believe Brenda is attempting any such thing. She is simply doing what is right for her own child.'

'We have absolutely no evidence that he really is Jack's son,' her sister staunchly repeated. 'And Mama did once write to say that this strip of a girl accepted an invitation to join a brothel. So we're perfectly well aware she's a whore.'

Brenda gasped, shock reverberating through her as she met the scathing gaze of this snobby young woman. 'How dare you accuse me of such a thing? I did nothing of the sort! Yes, a man did offer me a job in what I presumed to be a hotel. But when I found out exactly what it was, I immediately left. I ran away as fast as I could, in fact.'

Melissa gave a caustic little laugh. 'You expect us to believe that too, do you?'

'It is the truth.'

'You no doubt bestowed your favours upon the Germans like the harlot you clearly are. Otherwise why would Mama mention that fact in her letter?'

'I do not for a moment believe that dear Camille accused me of being such an immoral creature. She would simply have been describing how difficult life was in France back then. And how the Nazis were so against the British, it put me in grave danger.'

'She's just making excuses,' Melissa retorted, turning to her brother. 'Blaming the war and everyone else for her own stupid mistakes.'

Hugh stepped forward to confront Brenda with a weary sigh. 'I'm afraid my sister is making a valid point. This child could well be the illegitimate son of a German, and not our brother's at all. Having chosen to stay in Paris and live with the enemy following Jack's death, you were probably willing to spread your favours in order to remain free of internment, although it clearly didn't work.'

'I did *not* choose to live with the enemy, nor give myself to them!' How dare they accuse her of such behaviour? No wonder she'd found it difficult to admit she'd given birth to Jack's child after his death. Yet Brenda did still need to find her son, and then consider his future. Even Camille had insisted that she make a rightful claim for Tommy's inheritance. Oh, if only the poor lady were here to support and welcome her.

Giving a disdainful little smile, Melissa set down her empty glass and smartly folded her arms. 'You are no longer welcome here.'

Brenda almost laughed. 'I never was.'

'Then please leave now,' Hugh ordered, and firmly pressed the bell to call Carter.

The butler instantly appeared, his expression looking very much as if he'd been listening outside the door to the entire conversation.

'Show this madam out, please, Carter, and do not allow her to enter the house ever again.'

'Oh, for goodness' sake,' Prue cried, looking shocked. 'You can't do this to her.'

'It's all right, Prue,' Brenda said, blinking back tears. 'I need to return to Manchester anyway in order to find myself a job. We can deal with this matter some other time.'

As Carter held open the door to show her out, Prue stepped up to her brother with anger etched into every line of her lovely face. 'What on earth is happening to you? You're turning into a real bully, just like Papa. You've no right to treat dear Brenda in this cruel fashion.'

'I can do what I damn well please. *I'm* in charge here, not *you*! And we're all aware of your love of rebellion. This is no longer even your home, as you chose to occupy one of the cottages we should be letting out to a tenant.'

'Thank goodness I did, since I have every right to my independence and not be ruled by a tyrant like you. Like me, Brenda is a widow and she too has rights, namely to see her late husband's will.' And smartly spinning on her heel, Prue stalked out of the room in the wake of her friend.

They met up some ten minutes later in the kitchen where Brenda was putting on her coat, hat and scarf. Carter the butler fetched her brown suitcase and Mrs Harding quickly packed some food into a paper bag for her journey.

'You surely don't have to leave this very minute,' Prue said.

'I'm afraid that's what I've been instructed to do. Don't worry, Carter is taking me to the station and I'm sure there'll be a train along soon. I'll be able to stay with Cathie in Castlefield. If not, I'll sleep in the waiting room,'

Brenda assured her. Wrapping her arms about her friend as they said goodbye at the kitchen door, Prue whispered in her ear: 'Fairhurst and Emmerson is the firm of solicitors used by the family. You'll find them in John Dalton Street. Do remember you are welcome to come and stay with me in my little cottage any time you like. Please do, lovey.'

Nine

Watching from the dining-room window as the girl was driven away by Carter at dusk, a wave of guilt washed over Hugh. Where on earth would she go at this time of night? Had he become so torn by personal anguish that he'd ceased to show any concern for others? Had he done the wrong thing, he wondered, by being so dismissive towards her? He surely had the right to protect the family's future, although admittedly he'd been in something of a state on the day she'd arrived, having only recently buried his beloved fiancée.

But then nothing seemed to be going right these days. He felt beset by problems.

As if he didn't have enough family issues to deal with, he'd spent the entire afternoon caught up in a dreadful union meeting doing battle against impossible demands. When he'd refused to comply with his workers' requests, a strike had been called and they'd all walked out. They were objecting to everything: the number of hours they worked, the level of their pay, the shortage of staff and even the limited time allowed for a tea break, assuming there was any tea available. Had they forgotten there was a war on?

There'd been a considerable growth in trade unions and strikes, workers unwilling to put up with difficult conditions, many of them obstinate women, almost as if they possessed more rights than soldiers.

Men had gone to fight while women had taken on their work. This had, of course, given them a huge sense of independence, which would soon come to an end once the war was over and the fighting men returned home. There were some tasks, such as management, Hugh was still reluctant to offer them. Yet male managers were hard to find, so all responsibility fell entirely upon him.

Now, despite having more bills to pay and higher wages to find, the factory was at a stand still. The bank, too, had put a stop upon any more loans to help tide him over. No wonder he frequently lost his temper whenever creditors and employees bitterly complained, let alone stupid girls with no morals making claims upon his brother's inheritance. People constantly seemed to be making demands upon him. Did they imagine he was the richest man in the kingdom?

*

'What on earth possessed you to defend that chit of a girl?' Melissa truculently remarked. She'd tripped across the kitchen garden the following afternoon in her high heels to present her younger sister with a mug of Camp coffee, wishing to take the opportunity to give her a good telling off, as she so liked to do. 'You never think things through properly, just follow your heart and not your head.'

'Not a bad policy,' Prue said with a wry smile as she took a grateful sip. 'Brenda is my friend, has been from when she first came to work here, so why would I not be fond of her?'

Her mind flew back to the day they'd met, making her smile at the memory of how Brenda had chased and stalked the hens one evening, pounced and dashed about in an attempt to grab them and shoo the little creatures into their hut. Tripping over a bunch of flapping hens she'd fallen flat in the mud, then watched in amazement as they'd formed an orderly queue in their correct pecking order, hopped through the pop hole of the hen hut and settled on to their perches for the night. It was then that she'd heard old Joe laughing his head off.

'They know what they're doing better than thee, lass,' he'd said with a chuckle as he'd helped to pull her out of the muddy mess.

'Oh, how clever they are. I didn't know they could do that, having lived in a city all my life. Thank you.'

'You're welcome, lass,' and he'd walked away still chuckling.

Laughing too, Prue had gone to show Brenda how to lock the hut doors with a padlock. 'That was very brave of you, not to cry when you fell.'

'I think I've a lot to learn,' Brenda had woefully remarked.

'Well, I've learned a lot from old Joe too, not only about hens but also sheep and cows. Best of all, how to grow fruit and vegetables, which is what I love doing most.'

'I'm not even as good at cooking as I'd thought, or not according to Mrs Harding. So I've a lot to learn from her too,' Brenda had admitted.

'Don't worry, you'll get there. And Joe will help. He's worked on our farm for most of his life, ever since he was a boy of fourteen.'

Now the old man was crusty and bent, his face brown and lined as a leaf, his small frame battered by wind and weather. Prue still felt a great fondness for him, as if he were her grandfather, having always felt much closer to him than her domineering father. Fortunately, the responsibility for the farm had been left in old Joe's hands, and Hugh's, of course. Although how her brother was going to manage to run both farm and biscuit factory in future, Prue really had no idea. She did not envy the pressure placed upon him, which seemed to be stressing him out.

Turning to smile now at her equally bossy sister, Prue stoutly stuck to the defence of her friend. 'I'm sure Brenda *was* married to our Jack.'

'We have only her word for that.'

'Hopefully that situation will change, once she has spoken to the family solicitor and he's recovered the necessary documentation. Then you and Hugh will have to accept the truth.'

'Don't be silly,' Melissa snapped. 'How can she ever get back papers that don't exist? No wonder she claims that the alleged son of our darling late brother is lost. She's a confidence trickster, hell-bent on defrauding us.

Fortunately, Hugh and I made a point of not revealing the solicitor's name.'

'Well, *I* did,' Prue said with a big grin. 'Someone needed to, and since you two were busily condemning her for all manner of atrocities, finding her guilty without trial, I stepped in to help.'

'You bloody idiot,' said Melissa, hot with anger. 'Why do you never think things through properly? Don't you realise our family is nowhere near as wealthy as we were before the war, so we have to hang on to every penny we've got?'

'Oh, really?' Prue said with a scornful smile. 'And there was me thinking you'd hopped off to live in London just so you could more regularly visit Harrods to indulge yourself using your allowance.'

'Damn you, I am entitled to some fun, and more importantly, my children deserve their heritage to remain safe, particularly Ross.' Glancing round, she spotted her small son splashing about in a puddle, getting himself soaking wet. 'Oh no, the stupid boy.'

Prue laughed. 'He's just having fun.'

Melissa wagged a furious finger inches from her sister's face. 'I warn you that if Fairhurst hands over any money to that chit of a girl, this family will be in serious difficulties, which will be all your fault. And we all know what a defiant little idiot you are.' Spinning around in her high heels she almost tripped over a row of rhubarb. Then grabbing her son by the collar, she dragged him into the house.

'What an unfeeling family I have,' Prue said with a sigh

to the hens as she began to count them. She did this each evening to make sure none had gone missing, been attacked by a fox or become lost as they happily meandered about the farm. They needed to be safe, as did everyone in this frightening world. Her heart went out to poor Brenda if she really had lost her son. As a mother herself, why couldn't Melissa feel some sympathy for her too? There were times when it felt as if her sister was worse than a fox, always keen to bite someone.

Prue had to admit that she did sometimes make hasty decisions, generally out of affection and sympathy, or to stubbornly prove she could please herself as to what she did in life. Which was perhaps why she'd rushed into marriage without proper thought.

Watching the hens line up to pop into the hen hut, the memory of how she first met Cecil Weston came back to her. It was at a dance at the local co-operative rooms. He was tall with dark, wavy hair, really quite good looking. 'He's a bit of all right,' she'd said to her friend. Something in the way he'd looked at her had lit a spark within her and she'd happily slipped into his arms to dance the entire evening with him. After that they would secretly meet to go for walks and kiss in the woodlands, and being young and inexperienced, Prue had loved the attention he was giving her. Within weeks he was called up, and freely admitted he felt filled with fear.

'Will you write to me every day?'

'Of course,' Prue promised.

He'd gladly agreed to come but it proved to be a total disaster. Her father had instantly set about questioning him about his income, family and place in society, making it very clear he was unimpressed to discover he was a mere mechanic at a local factory. 'So you're working class,' Sir Randolph had dismissively remarked. Not at all the kind of husband with money and high ranking he'd planned for Prue to marry.

As they walked out together later that afternoon, she'd apologised to Cecil for her father's attitude. Smiling, he'd pulled her into his arms and kissed her with even greater passion. 'My parents are equally neglectful. They don't care a jot about what I think or wish to do. Marry me, darling. I need to know I'm not alone in the world; that someone cares about me.'

Prue had felt every sympathy with that sentiment, since Sir Randolph did not consider her to be as important as her brothers, or as glamorous or clever as her sister. And she certainly had absolutely no intention of being married off to some rich idiot even more controlling than her father. 'Why not?' she'd thought.

Being only eighteen at the time, she'd needed her parent's permission, which Prue was only too aware she'd never get, so they'd eloped to Gretna Green. Sadly, within days she'd realised Cecil was more obsessed with himself and his own safety, not her. He hadn't even been very exciting in bed. It had almost been a relief when he'd left for army training and was then sent overseas, even though she'd had to return home as she'd nowhere else to live.

Prue had promised herself never to make such impetuous decisions ever again.

Yet perhaps being impulsive and a bit reckless was a part of her she found hard to repress. Now, Prue felt a nudge of regret at admitting to Melissa what she'd told Brenda. Perhaps she should have remained silent. Would her arrogant sister now make even more problems for her dear friend? She did hope not.

*

Brenda stayed at first with her old school friend, Cathie, and quickly found a job working side by side with her at the local rubber factory, which produced tyres for motor cars, army vehicles and trucks. Then she found a flat to rent in Castlefield, overlooking the canal. It was quite small and shabby, with two tiny bedrooms, one nothing more than an empty box room; a combined kitchenette and living area, and a small bathroom. It was sparsely furnished with the odd chair, no wardrobe or set of drawers, but did possess one comfy bed. Here at least was somewhere to rest and lay her head in peace and tranquillity. She felt safe, at last.

The moment came when Brenda decided it was time to speak to the family solicitor. She found the office in John Dalton Street, as Prue had said. Staring at the gold lettering, *Fairhurst and Emmerson—Solicitors*, on the glass panel of the office door, she summoned up her courage and stepped into the dusty and dim interior. She asked the young woman tapping away at a typewriter if she might speak with a solicitor.

'Do you have an appointment?'

'I'm afraid not.'

'Both gentlemen are very busy people. Whom do you wish to speak to, and about what?'

'I really don't mind, but it's a private matter,' Brenda said, feeling slightly flustered and out of her depth.

Reaching for the office diary, the young lady made an appointment for her the following evening, soon after Brenda finished work at six o'clock, with Mr Fairhurst. Feeling highly relieved Brenda walked away, heart racing, but then spent a sleepless night worrying over how much she should tell.

Sitting in the solicitor's office the next evening, hands clasped nervously in her lap, and breathing in the scent of dusty law books, every word Brenda had planned to say went out of her head. Perhaps the blank expression of disinterest in the solicitor's faded brown eyes as he shuffled papers about on his desk was putting her off. His ears were large, rather like a dog's, sticking out from an angular-shaped head, a frown creasing his bushy eyebrows. Brenda knew she would not find it easy to reveal the traumas she'd suffered to a complete stranger, and could but hope he didn't ask too many questions.

Steepling his fingers and propping them against his wide mouth, he leaned back in his chair to stare at her. 'So what is your problem, Miss-er—um—Stuart?'

'*Mrs* Stuart,' Brenda corrected him, presenting him with

the basic facts of her short married life, without attempting to go into too much detail. 'I believe my late husband did send you a copy of his will.'

The fingers tapped and the frown deepened as if he was struggling to capture a wayward memory. 'Ah, yes,' he said at last, and calling upon his secretary, he instructed her to locate the will in the archives. Some long moments later she bustled back in to hand it over to him, the document looking far more formal than the paper Jack had posted. Putting on his spectacles he flicked through page after page, and began to silently read it.

Brenda was instantly irritated that she was not presented with a copy, or told what it said, but carefully held her annoyance in check as she awaited his response. At last he set the document down on the desk, clasping his hands upon it. 'Master Jack did leave you a sum of money, quite small, but then the family is not as well endowed with cash as it once was.'

Taking a quick swallow in her dry mouth and thinking of her precious son, Brenda asked, 'How small?'

Glancing again at the will, he pursed his wide lips. 'It would be a certain percentage, possibly amounting to around five hundred pounds.'

'Oh, my word, that's not small at all. Amazing!'

'I would, of course, need proof of your wedding before any money could be granted to you.'

Goodness, had her brother-in-law already warned this man not to believe a word she said? Or was this a legal requirement? 'I assume you are speaking of a marriage certificate?'

'Indeed.' He gazed upon her again with bland indifference, his fingers tapping together.

'I was hoping that you could help me with this problem,' Brenda said, and went on to explain where and when they had married at the Eglise Saint Roch in November 1939, and how she had come to lose all her papers a year later when arrested. 'I have written to the priest there, but had no reply. Possibly you'll need to contact someone in authority in the Catholic church, or the city hall. I've really no idea how to resolve the matter.'

'We'll do what we can,' he said with a resigned sniff. 'Although with the war still going on, it won't be easy, even assuming what you say to be true.'

'It most certainly *is* true. I'm not expecting a penny for myself, but my son surely has that right.'

'You have a son?'

'I do.'

The solicitor's interest perked up at this news, and he glanced again at the will. 'Ah, well, Master Jack has left his portion of shares in the business to be divided between you and any children you may have.'

Brenda stared at him in stunned disbelief. This was the last thing she'd expected. 'Shares in the family business? Oh, my goodness, I can't believe it! So darling Tommy will have a future, after all, once I find him.'

Now he frowned at her. '*Find* him?'

Brenda told him all about her missing child and how she'd come to lose him, her heart slowly pounding as she did so. 'I also need some assistance to locate the address of Camille's cousin, Adèle Rouanet, as I'm hoping he is still with her, now that dear Camille is sadly departed.'

His gaze softened with sympathy as he studied the sadness haunting her brown eyes. 'I suggest you give all the details to my secretary, Miss Dobson. She can then apply to the authorities in Paris for the necessary paperwork, and make suitable enquiries to discover the address of this lady.'

'Thank you so much, sir. You've been most helpful.' Shaking his hand with vigour and gratitude, Brenda hurried off to speak to the young lady in question with hope in her heart.

But once back in the flat, Brenda still felt that a part of her was missing, as if someone had reached behind her breast-bone and wrenched out her heart. All she could do was try to keep herself fully occupied and not dwell upon her loss, filling her days with activity. She would slip from high optimism to dismal depression from one day to the next, as if tumbling once more into that deep dark pit. It did occasionally cross her mind that there might be similarities between her own situation and that of her mother. Then she would remind herself that she had *not* deliberately abandoned Tommy. She'd left him in a safe pair of hands when finding herself faced with a horrific situation, and fervently believed she would find him one day.

She spent every evening after work writing letters to any friend or contact she could think of, as well as various family members suggested by Prue, asking them to help find Tommy and Adèle. It felt good to be back in her home city, even if a part of her heart was still in France, missing her son.

Ten

If they'd been hoping for warmth and comfort on arrival, reality soon kicked in. 'My lord, what a filthy mess. Don't take off a single item of clothing, or we'll freeze to death,' Emma warned, as they were shown into a shabby attic-type room at the top of the building which stank almost as badly as the train. There were no beds for them to sleep on, merely straw-filled mattresses with a single army blanket. Not even removing her glamorous fur coat, Emma lay down, closed her lovely blue eyes and was almost instantly asleep.

Equally exhausted after the long journey, Brenda fell on to the palliasse also fully clothed, gazing around the grim room in horror. There were bugs and vermin everywhere, brown marks on the walls she preferred not to investigate, and one small wood-burning stove puffing out more smoke than heat, as there was very little fuel in it. Neither was there any hot water to wash in, just one cold tap standing in a corner next to a bucket evidently meant for them to pee in. The place stank of faeces, decaying flesh and vomit, even though there were lavatories outside in the yard.

At supper that evening they queued for ages to receive a small bowl of soup containing what might have been a few flecks of barley, although she couldn't be certain. Nor was it any better the next morning when they were woken at 7.30 and offered nothing more than bread and water for breakfast.

The food was generally boringly monotonous, mainly comprising soup, stewed beans or mangy potatoes. Occasionally there might be a few scraps of tough horse-meat included. In the evenings they were again given a slice of bread, this time with jam or cheese, frequently green with mould. As a result of the foul quality of the food, diarrhoea and malnutrition became all too common.

From the very first day they spent hours cleaning the filthy room and washing the few clothes they'd brought with them in a horse trough in the courtyard. And emptying the bucket, which was never a pleasant task.

'We're also ordered to clean and empty the lavatories twice a day, and sweep away the snow,' Emma told her, cringing in disgust.

'At least that way we know they too are clean,' Brenda said as consolation.

These tasks and many others became a regular routine. In the afternoons they would take some exercise, play games, or sports, or even dance to help keep their spirits up. Lights had to be out by nine.

Brenda's chief concern was missing her darling Tommy.

How she ached to hold him in her arms again. Her periods had stopped, which was almost a relief, but milk continued to leak from her breasts for some weeks, until the lack of food resolved that problem too. Day and night she carried in her head the image of his baby-blue gaze locked onto hers as he suckled. She could see the flutter of his eyelashes, feel the touch of his tiny fingers, and smell the sweet tang of milk and talcum powder on his soft skin. She felt a desperate need to know that he was well.

Letters could be sent to family, although they had to be kept brief and with no mention of the war, or where they were being held. Even then censorship was so strict that many sections of a letter were blacked out, which meant the ones sent could only state: 'I am fine and well.' No other information was permitted, save for comments on the weather.

But how would Camille know where she was being held? And how could Brenda contact the two cousins without an address? She wrote to every neighbour she could think of in Paris, including the boulangerie where she used to buy their bread, asking if they knew where Madame Stuart was now living.

Emma was equally concerned about her husband, and frequently wrote to her parents in England, hoping they might have heard from him. The two friends would take turns to queue up at the office each morning, hoping for replies, but it took months before Emma heard back from them, no doubt because some letters got lost.

Brenda received no response at all to any of her letters.

Pain filled her heart and soul as weeks and months slid by and still she heard nothing, causing yet more sleep problems, heart palpitations and depression. 'What am I going to do? How can I find my child once I'm allowed out of here?' she would wail, and Emma would give her a comforting hug.

'Think of all the poor infants who have died here already, from being malnourished or picking up some dreadful disease or other. At least your son will be safe and well.'

Brenda reminded herself of that fact constantly, which did help a little. But she longed to know whether the two cousins were safely settled in the Loire Valley. And if so, where?

*

The war trundled remorselessly on and the two friends spent the next two years suffering near starvation and enduring a most difficult time. Brenda was still grieving for her husband as well as badly missing her child, even though she was deeply grateful for Camille and Adèle's care of him. Having been brought up in an orphanage, she found that she coped better than most of the women. She'd also made a private resolve following her recent traumas, to keep busy and concentrate upon dealing with whatever was going on in life now, not allowing herself to dwell on the past. She certainly made fewer complaints than her new friend, Emma. Being a smart girl from a fairly wealthy family, she hated being so confined and constantly fretted and made objections to the sorry state of the place. And there were still a great many problems.

'Why is it that now food parcels have eventually started to be delivered from the Red Cross, we don't always receive them? I think these bloody German guards must nick them.'

Feeling starving hungry, Emma handed over one of her beautiful diamond rings to buy one of these food parcels back off the guards. The women were delighted to find it contained powdered milk, corned beef, Spam and cigarettes, which she happily shared between them all. It was such a relief to at last have tasty food that she did this time and time again until she had no more rings, trinkets or possessions of any sort to use by way of payment. Not even enough to buy jam or marmalade.

Grateful as she was for Emma's generosity, Brenda felt thankful her own ring was still safe with Camille.

Hot showers eventually became available, if only twice a month, except when the water had been switched off, which it frequently was. Finding enough fuel to keep them warm also became increasingly difficult, and the freezing cold would bring on coughs and colds. Brenda suffered frequently from bouts of influenza, always anxious it might turn into pneumonia, as happened with several of the women.

'We need to get out of here,' Emma would mutter, particularly when someone had died of hypothermia, dysentery or some other dreadful disease. 'Perhaps we can persuade the guards to let us take a walk outside on occasion, in order to keep fit. If they did, we could then do a runner.'

Brenda gave a wry laugh. 'They'd never allow that. Women internees are viewed as enemies. Besides, I doubt

I'd have the courage or energy to try. We have no choice but to endure whatever starvation and misery is thrown at us, although I agree they've no right to treat us like this. We aren't criminals, nor were we involved in fighting the war. This is all about bloody revenge.'

'I know, honey, but it would be far too dangerous to complain to the Kommandant. We might find ourselves transported to a harsher prison and subjected to torture, or even executed,' Emma admitted, scratching one of the itchy bites on her arm. 'Though I'm sorely tempted to tell him exactly what I think of their treatment of us.'

Brenda shivered, from fear as much as the cold. 'Don't take the risk. Far too terrifying a prospect.'

Visiting the lavatories in the snow-covered courtyard was always a problem and deeply embarrassing, as they were little more than open trenches with no doors, in full view of the guards. Going at night was not recommended as rats would be rabid in the stinking sewers. As dusk fell, the women would queue and take their turn before retiring to bed.

One evening in autumn 1942, Brenda was last in line, as she'd found herself vomiting in the bucket. Whether that was caused by the flu or the dreadful fish stew they'd been given for dinner, she had no idea. Fearing she might be sick again, she waited her turn with some impatience. Fortunately, by the time she was able to relieve herself, her stomach seemed to be settling. Thankfully she was not developing diarrhoea, which was another worry.

It was as she emerged from the lavatory area to step

around the puddles filling the courtyard as a result of the pouring rain, that a dark figure suddenly appeared before her. 'Hello, my beauty.' The voice was flat and gravelled, sounding very German despite speaking in French.

Making no comment, Brenda took a quick jump to one side to avoid him.

'Don't attempt to run away, girl,' he growled, grasping her arm. 'If you don't comply with what I want, I shall tell the Kommandant that you attempted to escape and I managed to stop you. He would then move you to a far more secure prison, and you know what could happen to you there.'

'Please don't do that,' she begged, but he simply laughed.

'Then let me have you,' he said, pushing her back against the wall.

With no one around to save her, Brenda made a valiant attempt to escape by giving him a shove. Laughing out loud, he grabbed her by the shoulders and knocked her flat. Smirking with pleasure, he pinned her down on the wet earth, holding her firmly with one arm across her neck. The pressure nearly choked her, cancelling out her small whimpers of protest. Unable to move or escape, Brenda gritted her teeth, making not a sound as he yanked up her skirt and thrust himself into her, pounding so hard the pain was horrendous. Somewhere in the courtyard behind him she could hear snorts of laughter from his colleagues as they watched. The moment he grunted and released her, terrified his comrades might decide to join in the game and do the same to her, Brenda leaped up and flew up the stairs as if the devil was yet again on her tail. Only this time he'd won.

Falling into bed, she sank her face into the straw palliasse in a valiant attempt to smother the sound of her weeping. This was not uncommon in a room packed with distressed women and children. As if she hadn't suffered enough trauma during this blasted war, now she'd been forced to endure something even worse.

Brenda scrubbed every part of herself, inside and out, but was still suffering from chronic pain and felt as if she'd fallen back into that dark pit. Would she ever be free to live a normal, happy life? If so, Brenda surmised she'd never want a man to touch her ever again. Just the memory of the stink of that brute, let alone his violation of her, had left her traumatised.

She felt the need to constantly assure herself that she'd done nothing wrong, just visited the lavatory alone because of the sickness she'd been suffering from. But that cruel bastard had assaulted her out of pure hatred and a desire to prove his power over her. How many other women had he attacked? She could well understand how such incidents were rarely spoken of. Just getting through the routine of a normal day at this camp was stressful enough when a part of you felt locked and caged in a disturbing world.

Eleven

1944

A day or two later Hugh was taking a brisk walk to give himself the opportunity to clear his head with some fresh air and hopefully calm himself down. Perhaps then he could approach the problems he was facing with more ease. He could remember how, before the war, he would walk for miles every weekend over the hills, following trails that were part of the Pennine Way that ran from Derbyshire to the Scottish Borders, along the beautiful backbone of England. Not that he'd ever walked that far, but would love to one day. He enjoyed exploring these moors, as well as walking alongside local streams, rivers, and the Huddersfield canal. Now all the fun seemed to have gone out of his life.

As the sun lit the sky with a pink haze of dawn, he gazed out upon the crisp shards of bracken covering the hillside, as silent as ever save for the carolling of a lone blackbird. But beyond this wonderful world lay another one entirely fraught with difficulties, not least because of this dreadful war.

He was feeling even more highly irritated and impatient than usual. If he could think of a way to improve the situation the company was in he would do so, but a part of him really didn't care. He'd never been kept properly informed about the state of the business, which was in a far worse situation than he'd realised. As a consequence, Hugh had completely lost interest in the estate and the business.

But then he'd grown up with a father who strongly disapproved of his children expressing their feelings or opinions. They were expected to do as they were told, never permitted to take responsibility for anything in their lives. Any display of emotion or an opinion of their own would be ignored and dismissed. It rarely paid to disagree with Sir Randolph. His reaction could be devastating, as Jack had sadly discovered. But then they'd never received the love they deserved from him, or developed any respect for their father as a result.

Hugh had hated the way his father had treated his lovely wife too. Mama had been absolutely adorable, a wonderful mother. No wonder she'd finally left her husband. Too many people had resented or even been afraid of Sir Randolph; few showing any liking for him, despite his title. Being this arrogant man's son, that could well be the reason the workers were so against him. Yet Hugh really had no wish to replicate his father's attitude, so he should try to calm himself.

The solution to his problems did not lie in bullying or harassing others. He'd ranted on about the war and the effect it was having upon business at some length to union members, pointing out they should feel relieved that their factory had not been bombed, as so many had. But it had done no good at all. They hadn't even properly listened. Shortages might present difficulties but at least rationing prevented the greedy rich from buying all the best food. The union did eventually acknowledge that fact, but after hours of dispute Hugh accepted defeat and resolved the strike by promising to look again at wages and the daily work routine.

Hugh told himself he needed to treat people with more respect in order to build better relationships, achieve new goals, and lead a fuller, more satisfying life. Learning to control his anger caused by all the traumas he was facing was not, however, proving to be easy. He could barely sleep or eat, suffered badly from insomnia and spent much of each night pacing the floor in despair. Was this a form of depression?

Yet people would be more inclined to listen to him and accommodate his needs if he behaved in a more respectful manner towards them. He had no control over the horrors war created, nor could he easily resolve the difficulties the business was in, but surely he *could* control how he reacted to these problems. He made a private vow to attempt to improve his patience and mask the sense of insecurity, hurt and vulnerability created in him by the war and his over-powering father.

Turning back down the track to the farm, he waved at old Joe as he appeared leading the horse and cart out into the farmyard. Dressed in a suit, collar and tie, his gaiters polished to perfection, he looked remarkably smart, as he always did when doing the morning milk round. Hugh went over to help him lift the cans into the back of the cart.

'Morning, sir.'

'Morning, Joe. How are you?'

'Fair to middling.'

Hugh smiled, knowing this was his usual response. The old man had worked on this land for the last fifty years or more, and never complained of the long hours he spent labouring over seven days a week. And finding people to help was not easy. Trowbridge Hall farm was a long walk from Uppermill, Mossley, Greenfield and other local villages, although a few youngsters would gladly cycle over from Trowbridge itself, in order to earn a bit of money at harvest time. Wages for farm hands too had gone up. The Land Girls had made a very valuable contribution, despite it being the first experience of agricultural work for many of them. But now they'd moved on elsewhere and the farm had been left with just one PoW. Yet farmers were being asked to produce more and more food with fewer workers, and food for pigs, cows and poultry was increasingly scarce.

Sadly, Hugh had little time to help on the farm these days, largely finding himself confined to the office worrying over how to bring the business back into profit. He missed working on the land, but what was it he wanted out of life? If only he could decide. Everything was becoming irritatingly difficult.

Old Joe cleared his throat. 'We've been using the Bamford mowing machine ever since we bought it back in the early thirties, but in view of all the extra sections of land we've had to turn over to food production and now have to plough, we should really buy a tractor.'

'I believe you've mentioned this before, Joe.'

'Aye, I have. Hiring a tractor isn't always easy, and using our Dobbin here to pull the Bamford mower does work, but it's slow.'

Hugh sighed at yet another demand upon him, but could see no way to refuse this request, bearing in mind farmers were forced to comply with an endlessly growing list of regulations. The government had taken complete control of the economy and massive debts had accrued as a result. How they would ever recover from this war didn't bear thinking about. The plough was now something of a decrepit mess. Old Joe frequently attempted to borrow a tractor from neighbouring farmers, but wasn't always able to do so when they needed it themselves. And this was a request Hugh had ignored for far too long.

'Very well, Joe, I'll look into it.'

'Thank you, sir. Every scrap of wasteland and even flower gardens might well have been turned into vegetable plots. I know backyards are alive with chickens, rabbits and the odd pig, largely fed on scraps. Tomatoes are grown in window boxes and even childer at school are Digging for Victory. But we still provide the lamb, milk, cheese and best food available. That's our duty.'

Hugh supposed he should consider himself fortunate to have this man working for him, as well as access to such good food. 'It is indeed, Joe. Have a good day.'

'And you too, sir,' he said, tipping his cap with respect.

Hugh watched him climb up on to the cart and flick the horse into action, feeling a warmth inside himself at last. Things might gradually improve.

But how to handle the squabbles within the family would not be easy either. Prue seemed to resent every aspect of life at the Hall, insisting on working like a slave and living in a humble cottage. As for Melissa, she was a most difficult woman, her head filled with her own self-importance. It was all very well to make these promises to remain calm and supportive towards everyone, but carrying that out effectively with his sisters was another matter entirely.

*

Melissa wasted no time in calling at the solicitor's office, driving to Manchester in her smart grey Humber car. 'Ah, Miss Dobson, I'm hoping you may be able to help me,' she said, as she was shown into the secretary's office.

The young woman instantly leapt to her feet to draw up a chair for her high-class visitor. 'What is it you require, milady?'

Melissa smiled. How she loved to be spoken to with such respect, although strictly speaking she was not entitled to be so addressed not being the daughter of an earl or a duke. Her father had been granted a knighthood simply for his success as a businessman and farmer. 'I believe you have been visited by a girl claiming to be my sister-in-law. I'm sure she made her case sound most convincing, but you need to be aware that neither my brother nor I believe a word she says. She is making this claim out of greed, which will rob my children of their inheritance.'

Mary Dobson's cheeks flushed crimson. 'Oh dear, but I've already written to the church where she says they were married, and to the mayor of Paris, hoping for help to find your Mama's cousin, whom she claims to be in charge of her son.'

'Have you indeed? Well, that is another issue. This child may be *her* son, but there is no proof he is my *brother's*, as Jack died some time before he was born.'

'Oh dear! How long, exactly?'

'Long enough to prove this chit of a girl to be a liar and a fraud,' Melissa snapped. 'Please ensure that any response you receive is transmitted directly to me, and not to that little madam. Do I make myself clear?'

The young secretary was briskly nodding, clearly fearful of causing offence to one of their most valued clients. 'I had no idea there was such a problem,' she said. 'But I most certainly will keep you fully informed, milady.'

Melissa rose to her feet. 'Excellent. I look forward to hearing from you. Good day.' Having made her point, she elegantly strolled away, returned to her car and drove to the Midlands Hotel for lunch. She felt really pleased with herself, determined to do everything necessary to prevent that scraggy little whore from taking a penny of their money, let alone probing into family matters over which she had no rights.

*

'I have to say that the way you treated Jack's widow was quite appalling.' Prue confronted her stern-faced brother with defiance strong in her heart. Despite their frequent disputes of late she'd always been fond of him, as at heart he was a kind and caring man, if not as broad minded or patient as Jack had been. When she was a young girl he'd walk her to school, taught her how to ride a pony, and even helped with her homework, as he was much better at arithmetic than she ever was. But his behaviour recently had considerably deteriorated. The sight of him so pale-faced and with bags under his eyes filled her with concern.

Tossing aside his pen, Hugh heaved a sigh. 'Let us not go into that issue all over again. It is perfectly reasonable to demand that she provide the necessary proof before she gets a penny off us, or has any say over the business.'

'Ah, so that's your major concern, is it? Has Jack left her some shares?'

'Not that I am aware of, why would he? Yet she may consider she deserves that too, since she's a madam of the first quarter.'

'Oh, for goodness' sake, Brenda is a lovely young woman with a kind heart. Stop being such an arrogant bully. What has happened to you, Hugh?'

'Life!' he growled.

Wrapping her arms about him, Prue gave him a hug. 'I know, but Brenda too has suffered from this war and a difficult childhood. She needs our help. Please do find it in your heart to be a little more tolerant and forgiving.'

For a moment his face softened as he looked up at her. 'I

was coming round to that conclusion until Melissa related what Mama had said about the girl working in a brothel.'

'You've no proof of that either,' Prue calmly pointed out.

'The subject is closed,' he coldly informed her. 'Now, unless you have some other reason to be here, I have work to do. As, no doubt, have you, picking rhubarb or whatever.'

Taking a breath, Prue pulled up a chair to sit beside him. 'There is actually something I need to tell you. I thought you should know that Dino has asked me to marry him, and I have accepted.'

'What! Who is this Dino? Not that bloody PoW?'

'He won't always be a PoW, and it wasn't Dino's fault that he was arrested just for being Italian.'

'You've already made one mistake with a hasty marriage in this blasted war. Why on earth would you risk doing it again?'

'Because I love him.'

'That's what you said the last time, but it wasn't strictly true, was it? You were merely being impulsive and rebellious.'

'I admit, I did make a mistake. But this is different. We truly love each other, and that's all that matters. We've felt this way ever since the moment we first met and his nationality is not an issue between us. Once the war is over and Dino is released, we will acquire a special licence and get married.'

'You have no right to do such a thing without my permission,' he growled.

'Don't be ridiculous.' The furious way he was regarding

her as he sat at her father's desk made Prue feel almost as if she were a young girl facing yet another stormy lecture. 'Why would I have to ask your permission? How many times must I remind you that I'm a widow and over twenty-one, a grown woman?'

'I'm the one who provides you with a home and income,' he reminded her, stabbing himself in the chest with his thumb. 'You never think things through properly, too easily moved by a few soft words or someone's needs. Would this fellow manage to get a job, as well as somewhere for you to live? Can he look after you properly? And why should I not damn well object when he's an enemy alien? You should be ashamed of yourself.'

Prue felt again that cloying sense of claustrophobia, the very reason she'd stopped living in the Hall and moved into the cottage, although at the time she'd been escaping from her father's fury over her elopement. Now she didn't react with a burst of anger, only a sigh of resignation. 'I am not in the least ashamed, and he is *not* our enemy. Dino has lived in England for most of his life, and doesn't even speak much Italian.'

'He certainly is according to the government, so you do need to take care. Italy signed a pact to ally itself with Hitler.'

'And has now surrendered to the Allies. But what has any of that to do with Dino? Nor is it anything to do with *you* whom I decide to marry. It's *my* life,' she insisted. 'I'm telling you this now, Hugh, as I thought it would be selfish of us to marry without even offering you an invitation.'

'Fraternisation with enemy aliens is illegal. Can't you see that I'm trying to protect you, Prue? Do listen to what I'm saying.'

Facing her brother with her usual stubborn defiance, she shook her head. 'It will happen the moment Dino is free, which could be sooner than you think, as he applied for repatriation some time ago.'

'I could always have the fellow sent back to that camp in the Isle of Man.'

The condemnation written in his face chilled her. 'That would not work. A large number of internees have already been repatriated, particularly those like Dino who are not pro-Nazi. Hundreds are now free, and he will be too soon. We've written again to the Commander in charge of the camps, making that request. But if you throw him out, then I'll go with him, just as Brenda did with dear Jack when our father packed him off to France. I'd be quite happy to live somewhere close to Dino on the island. May I also suggest it would be wiser for you not to follow in our father's footsteps. You are my dear brother, so why not show some concern about my happiness?'

'That is exactly what I am doing. Marriage is never easy, as you know from that of our parents, let alone the one that you stupidly rushed into. Had the poor chap not lost his life in the war, you would have regretted it for the rest of your life. So how do you know this one will work any better? It could be a total disaster.'

The bitterness in his tone cut right to the heart of her. 'So you don't care about anyone's feelings but your own?

No doubt you wish me to marry money, as did Papa. I'm sure Melissa would agree with you there, although she might be deeply disappointed if she was not invited to my wedding. She does love any excuse to buy herself a new outfit and show herself off. Isn't glamour and money all she cares about too?' Prue caustically commented.

'Don't talk nonsense. Neither Melissa nor I would have any wish to attend such a wedding. This man is *not* for you.'

A telling silence followed these harsh words, one which went on far too long until Prue felt calm enough to break it. Reaching out, she stroked his hand as his fingers angrily drummed upon the desk. 'I can understand that losing your would-be bride only weeks away from your own wedding can't be easy, but wouldn't you be prepared to give me away?'

'Never in a million years. Now get back to work and stop talking nonsense.'

She was all too aware that some of the points Hugh was making were perhaps valid, certainly with regard to her first, disastrous marriage. But this one would be entirely different, and Prue felt desperate to put an end to this conversation before she said something she might live to regret. Fighting back tears, she did as she was bid and returned to the greenhouse, leaving him to get on with his paperwork.

Twelve

Brenda worked hard in the weeks and months following, concentrating fully upon her job at the rubber factory, and meeting up regularly with her old school friend, Cathie, for a coffee or snack at Campfield Market. There was still an ongoing barrage of V-1 flying bombs, known as doodle-bugs, and air-raid sirens frequently heard, but the war was at last coming to an end. Ever since D-Day many German armies had surrendered; Rommel had committed suicide; and France had recaptured many of her territories. Peace was expected to be declared any time soon.

Even the blackout had eased a little in towns and cities. On Christmas Eve Brenda visited the local church, which was allowed to set lighted candles next to its stained-glass windows. She then spent Christmas Day alone in her flat, a sad experience. Cathie had invited her to join her family. But as her friend's sister was pregnant, and had lost her beloved husband who'd gone down with his ship in August when it had been sunk by a U-boat, Brenda really did not feel she could cope with such trauma right now.

Always at the back of her mind lay her anxiety over her son. Where was her darling Tommy? She could still hear the sound of him crying whenever he was hungry, feel his chubby little body in her arms and smell the baby soap on his soft skin. What would he be like now that he was so much older? How she wished she knew and could hold him again. Brenda never mentioned him to Cathie, as she still found it far too painful to speak of her loss.

It had taken the best part of a year to find the necessary help and transport to escape through France and Spain, and endure a long and arduous sea voyage in order to return to England. Even longer to search for little Tommy. In the end she'd had to abandon that in the hope he'd already been returned home, which sadly was not the case. Oh, and she missed her beloved husband too.

What a mess her life was in. Hugh might blame her for what happened to Jack, but had his father not thrown them both out simply because they fell in love, he could still be alive. Brenda had few details of the projects Jack had been involved in with the Resistance, but he was a brave and honourable man who did much for the cause. She was so proud of him, which helped her to cope with her grief. She must be brave too, and keep on searching for their son.

Spring slowly dawned and Brenda would frequently choose to walk out along the canal banks for a breath of fresh air to enjoy the sight of primroses and snowdrops, and later the heady scent of garlic flowers and bluebells. She loved watching the boats and barges going about their business. The vast waterways network was such an important part of Manchester, carrying goods all over the country. But Brenda missed the dramatic glory of the Pennines and vowed to return to see Prue sometime soon, as she missed her too.

In April, Adolf Hitler took his own life instead of being prepared to face surrender. Hopes escalated that this would be the beginning of the end, everyone listening to the wireless with growing impatience for the news they'd been awaiting so long. But the phoney peace seemed to linger on almost as long as the phoney war had done years before.

Gritting her teeth with resigned patience, Brenda kept her mind focused on what really mattered to her. Once a week she would visit the solicitors, Fairhurst and Emmerson, and speak to the secretary. The young woman would shake her head, barely lifting her gaze from her typewriter, and calmly inform her that there was no news.

Would they ever find Adèle's address?

'It's taking so long. Is there nothing more you can do?' Brenda begged, all too aware that once they did, she might then have to return to France to fetch Tommy home, although it probably wouldn't be safe to do so until this war was finally over.

'We are doing our best,' the young woman sternly remarked. 'There's really no need for you to keep calling. We'll be in touch if we hear anything.'

'*If*?'

'I mean when,' the secretary said, her cheeks flushing a little in apparent embarrassment.

'I appreciate that even though you are in touch with the

authorities in Paris regarding my paperwork, a response might well not happen until this war does at last end. But have you also contacted the local authorities in Orleans, Tours or Angers? I really have no idea in which part of the Loire Valley Adèle resides, but the authorities there may know something.'

'As I say, Miss Stuart, we will keep you informed.'

'*Mrs* Stuart,' Brenda retorted. As she left, feeling grim with disappointment, she made a private vow to send out more enquiries of her own. Many evacuee children had lost track of their parents too. How would those poor little souls survive if their mum and dad had been killed, or had deserted them? Rumour had it that more than a million Jewish children were now dead. Could darling Tommy have suffered a similar fate? It really didn't bear thinking about.

*

Still in the midst of dealing with his father's probate, Hugh was deeply curious about how much money Jack might have left the young woman claiming to be his widow. She obviously imagined it to be a tidy sum, otherwise why would she make up such nonsense? Not for a moment did he imagine his brother would marry without telling him, let alone leave her a penny from the estate just because he'd enjoyed sleeping with her. Unless they truly were man and wife, of which there was no proof. As the secretary showed him into the solicitor's office, Hugh wondered if he might be able to persuade Fairhurst to show him his brother's will. Surely he had a right to see it? In the meantime, there were more important issues that needed addressing. Taking a seat, he exchanged a few polite words about the weather, then clearing his throat, admitted a grim truth.

'The fact is, Fairhurst, I don't have the necessary funds to pay this exorbitantly high death duty. Unless you can think of some other solution, I am going to have to sell a sizeable chunk of land.'

A frown creased the lawyer's bushy eyebrows. 'I'm sorry to hear that, Mr Stuart. I thought the farm was doing better.'

'Profits have gone up, although these are still hard times, and we've had to invest in a tractor and other new equipment. We're also very dependent upon the government for decisions on prices, and can but hope they won't decide to drop them, as they are still in need of an increase in food production. Nor do I feel able to raise the level of rents, even though the number of tenants has reduced over the years. This huge sum of money demanded upon the death of my father could destroy us. I also have a problem with the biscuit factory, which is not doing at all well.'

The solicitor gave a grunt of a cough. 'Have you considered finding yourself a rich heiress to marry?'

Hugh gave a sardonic little laugh. 'Absolutely not. Those days are long gone. These bloody taxes, based on the value of the property and all our possessions have inflated beyond belief, not taking reality at all into account.'

'Then I agree you have no choice but to find a tenant willing to buy his piece of land. It will, of course, need to be at a favourable price, particularly if his family have occupied it for some considerable time.'

Hugh nodded. 'I do appreciate that and have no intention of over-charging anyone, but it isn't going to be easy to find a resolution.' Getting to his feet, he gave a sigh. 'I merely wished to warn you in the hope you can delay this demand for payment. I'll let you know when a sale takes place.'

'I will do my best,' Mr Fairhurst assured him, rifling through papers on his desk. 'You do realise that if we find the necessary papers for your brother's alleged widow, she will be granted a say on this decision, and even on the business?'

Hugh stared at the solicitor in stunned disbelief. 'Are you telling me that Jack has left this madam shares in the company?'

The solicitor stroked his pointed chin. 'He did indeed. He made a will at the British Embassy when war broke out, fairly basic, but it served his purpose. Of course, the Embassy was closed down once the Nazis occupied France. However, he wisely sent a copy to me.'

'Does that prove they really were married?'

'Not necessarily. Were it ever to come to court, she would need to prove her identity and produce a copy of her marriage certificate. The girl could well be speaking the truth, but we need evidence of that fact.'

'Please let me know, should you ever find it,' Hugh sternly remarked.

'My young lady secretary already has instructions to do that.'

'Then good day to you, Fairhurst.'

'Good day, and good luck, sir.'

*

It was on Monday, 7 May, around 7.30 in the evening, as Brenda was listening to a piano recital on the radio that the BBC interrupted the programme to make a public declaration issued by the Ministry of Information. It stated that the following day was to be treated as Victory-in-Europe Day and would be regarded as a holiday. An official announcement would be broadcast by the Prime Minister at three o'clock. The civil servant went on to say: 'His Majesty the King will broadcast to the people of the British Empire and Commonwealth tomorrow, Tuesday, at 9 p.m.'

Brenda leapt out of her chair to run out into the street, where she met dozens of her neighbours also jumping about with joy and excitement.

'The war is over at last! Germany has surrendered and the Third Reich is defeated!' yelled one old man, and everyone cheered.

The next day, flags and bunting sprang up everywhere like blossom in spring. There were posters of King George VI and Winston Churchill, reminding Brenda of how in France she'd seen so many put up to insult the British. What a relief it was to see these declaring victory. They held a street party, and celebrated by eating all the precious food housewives had been secretly stowing away for exactly this purpose. Then the women picked up their skirts and danced, singing 'I'm Looking Over a Four-Leaf Clover' and 'There's a Long, Long Trail A-Winding'. All popular songs from the First World War, plus many more recent ones including 'We'll Meet Again', finishing with a conga along John Dalton Street through to Albert Square and down Deansgate. What a joy it was.

The whole of Manchester, as well as London and every other city, rang with the sound of music and laughter, pausing only to listen to the King's speech at 9 p.m. Bonfires blazed, fireworks exploded and the lights were on again. Peace was with them at last.

Yet beneath all this excitement, the mood was more sombre as people recalled their losses, some nursing their injuries with tears in their eyes. And as Brenda queued up for a loaf of bread the following morning, not even certain there would be one available, nothing seemed to have changed at all. The war might be over but the pain she was suffering never would be. But whatever she might have to face, she must learn to live with it.

*

Peace having been declared, Prue and Dino decided to join the local celebrations in Trowbridge village. They'd carefully kept their relationship secret until now, confining their meetings to a short stroll in the quiet countryside where no one could see them, holding hands and kissing as they fell in love. But now they felt everything had changed.

'Are you sure this is a good idea?' Dino asked.

'Why would it not be? I've told Hugh about our plans

to marry, and as the war is at last over, you should be free soon.'

She was horrified to find old friends and neighbours shunning her as they walked together down the village street. They were clearly shocked and disapproving to see her accompanied by a prisoner of war, even though the pair of them were careful not to touch each other or hold hands. Prue made a point not to so much as glance or smile at him, dutifully acting as his employer, not his sweetheart. But they must have displayed some evidence of their relationship, as the reaction to their presence together was quite chilling.

'Isn't an English lad good enough for thee?' yelled one woman.

Another ran over and tossed a bowl of washing-up water over her, soaking her to the skin. 'Tha needs to clean theeself,' she said, and spat in Prue's face.

'How dare you fraternise with the enemy when our dads, husbands and sons have been killed by the Germans?' yelled one young mother as she rocked her child in her arms.

'He's Italian, not German.'

'Makes no difference. They let them buggers kill any of our lads they could find, once they'd surrendered to the bloody Nazis.'

The day proved to be a dreadful experience, not a celebration at all. The war was over but fraternising with PoWs was still forbidden.

But in her heart Prue refused to allow anyone to spoil

her happiness. Surely this nonsensical rule would come to an end soon. As they walked slowly home along the riverbank, this time arm in arm, she smiled up into his beloved eyes. 'Listen to the rush of that little waterfall. Isn't it wonderful? Come on, I'm wet through anyway,' she said, pulling off her shoes. Like children in a magical world, they paddled in their bare feet through the fast-flowing waters, loving the tingling spray of icy water on their faces.

Finally tired from their exertions, they climbed out to sit beneath the wide, swaying branches of a sweet chestnut tree.

'I used to sit here as a child to listen to the birds,' she told him. 'Sometimes I would tell them my problems while I gazed over the majesty of these wonderful hills. I love this place, but now things are all going wrong. Should we leave and go and live somewhere else?'

He shook his head. 'You'd miss it terribly.'

'So true. I enjoyed growing up here in these beautiful hills, but my life now is with you.'

'And soon we will be married,' he murmured, pulling her into his arms to kiss her.

How she adored being locked in his embrace, touching, tasting and kissing him. Her pulse beat wildly as he lay her down on the sweet green grass to nestle her between his thighs. Was this the moment she'd always longed for? He was so handsome, and with a lively sense of fun and adventure. What did it matter what other people said about him? He was her strength and she loved him. He was not an enemy at all.

'Why would we wait another day?' she whispered as she scented the intoxicating maleness of him. 'You are the love of my life.'

Thirteen

Days later Prue was surprised to find Dino packing his rucksack early in the afternoon. 'You're not leaving already? Why is that truck parked in the lane? Your transport doesn't normally arrive until six o'clock.'

'I'm being turfed out.'

'Why would anyone do that?' she asked, puzzled. 'Your help is greatly needed on this farm. You aren't saying you've fallen out with my brother, are you?'

He gave a wry smile. 'You could say that. It's true that I've learned a great deal working here: milking cows, ploughing, and many other skills. Let me show you something.' Dino led her across the farmyard and proudly pointed to a drystone wall he'd repaired. Each stone had been slotted into its appointed place as precisely as a jigsaw puzzle. 'It took me the best part of a day, but Hugh came over and told me I'd no right to be working on this alone.'

'Why would he say such a thing?'

'I thought at first it was because he'd discovered my disability, as has happened to me on previous occasions with other employers.'

Prue looked startled. 'What sort of disability?'

'I'm partially blind in one eye.'

'Oh, Dino, I'd no idea. Why didn't you tell me?'

'It's not something I like to reveal as it could result in my losing the job, and I'd no wish to be sent back to camp. Or lose you,' he added with a loving smile. 'Some things don't require perfect sight, the skill for repairing a wall being in a strong pair of hands. But I was wrong. That was not the issue at all.'

Prue frowned. 'Then what is?'

'Our outing together on VE Day. Someone must have told him that I'd accompanied you, and as fraternisation is still against the law, he tipped off the police. I'm now to be sent back to the camp in the Isle of Man, or possibly prison.'

Prue let out a gasp as she stared at him in horror. 'Oh no! Just for taking a walk with me to celebrate peace?' She made no mention of what had happened between them afterwards.

At that moment the local constable, PC Matthews, quietly approached. Touching his brow with a polite tap of his hand, almost like a salute, he gave a sad little nod. 'I'm afraid that is the case, Miss Prudence. This is not my choice, but I'm afraid I must follow the rules. Italian PoWs are permitted to speak to members of the public and accept invitations to visit their homes, but relationships with a young lady are prohibited. Excuse me.' And clipping handcuffs on to Dino's wrists, the policeman led him away.

Utterly devastated, Prue ran after him. 'This is completely wrong. The war is over and he's not an enemy.'

'Will you let my mother know where I am?' Dino

anxiously begged her as he was ushered into the back of the truck.

'I will, and I promise I won't allow my brother to get away with this,' she cried, her heart plummeting with fear as the vehicle drove away.

*

Relations with her brother had become increasingly strained over the last few weeks, and Prue made a vow to stand up to him all the more and do everything she could to get her beloved man released. After all, British soldiers were allowed to marry their German sweethearts, so why couldn't she marry hers, a perfectly innocent Italian PoW?

Bursting into Hugh's office, she slammed the door shut behind her and stood before him, hands on hips, defiance pounding within her. 'How dare you do this to Dino?'

Glancing up to meet the fury of her gaze, Hugh let out a heavy sigh. 'You know full well that fraternisation between prisoners of war and the local population is strictly forbidden in this time of crisis.'

'There is no crisis, the war is over.'

'Have you no sense of morality?' he sternly asked. 'Women are not allowed to involve themselves in undesirable relationships with PoWs. I expected you to behave more respectably. Not only are you bringing shame upon our family, you could well be charged and fined for engaging with the enemy.'

'Oh, that's ridiculous. Dino is a good man, and you were perfectly happy for him to work on our farm.'

'That had nothing to do with me,' he snapped. 'According to the Geneva Convention, officers cannot be forced to do any work but the lower ranks can, which is most certainly what he was.'

'If he's allowed to work on the farm, why could he not join me for the VE Day celebration? That attitude is so unfair. He's killed no one, done nothing wrong.'

'As I pointed out when we spoke of this before, sexual or social encounters with women are against the law,' Hugh coolly reminded her. 'Action had to be taken. Your so-called relationship had to be stopped before you were accused of fraternising with the enemy.'

Tears filled her eyes as she thought of Dino being locked up in prison when he so loved the freedom of the outdoors. 'Lord, I wish the government would lift this stupid ban.'

'It won't happen any time soon, so you'll just have to learn to live with it.'

'I most definitely *won't*,' Prue retorted. 'As a woman I have rights too, and I'll do everything I can to get him released. Then we'll marry as soon as possible.'

Watching her storm off, again slamming the door behind her, Hugh sighed, feeling filled with anguish. Had he done the wrong thing yet again, despite feeling the need to protect Prue?

He seemed to be at odds with both his sisters, if for different reasons. Melissa had made her objections to this Brenda person clear from the start, insisting that she would never accept her as a member of the family or hand over a penny. Admittedly, he too was reluctant to do so, or allow her any say in the running of the business. And not for a moment did he believe she would ever succeed in finding the correct papers.

Yet Fairhurst, the family solicitor, took an entirely different point of view. He'd pointed out that she could well be speaking the truth, and would do his utmost to resolve the issue. There was still no proof her alleged child was Jack's. German soldiers may well have been forbidden from having relationships with women, but according to reports, that was a rule difficult to enforce. So why would that little madam expect riches to be given to her if she really did join a brothel and bestow favours upon her enemy?

A thought occurred to him which brought forth a slight chuckle of amusement. Were she to offer him certain favours, would that tempt him to change his mind? She was, after all, a very attractive young lady.

Hearing a patter of heels clicking across the hall and seeing Melissa enter, his heart sank as he prepared himself for yet another dispute.

*

Prue called at the police station day after day to see Dino, then would speak to the local bobby to argue their case. She also visited the town hall as well as writing to every person she could think of in a valiant attempt to get him released. Sadly, without success. One afternoon when she called, PC Matthews told her Dino had now been returned to a camp in the Isle of Man. She was utterly devastated, but remembering her promise to him, Prue took the next train to Ancoats, determined to speak to his mother. She was also keen to hear more of his family's story.

Walking along Great Ancoats Street, packed with delicatessens selling pasta, the scent of spicy sauces made her feel quite hungry. It was an area known as Little Italy, although there were plenty of Irish living here too. It had always been a thriving community well respected by Mancunians because of the Italians' friendly charm and their skills with music, ice cream and good food. Sadly that had all changed now.

She found the small shop close to the Wharf, the window boarded up. But Prue smiled at a Union Jack hanging from an upstairs window. The family was clearly eager to prove their loyalty to Britain. Knocking on the shop door, she wondered why the business was closed.

The door opened a crack and a small face appeared. 'We not open, sorry.'

Prue smiled. 'I'm a friend of Dino's and he asked me to call. Are you his mum?'

The door swung wide open, revealing a small grey-haired woman standing with her clasped hands pressed to her chest. 'Ah, mamma mia. You knowa my son? Come in, come in.'

Seconds later they were seated together in a small kitchen as Mrs Belloni prepared a cappuccino for them. 'Tell me, how is *caro mio*?' she asked, placing a cup before Prue.

Taking a quick sip of the delicious coffee, Prue gave the

bad news, together with a brief explanation of how they'd been accused of 'fraternising'.

Sympathy focused in the older lady's dark eyes. 'He lovesa you?'

'He does, and I love him. We hope soon to be married, now that this dreadful war is over, although it could take a while. I am aware that your family has suffered badly, but I do hope you will welcome me.'

Giving Prue's hand a little pat, she smiled. 'We do nota blame the British for whata happened. Even when the polis came for *mio marito*, they were most gracious in their questioning. He was asked where he kept his private papers, and if he was a fascist. Then Bartolomeo was handcuffed and taken away to the polis station. I too was taken. We were separated, not knowing where the other was being held.'

'That must have been so hard.'

'*Sì*. The next day Dino too was arrested.' A bleakness entered her dark eyes, and clasping her cup with both hands, she savoured the coffee for some moments before continuing with her story. 'They were both interned in different places without any reason given. The authorities did nota take into account the facta we have lived here for years and are perfectly respectable people. We came from Campania in search of a better life and soon became very much a part of this community. For weeks I heard nothing until *mio marito* wrote to me from the Isle of Man. Later I heard from Dino. He was held at Warth Mill near Bury, sleeping on a camp bed in very bad conditions.'

'He told me once how he was taken to Liverpool, then

across the Irish Sea in the *Lady of Mann*, which they called a Prison Ship, escorted by a naval frigate,' Prue said.

His mother nodded. 'I was released almost at once, but ordered nota to go out of the city. I could nota go more than ten miles from my home. My wireless was taken away and the business closed. I tried to keep it going, but there were too many difficulties. I felt that we were being blamed for our nationality, yet we havea always remained loyal to Britain in this war.' Clenching her fists to her heart, she said, 'If I were a young man, I'd happily fight to destroy Mussolini. As do my other sons. They have botha been regular soldiers for years. Dino, my youngest, would have joined too, but his eyesight nota good, so he was rejected.'

'Dino admitted that problem to me only the other day when he was re-arrested. I did wonder why he'd never told me before.'

'Ah, he isa blind in one eye, but never likes to tell anyone, or they mighta class him as deformed and nota worth employing. He is a proud, hard-working man.'

Prue smiled. Listening to his family's story, she realised how little she had previously known about Dino. Not that it made any difference to her if he suffered from a disability; she still loved him with all her heart. 'He is very good at his job on the farm, and so keen and willing to learn more. What did he do before the war?'

'He trieda different jobs, but in the end worked in the family business doing terrazzo tiling and mosaics.'

'A business that is now closed. How sad. And what about your husband, is he free yet?'

'Bartolomeo was released back in 1942 and has been working for the Home Guard ever since,' she proudly announced. 'Now he isa busy helping to clear up bomb sites. He did try to start the business again but distrust has grown and somebody broke the window, so we boarded it up. He was nota fit enough any more to cope on his own with no one to help him. And there were few orders to be had, now that people had turned against us. Too many innocent Italians have been held in the camps.'

'I believe most PoWs are now being released, so it irritates me all the more that Dino has been taken back, even though the war is over. I really feel the need to be with him and try to get him released or repatriated, whatever they call it.'

'Oh, that woulda be so wonderful, if you could,' Mrs Belloni said, again grasping Prue's hands to give them a warm squeeze. 'You are a lovely girl, pleasea help him.'

Determination ricocheted through her. 'That is what I fully intend to do,' Prue firmly stated. 'And I'll keep in touch to let you know what happens.'

Fourteen

Mrs Harding was busily cleaning the oak mantelpiece with dregs of tea leaves, as she generally did every Thursday morning when Brenda popped her head around the kitchen door. 'Can I come in?' she softly asked.

'Eeh, lass, good to see thee. I'll put t'kettle on again. I'm ready for a sit down and a bit of a chin-wag.'

'I'm fully aware that I'm no longer allowed in this house, but it's Wakes Weeks, as we Lancashire folk call our summer holiday. And as Prue said I was welcome to stay with her at any time, I wondered if I could spend it here. I can see no sign of her right now. Do you know where she is?'

'Sit theesen down and I'll tell thee what's happened.'

The tale of how Dino had found himself arrested simply for walking down into the village with Prue filled Brenda with horror. It sounded so unjust. She understood exactly how it felt to be treated as an enemy, as she had been in France, and suffered badly as a result. 'Poor man, and poor Prue. She must feel utterly decimated.'

'Aye, but she's a determined and very positive-thinking young lady, so is out most days talking to local councillors,

Members of Parliament, the mayor, vicars, anyone she can think of who might offer some support to help get him released. We can but hope she succeeds, as he's a nice young lad. Anyroad, how about you? Have thee found out owt about your little one?' Mrs Harding asked, placing a mug of tea before Brenda.

'I'm afraid not, but like Prue I'm writing and calling upon everyone I can think of, so far to no avail. At least I have a good job in Castlefield and can afford to rent a flat and the cost of this search, but feel in sore need of a little break and a change of scene. And Prue is such a good friend, I've missed her. If she's busy with this task I'd be happy to help her in any way, and you too, while I'm here.'

'Tha'd be most welcome, lass. You're a right little treasure in any kitchen. Most of the servants once employed here joined the forces, or went to work in better-paying jobs. None seem eager to return, so there's far too much for me to deal with looking after this big house.'

'I'd be most happy to do my bit, Mrs Harding, were Hugh willing to allow it. Although why would he object when he treats me like a servant anyway?' Brenda said with a laugh. In her heart she felt a little nervous of his reaction, her main motivation being to attempt to win him round so that he might start to believe in her. And if that meant doing her bit in the kitchen, it was a small price to pay.

The housekeeper gave a wide toothless grin, her false teeth currently sitting in a glass bowl on the kitchen sink. 'He happen wouldn't agree to pay thee much, if owt at all, but at least tha'd get well fed, and could go for a walk whenever it takes tha fancy. It'd be grand if tha could make some cakes and puddings.'

'I'm not asking to be paid. I'm on holiday. Just glad to do something useful instead of sitting about doing nothing. How about if I start by making you a fruit cake?' Brenda suggested with a smile.

'Eeh, we've no dried fruit, save for a few sultanas. They're a bit hard to come by.'

'I could soak some prunes instead, if you have any of those. The cake would be a bit more solid, but still tasty and filling.'

'Aye, we've plenty o' them. Eeh, tha's a clever lass.'

'I'll start right away,' Brenda said, reaching for an apron.

Following the afternoon tea when the fruit cake was served, Carter the butler brought them a message as he carried back the empty trays. 'Master Hugh wishes you to know, Mrs Harding, that the cake was delicious. He sends his compliments.'

'If only he knew it weren't me what baked it,' she chortled.

'Best not to tell him,' Brenda said, and they all burst out laughing.

*

Brenda was eagerly welcomed to stay in the cottage by Prue. That evening she sat happily crocheting a bag out of string, since she couldn't afford to buy one, while her friend told her own version of Dino's arrest and what she'd learned from his mother.

'It is so wrong to treat him as an enemy, a feeling I know well,' Brenda said. 'But are you saying it was Hugh who reported Dino to the police? Why would he do such a thing?'

Prue sighed. 'Oh, my darling brother is in something of a state himself. He's lost all his usual patience as a result of the low profits coming from the sale of biscuits, as well as struggling to find the necessary money to pay death duties on Papa. Bit of a nightmare, so he has my sympathy, even though I was hugely cross with him.'

'Is there anything I can do to help?' Brenda asked.

'Bless you, not really.' Pausing for a moment, Prue frowned as tears filled her eyes. 'The trouble is, Dino's now been returned to a camp on the Isle of Man. Not good news.'

'It's better than being confined in a police cell,' Brenda gently pointed out.

Giving a little nod, Prue sadly agreed. 'I once told my brother that were he ever to arrange for Dino to be sent back to the island, I would go too. At least then I could visit him regularly and help to persuade the camp commandant to release him.'

'Sounds like a good plan,' Brenda agreed.

'His dear mother thought so too.'

'Take care how you go about it.'

'I most certainly will. I learnt quite a bit more about his family, which should help. Oh, and I'm longing to see him again. The only snag is that it would mean abandoning my work here. Who would keep the garden weeded, tend to the fruit and vegetables, the tomatoes in the greenhouse, not to mention look after the chickens and Kit while I was away?' she said, glancing across at the collie snoozing in his basket.

'I'd be happy to do that. I've a couple of weeks free but do like to keep busy, so why not?'

Prue blinked. 'Even though it's your holiday?'

'There's nowhere else I want to go, even if I could afford to,' she laughed. 'And I'm sure I can cope. I helped deal with quite a few of those jobs in the past, so why would I not?'

'Oh, that would be wonderful! What a dear friend you are,' Prue cried, wiping the tears from her cheeks as she jumped up to give Brenda a hug. 'Thank you so much. I'll speak to Hugh first thing in the morning and tell him what I've decided to do, and that you've offered to take my place for a while.'

'It might be better if you catch the early train and leave Hugh to me, otherwise he could create more havoc and stop you from going. I very much doubt he'll be pleased by this decision. Carter can take you to the station and I'll persuade him not to say a word. Then I'll wait till late in the day before giving Hugh the news. By which time you'll be crossing on the ferry from Fleetwood, so it won't be worth his while to chase after you and attempt to drag you back.'

'Hmm, good point.' And the two girls grinned at each other in agreement.

*

Hugh was suffering yet another difficult day at the factory. Nothing seemed to be going right at the moment. Despite the strike being over, tension remained high and complaints rumbled on. He had to admit that there were problems. Deliveries were slow, not coming at the right time of day, which badly affected the work schedule, and finding sufficient coal or wood to feed the ovens was an absolute nightmare. Then when they did finally succeed in getting them fired up again, one woman fainted, hitting her head against the kitchen table as she fell. She fortunately came round fairly quickly but blamed the accident on the intense heat.

'I told her the ovens have to be hot in order to bake,' the chap in charge said when Hugh questioned him on the subject. 'She should have kept well away from the ovens instead of coming over to speak to me again and again.'

'What did she wish to speak to you about?'

'She was fussing about wanting a drink of bloody water.'

'I see. Did you give her one?'

'Nay, it's not my job to run errands for them womenfolk. I told her she could get a drink at dinner time. Right now she had to get on with her work and prepare them biscuits for cooking.'

A few days later a woman carrying a bag of flour from the stock room on the first floor slipped and tumbled down the stairs, the precious rationed contents spilling everywhere. Hugh heard her scream as she fell and ran to catch her, but reached her far too late and had to quickly call an ambulance.

'It was far too heavy for her,' yelled her friend, as the woman was taken away on a stretcher, having broken her ankle. 'Even dragging it made her lose her balance.'

Damnation, he thought. What disaster would happen next? Men would have no problems carrying a bag of flour. Was employing all these women creating yet more problems? And with the war now over, that could be changed, although as women were so good at baking, would it be the right thing to do or not? Feeling the need to discuss these issues, he went in search of Prudence, only to feel even more furious when he found Brenda picking the strawberries. His sister was nowhere around, and he was calmly informed that Prue had left for the Isle of Man.

'How dare you encourage her to do such a stupid thing?' he roared. Feeling so frustrated, Hugh certainly felt no urge to discuss his private problems with this madam, even if he did find the way her mouth curled up into a gentle smile very comforting.

'It was Prue's decision, not mine. I just offered to deal with her jobs while she was away,' Brenda firmly responded.

'Didn't I make it clear that a hussy like you has no right to even be here? I banished you from Trowbridge Hall because of your immoral behaviour and lies.'

Her eyes widened, showing a spark of anger at his choice of words, but her tone of voice remained studiously calm. 'Banned for something I did not do? And I thought I had made it clear that the only reason Camille decided to say nothing about our wedding was because she feared your father might decide to cut Jack out of his will and abandon him completely.'

'We have only your word for that.'

'It is nonetheless true, if very sad that she can't be here to explain it herself. I am prepared to help, Hugh, and you did compliment me on the cake I baked yesterday.'

He felt momentarily stunned by this remark. '*You* baked that fruit cake, not Mrs Harding? I didn't realise you were capable of such things.'

Brenda almost laughed out loud at this remark. 'I did indeed. She's a really kind and friendly lady but dreadfully overworked. Prue is very anxious about Dino, so as your brother's widow, why would I not wish to help them both? I do have quite a bit of spare time on my hands.'

He glared at her, noting the twinkle of defiance in her brown eyes and the way her full lips pursed with stern determination, the kind of mouth any man would love to explore. After some long seconds of silence, he slowly responded. 'What a puzzling lady you are. Feisty and rebellious, but…'

'A good cook, and a dear friend to your lovely sister.'

'I was about to say you are a liar and a fraudster, as we still have no proof of the claims you are making about your relationship with my late brother.'

'As you are fully aware, the matter is in the process of being dealt with,' Brenda calmly insisted. 'Although I do feel a slight irritation over how long it is taking for the solicitor to retrieve the necessary papers.'

'Until that happens you will continue to be treated as

a servant, not a member of this family. I'll pay you five shillings a week,' he growled. 'Not a penny more. And in future please address me by my full name, not Hugh. Is that clear?'

She gave a little chuckle. 'Ooh, yes *sir*. Sorry, *Mr Stuart*. Of course I'll act as a servant, *sir*,' she said, bobbing a little curtsey. 'But I'm doing this for Prue and Jack, so I'm not asking for any wages. Not a single penny need be paid.'

Despite his grumpiness, Hugh couldn't help but look her over with a glint of humour in his own gaze. What a fascinating young woman she was, and really quite attractive.

*

The next morning, while Mrs Harding was listening as usual to *Kitchen Front* on the radio while she prepared breakfast, Brenda mentioned that she needed to pop back to her flat in Manchester to collect her things. 'I've fed the hens and will be back in time to see to them later in the day. I've spoken to old Joe and he's quite happy with that, and to give me a lift to the station.'

'Right then, lass. Have a bit of sausage before tha goes, and I'll make sure there's some supper waiting when tha returns.'

Catching an early train, Brenda went straight to her flat and soon packed her few possessions. Then decided she should call again to speak to the solicitor's secretary. This time the young woman greeted her with a dry little smile.

'Ah, *Mrs* Stuart, good of you to call. Sadly, we are no nearer to finding your paperwork, but have received some news from the Mayor of Angers to say that the lady you are seeking, Adèle Rouanet, probably crossed the border into Switzerland. I'm afraid we've no idea where exactly she ended up, but does that help?'

Brenda felt her heart sink. 'Not really. We've always known the dear lady might have done that in order to be safe, as did many other people. But without proper proof, how can we be sure?'

Wasn't this what she and Emma had feared might have happened? If it was true, how infuriating to have spent all those months interned in a camp so close to that beautiful country without knowing her son and Adèle might be somewhere nearby. But as the dear lady had no idea where she'd been interned, how could they ever have got in touch?

Brenda wrote to her friend Emma that evening to tell her what she'd heard, adding her doubts and hopes that it wasn't true.

*

'I keep wondering if I should go once more to search for him? If only I'd some idea of where to look, then I most certainly would. What a time we had, spending well over a year searching for him. But though we found no trace, it did prove to be an interesting experience, and I'm sure I could never have coped without your help. I wonder what you suggest I do now?

Fifteen

France 1942

On the morning following the rape, Brenda made no mention of what had happened, desperately attempting to block the attack out of her mind as she scrubbed and cleansed herself one more time. In the days following she took much greater care not to be left alone any place, certainly not the lavatory area, and kept her head down whenever that brute of a guard or any of his mates were stalking around. Her distress slowly began to change into a feeling of anger, the one thing on her mind now being to escape this dreadful prison.

Emma seemed to be keeping a close watch upon her, an anxiety clearly evident in her troubled gaze. 'You seem not at all yourself, a bit withdrawn. Are you all right, honey?'

'I'm doing the best I can as I'm sure we all are,' Brenda snapped, wondering how she could ever be herself again when the situation felt so dangerous, unpredictable and threatening. Then realising she sounded irritable, took a calming breath and made a personal resolve to be honest and open. 'You're right about devising a plan of escape. We do need to get out of here.' And finally feeling the need to share her trauma, confessed to Emma what had happened.

'Dear lord, that must have been dreadful.'

Brenda nodded, fighting back another wash of tears. 'I'm terrified it could happen again at any time. Have you any notion how we could get out of here?'

'I've one or two ideas,' her friend quietly remarked, glancing around to check no one was listening. 'I'll follow them up and let you know.'

Days later they were listening to a choir practising Christmas carols, one of the many groups set up in order to help the internees relax. Whispering softly, Emma shared her plans. 'I told a woman in the Red Cross what had happened to you and she has agreed to find us a couple of nurses' uniforms. The next time they come, she says we can put them on and leave with the Red Cross team.'

'Oh, my goodness, do you think that will work?'

Emma smiled as she clapped when the song ended. 'We can but hope so.'

'But we have no papers or documents of any sort.'

'We'll worry about that later. Nor can we take any personal possessions with us. We just walk out, right? They'll be coming again in early January, so be ready.'

*

When the day of escape dawned, Brenda felt sick with fear. If it didn't work and they were caught, they could be sent to a security prison, beaten or even executed if accused of being spies. And how could they defend themselves against such a charge? As women and children queued up to be seen by the three Red Cross nurses, one quietly slipped Emma a bag containing two uniforms. While the guards chivvied the women into some sort of order, allowing each only a few seconds to discuss whatever health problem they were suffering from, the two of them kept well hidden in the midst of the crowd. Friends helped shield them as they pulled the uniforms over the clothes they were wearing. They then quickly adopted the role of first-aid workers, bandaging or treating wounds inflicted through laborious jobs, and handing out food and medicines as quietly instructed to do by the real nurses.

Brenda's heart was pounding as loud as a drum when they finally packed their first-aid bags and prepared to leave, the nurses happily chatting to the guards that their day of duty had been done. Keeping their heads down, just in case one of the guards recognised them, the two friends walked quickly out with the nurses, keeping close to the one who had assisted them in this escape.

It was as they reached the main gate that one of the guards came hurrying over, to speak rapidly to Brenda in German. She stared at him in shock, not understanding a word. What was he saying? Had he recognised her? The Red Cross nurse standing beside her reached into her bag and handed him a jar of ointment.

'*Danke*,' he said, giving a grateful smile.

'He's been bitten by some creature, probably a rat,' she murmured to Brenda, who found herself starting to shake. Grasping her arm the nurse pushed her gently into the ambulance.

'Dear lord, that was a close shave,' Emma said, as the gate opened and they slowly drove away. Heart still trembling, Brenda said not a word.

They were driven some distance over the mountains before the ambulance finally halted in a quiet area of woodland.

'Good luck and take care,' the nurses told them as they climbed out and waved goodbye.

'Thank you so much for your help.'

'Don't tell a soul what we did,' they warned.

'We won't, that's a promise.'

'So now what?' Brenda asked, as they watched the vehicle disappear into the distance.

'We walk home,' Emma said with a grin, 'keeping well off the road.'

'I need to go to Paris first to enquire about my son before finding my way back to England,' Brenda explained. 'So if you need to head south, then please do so.'

'I am keen to get back home, as Mum isn't too well, but let's stick together for as long as we can,' Emma said, with which Brenda was happy to agree.

They walked and walked, day after day after day. They slept in barns and under hedges and haystacks, eating the food they'd managed to steal and bring with them, restricting their meals to only a small amount at a time in order to make it last as long as possible. They also ate any wild fruit and raw vegetables they found growing.

They finally reached a railway station, hungry and exhausted but hugely relieved. And being dressed in nurses' uniforms, able to show the passes the Red Cross nurses had given them, they managed to avoid being searched by a German officer by going through the barrier with a whole party of noisy soldiers. But then they were halted when one young man asked for assistance, as he had a deep wound in his leg. Thankfully, the nurses had provided them with a small first-aid bag too, so Brenda dutifully cleaned and bandaged his leg.

'*Merci*,' he said with a smile and a nod, and she exchanged a flicker of anguish with Emma as they climbed on board.

'Papers,' a guard demanded, and Brenda felt her heart plummet. Was this the end? Would they now be arrested yet again? But the young German soldier they'd helped spoke quickly in French to the guard, explaining that they were Red Cross nurses and were looking after them. Brenda and Emma happily spent the entire journey tending to their wounds, as well as laughing and chatting with him. It felt such a relief to be on a train and free at last, this time one that was fairly warm and clean, if very crowded.

On their arrival in Paris, Brenda found no sign of Camille. Her mother-in-law's once elegant apartment was a shambled mess, the roof smashed in and heaps of stone and rubble everywhere, clearly having suffered a severe bomb attack. According to a local shopkeeper, that had happened back in 1941, most of the occupants having been killed or injured; others had escaped and not been seen since. As

Brenda still had no address for Adèle's house in the Loire Valley, depression hit her like a rock.

Tommy was missing, and she had no idea where or how to find him.

Brenda searched everywhere for her son, but there was no sign of him anywhere, or either of the two dear ladies. She talked to any neighbours and locals she could find. Unfortunately, most of them had vanished too. Even the boulangerie had closed down.

'There's nothing for it but to go to the Loire Valley and search for them there,' she announced to Emma. 'Although heaven only knows how and where I should start looking. I've no intention of giving up.'

'I'll come with you to help.'

'You don't have to. I know your Mum isn't well and you are desperate to get home to see her. I'll cope somehow.'

'We'll cope together,' Emma announced, in that brave, regal tone of hers that Brenda admired so much. 'I've no wish to travel alone and I don't suppose you have either. And as we will have to make a journey through Spain to reach England, we can look around on our way south.'

'That is so generous of you.'

'Nonsense, it's common sense. I keep hoping Paul will be released or somehow manage to escape, but now we're on the run he can't possibly contact us, so I'll just have to be patient. I need to write and give him a few clues about where I am.'

Brenda nodded. 'I do understand, but that won't be easy,

as we should do our best to keep where we are a secret, at least until we get out of France.'

'True. Don't worry, honey, I will,' Emma agreed. 'I'll tell him the birds are flying south, and he'll hopefully get the message that we are free.'

Holding each other close for a moment, then wiping the tears from each other's eyes, Brenda gave her friend a smile. 'We've got this far, so let's go forward and stay brave. First I need to speak to Alexis, a very kind young man who was a friend of Jack's in the Resistance. I'm hoping he'll be able to find us some transport.'

*

The small lorry rumbled along rough, broken roads and through acres of green meadows, the two girls singing along as Alexis taught them the words of Bing Crosby's new hit 'White Christmas', a season that had gone by largely unnoticed so far as they were concerned. He drove past many ramshackle cottages, damaged tanks stuck in fields, and a great deal of rubbish lying about everywhere. Yet despite it being February, the winter sun shone brightly over the gardens, vineyards and pretty little villages, as well as on the glorious châteaux perched here and there upon rolling green hills. Finding one town awash with army vehicles and German soldiers, Alexis did a quick turnaround to avoid it and chose a different route.

'Well done,' Emma told him, as he made a speedy exit. 'The last thing we need is to be strip-searched by the enemy on a cold day like this, although at any other time it might be quite exciting.' And they all laughed at her weird sense of humour.

They'd disposed of the Red Cross uniforms some time ago, beneath which were the shabby dresses and jumpers they'd been living in for the last two years. Sadly, all of their other belongings, including Emma's beautiful fur coat, had to be left behind. And of course she no longer possessed any of her diamond rings either.

'What lovely countryside,' Brenda commented, as they drove past a field lined with vines, rows of beech and oak trees dotted on the hills beyond. 'I almost feel like I'm back in the Pennines, save for the fact we can't grow grapes in Lancashire as there's far too much rain,' she said with a giggle.

Reaching the Loire, the lorry drove alongside the river for some miles, stopping whenever they found a village to ask the vital question: 'Do you know Adèle Rouanet?' The locals would give a puzzled frown or shake their head in disinterest.

Towards the end of the day Alexis warned that he was running out of petrol. 'I'd love to stay and help you, but I have only one can of fuel left, and there's a limit to the time I can offer.'

'We do understand that,' Brenda said, worrying how far they could manage to walk. Depression was again sinking into her, causing odd palpitations in her heart. 'I'm beginning to think we're wasting our time doing this search. Apart from the fact that the Loire Valley is a huge area to cover, we've no proof that Camille and Adèle will still be here. They could be anywhere.'

'They might even have escaped to England,' Emma suggested. 'But if they haven't managed that yet, wouldn't some member of the Stuart family know where they are, or where Adèle lives?'

Brenda heaved a weary sigh. 'I wish I knew the answer to that one, although I would expect them to know something. Those dear ladies might well have decided that England was the safest place for baby Tommy, being heir to Trowbridge Hall. On the other hand, they might have hidden him away some place, as Jews do with their children when they're in danger of being captured. Who knows where they may have gone?'

'We could try to find a train heading south, and keep searching as we progress towards England,' Emma suggested. 'Never give up.'

'That makes sense,' Brenda agreed.

'What if they crossed the border into Switzerland?' Alexis suggested. 'Many people are doing that. Even the Vichy government has been hounding and persecuting Jews. Some Jewish children have become separated from families who've been captured, as were you, only they suffered far worse. Various groups are attempting to help by hiding them, then sending the children on to safety in places such as Switzerland or the United States.'

'Switzerland! Oh, goodness, that would be so frustrating, considering we've just come from near there,' Emma replied, glancing at the anguish on her dear friend's face.

'Let's hope these two ladies are indeed on their way home to England.'

'If not, then the people to ask for help are the *Oeuvre de Secours aux Enfants*, known as the OSE,' Alexis told them. 'They run orphanages for children whose parents have been imprisoned in concentration camps, or executed. They operate secretly, like the Resistance, but I can give you the address of my friend Jeanne, who works for them in Tours,' he said, fishing in his pocket for a pen. Unable to find even a scrap of paper, he wrote it on the back of Brenda's hand.

'Thank you so much, Alexis. However difficult it might be, I'm not prepared to give up searching yet,' she staunchly insisted. 'But if I fail to find Tommy soon, then I agree it makes sense for us to go back to England.'

Sleeping that night in the back of the lorry, Brenda examined her hand, going over all that Alexis had told them, her heart once more in anguish for her missing son. She felt as if she'd lost a limb, and her entire reason for living. There had been a time, not feeling too well after the rape, when she'd feared it might result in further anguish. The last thing she wanted was to give birth to a child of that Gestapo brute. And as her monthlies had long since stopped, how could she be sure she was safe? Fortunately, Brenda was now feeling much better, so hopefully all would be well. And finding Tommy was much more important.

Surely the two cousins would be more likely to go to England than Switzerland. But Camille was not a well woman, so what if something had happened to her? What would Adèle do then? Would she take Tommy home to his family, if that were at all possible, or would she seek help in order to do so? In which case, she might well go to these OSE people. It was an interesting thought. Again reading the address on the back of her hand, Brenda carefully copied the details on to a paper bag she happened to have. Should they go and see this friend of Alexis's, or not? Sleep overcame her before she'd reached any decision.

The next morning they scoured one last village and the medieval town of Amboise, admiring the half-timbered cottages, the magnificent Château d'Amboise, and the view from the bridge over the River Loire.

'Adèle is a very grand lady, so this town would suit her perfectly,' Brenda acknowledged.

There was a market open so they took the opportunity to stock up a little on food, as well as asking the all-important question, which sadly brought forth the same negative responses. Finally accepting defeat, Brenda asked Alexis to drop them off at the Gare Amboise. She thanked him for his generosity and help, assuring him that she'd made a note of everything he'd told her, even though she hadn't yet made up her mind what to do with it. They waved goodbye as he drove off back to Paris, no doubt to face yet more dangerous duties. The two girls sat in a far corner of the platform to nibble on a sandwich and patiently wait for a train.

'Do we head south to Toulouse, then over the Pyrenees through Spain and back to England, or to Tours to find this Jeanne?' Emma asked.

'No idea. I wish I could decide which was the best option.'

Some hours later, when a train finally came puffing slowly into the station, it was not heading south to Toulouse, but indeed to Tours.

'I believe this must be an omen,' Brenda said. 'I do take Alexis's point. This group he mentioned, the OSE, sound like experts where lost children are concerned, so they might help me to find Tommy.'

'Right, let's go and ask them,' Emma said with a grin, and they quickly climbed on board.

Sixteen

Prue boarded the *Lady of Mann* quite late that evening. This time, as it crossed the churning Irish Sea, the ship was not escorted by a frigate, and unlike poor Dino, she was not going to be interned. But the boat was so packed with passengers that she had no choice but to sleep on deck. Fortunately it was a warm June night, so that was not a problem, although the tossing and rocking of the boat did keep waking her.

Arriving at Douglas early the next morning she at once took a train to Ramsey, where Dino had told her in his most recent letter that he was being held. It was a lovely ride through the hills and countryside in the early morning on the Manx railway. The excitement that she would soon be seeing him pulsated within her. She'd longed for him so much. But how she would set about achieving his release was still to be resolved.

The moment Prue arrived in the small town she set out in search of accommodation, carrying her brown suitcase and feeling deeply tired. The streets looked stark, with huge lengths of barbed wire fencing off sections of the promenade. She called at several boarding houses, failing to find any spare rooms available while other landladies would slam the door shut stating they didn't have anything to do with internees. Eventually one agreed to take her in, Prue having quickly explained why she was here. It wasn't exactly the smartest place she'd stayed at, with no sign of any carpets, and all personal items and ornaments having been removed from the sitting room. Perhaps because this landlady didn't trust internees either, or their visitors.

Being shown into a single room high up on the top floor, it felt small and sparsely furnished. But at least there was a wonderful view out over the sea.

'You're not allowed any visitors to your room,' Mrs Pickering, the landlady, sternly informed her. 'And you must be in by nine o'clock or you'll find the door locked. Lunch will be in half an hour.'

'Thank you, that would be lovely. It has been a long journey.'

Unpacking the few possessions she'd brought with her, Prue felt a tide of loneliness wash over her. What should she do now? How she wished her dear friend Brenda was here to support her. She was such a brave lady, despite having suffered so much trauma herself. Prue felt a little lost, as if her own courage was rapidly fading. Had this been another hasty decision she'd made, one she would come to regret? She really did hope not, but how could she possibly help Dino? Would anyone even be prepared to listen when she begged for his release?

'Who would you recommend I speak to?' she asked as the landlady placed a most welcome plate of sausage and mash before her.

'You'll need to ask the camp commandant that, love. Many camps have already been cleared out. Some of the police and guards in charge are also leaving, even though numbers are on the rise again now that German prisoners of war have started arriving. Is your fellow one of them?'

'Oh, no,' Prue quickly assured her. 'He's Italian.'

'There are still a few hundred internees here at Mooragh, and across at Peveril, and some women and married couples at Port Erin. But most internees have now left, many having been held for as long as five years.'

'Then why would my fiancé be brought back here?'

'No doubt they are classing him as a war criminal,' Mrs Pickering quietly suggested.

'He's not at all. He's perfectly innocent.' The prospect that Dino was being looked upon as a war criminal simply for falling in love with her, felt utterly soul destroying. How could she ever hope to save him if that was the case?

'Well, you have my sympathy, love. The transportation of aliens to this Island began back in 1940,' the landlady said as she sat herself down beside Prue to continue with her tale. 'The news was put out in the local paper that about thirty boarding houses on the promenade were to be requisitioned to form an internment camp.

'We'd expected the PoWs to be put in huts, but owners were given a week in which to gather up their personal possessions and move out, which was a bit of a shock.

They were even instructed to leave their furniture behind, although some took their favourite pieces with them, replacing them with second-hand misfits,' she said, giving a little chuckle. 'Some folk were quite in favour, as the money they were paid made up for the loss of tourists. Then day after day the men started to arrive, young and old, carrying their gas masks, luggage, fishing rods and even some fetching a dog. We thought they'd take over the town, but the selected houses were ringed off with barbed wire.'

'Which does look pretty dreadful. But I can understand why the military would need to do that, or the fascists and Nazi sympathisers could escape and create huge problems.'

'Indeed, as one or two tried to do, but generally failed. Why they bothered, I don't know, as they were all well fed. This island is not short of milk, potatoes, or other good food,' Mrs Pickering pointed out.

'I remember Dino saying he was treated well and not as an enemy. He was eventually allowed to come and work on our farm, which he greatly appreciated.'

'That's good. Some of the women were released early because they were pregnant. You aren't in the family way, are you, love?' she softly asked, seeing a slight flush appear upon Prue's cheeks.

'Umm, might be, not sure yet.'

'I did wonder if that might have something to do with why you've risked coming here. Well, bearing in mind the reason your fiancé has been re-interned is probably your fraternisation, I wouldn't recommend you using that as a plea for his release.'

Grateful for all she'd been told, Prue smiled. 'I take your point. Thank you.'

'And as your fellow is Italian, he'll be in the N Camp.'

Walking along the promenade, the sound of seagulls flying overhead and waves washing along the beach lifted her spirits a little, as did the beautiful sunshine and views of the hills beyond. The temperature felt much milder than in the Pennines. Ramsey was no doubt a really pleasant harbour town before the war. But once again the sight of the barbed wire enclosing a row of Victorian houses brought her back to reality. So this was the camp. How dreadful to be locked up here, particularly when the rest of the country was celebrating peace. She could see a group of men wandering about within the compound, clearly taking a little exercise. And suddenly there he was, strolling about with his hands in his pockets, looking slightly glum and depressed. Running over, she called his name.

'Dino, Dino, I'm here!'

He looked up in stunned disbelief, then glancing around to check he wasn't being watched, hurried over to gaze at her in delight. 'How wonderful to see you, darling.'

'I've come to try and help. Oh, and your mother sends her love.' She began at once to tell him about her visit to Ancoats, pushing her fingers through the wire in an effort to reach him.

'Best not to do that. We can't touch,' he warned her, again looking anxiously over his shoulder at the watchful guards. 'So long as you stay well back and keep walking we can talk, although we're only allowed out here for a short time.' These words were barely out of his mouth when a whistle blew and the PoWs were ordered back inside.

'I'll come again tomorrow, a bit earlier,' she promised, her heart flickering with joy that at least she had found him.

*

Every morning Prue would walk to and fro on the outside of the barbed wire compound on the seafront, while Dino walked alongside her within it. Sometimes windows would open and heads would pop out, as if the interned men couldn't resist gazing upon an attractive young woman. She even heard the occasional wolf whistle, which would make her giggle.

'Are you all right?' she anxiously asked him. 'Do they feed you properly? Do you suffer from any sickness?'

'I'm fine, *cara mia*, if hugely bored.'

'Oh, I can well believe that. What can I do to help?'

'Just seeing you here makes me feel far less lonely. We won't get long, so you need to know that I'm constantly called to be questioned and cross-examined, not least about my political status.'

'And presumably our fraternisation.'

He nodded. 'That too. Those who manage to convince the committee of their loyalty and friendliness to Britain have been released. I'm trying to do that, but it does seem to take some time. I need to give them a good reason.'

'Other than the fact we want to marry?' she said with a wry smile.

'I'm afraid so.'

An armed guard came over at that point and instructed her to leave as their allotted time had run out.

'Love you,' she murmured, as she watched Dino being led back inside.

Wasting no time, she went straight to the local admin office and requested a meeting with the camp commandant. The young officer in charge looked up at her blank-faced. 'He's a very busy person.'

'So am I, as I'm largely in charge of growing food on our farm,' she said, keeping her tone polite but firm. 'Nevertheless, I do have some information about Dino Belloni which may of interest.'

Prue's nerves jangled as she was shown into the commandant's office. He was seated behind his desk and didn't even glance up from whatever he was scribbling on a file as she stood before him. She waited with trembling impatience and had almost given up hope when finally he snapped, 'What is it you want?'

Clearing her throat, she politely asked the question hovering at the back of her mind. 'I am wondering why Dino Belloni has been re-interned, and when he is likely to be released?'

Silence again followed, then glancing up at her, he said, 'Name?'

'Prudence Stuart,' she said with a polite smile.

'I mean this young man you're referring to.'

Hadn't he even listened? 'Dino Belloni,' she carefully repeated. 'He has worked on our farm in the Pennines for some months. He is not an enemy, nor an alien, and certainly not a fascist.'

'Being anti-fascist is not sufficient reason for his release.' He glanced back at the file he'd been working on, engaging in a quiet conversation with the young man standing beside him as he handed him various papers. When he dashed off, the commandant finally turned to Prue to answer her question. 'This Italian prisoner of war has been returned to the Isle of Man to be interned on charges of fraternisation. As you are no doubt aware.' His expression was grimly authoritarian, making Prue feel like a schoolgirl being chastised by her headmaster. 'And here he will stay.'

'But he's done nothing wrong, save walk down to the village with me to celebrate VE Day.' She carefully made no mention of their relationship.

He gave a snort of disbelief. 'If you imagine you had any right to do that, you are very much mistaken, girl. Fraternisation with PoWs is very much against the law. Good day to you.' He thumped the bell on his desk, and a young guard came bustling in. 'Show this young woman out!' he snarled.

'Yes, sir,' the guard smartly responded, indicating Prue should follow him.

Ignoring him, she rested her hands on the desk to lean closer to the commandant. 'All right, I admit we do love each other and wish to marry as soon as he is free. But why is it considered to be a crime to fall in love with an Italian, even though British soldiers are allowed to marry their German girl friends? And why hasn't the law changed now that the war has ended?'

'It may well change eventually,' he frostily remarked, 'but not right away. Remove her now!'

Grasping her arm, the guard marched Prue out, almost as if she was a prisoner herself.

'I'll be back,' she told him as he pushed her out and slammed the door in her face. Realising she'd made a bad mistake by revealing how they felt about each other, it became clear to her that getting Dino released was not going to be as easy as she'd imagined.

Seventeen

Summer passed in a blur of hard work but as autumn 1945 approached, Brenda was shocked to be informed by her boss at the rubber factory that her job was coming to an end. 'How on earth can I continue to pay the rent without a wage coming in?' she said, as Brenda and her friend Cathie shared dismay over this news. 'I've no real wish to return to my late husband's family home out on the Pennines. Not that they would welcome me.'

Cathie gave her a consoling hug. 'I'm sure if we look hard enough we'll find other work, even if it's only part time. We do have considerable experience at our fingertips, after all. Surely all these years of hard work we've done must count for something?'

'I do hope so. We should have seen this coming, of course. Those brave soldiers do deserve their jobs back. I'd just never got around to thinking how that might affect me. Nor did I expect it to happen so suddenly.'

'Me neither. A little warning might have helped, or better still the offer of an alternative job here in the factory, one that involved us in work we know well.'

Sounding equally disgruntled their fellow women

workers expressed their opinion that other factories were
likewise laying off women employees, so a new job might
not be easy to come by.

'Seems they were right,' Cathie said, as they trailed
around Castlefield and other areas of Manchester, calling upon every factory, tea room and shop, in an effort
to find employment. They even tried the larger stores,
including Liptons and Maypole grocers, and the famous
department store, Kendal Milne, all to no avail. Brenda
deeply resented going through the same problems she'd
suffered back in Paris at the start of the war. When would
life ever get better? When she'd found her darling Tommy,
of course.

Failing to find a job, she felt a fresh determination
to again search for her son. Hugh had claimed to know
nothing about Adèle, nor did Prue, and Melissa had been
her usual haughty self showing not a scrap of empathy
towards her. But resolving to stay strong and never give
up hope, Brenda began to wonder if there might be some
other family member who might have answers. It would
be good to see Prue again and speak to her about this.
Would she have returned from the Isle of Man by now?
Hopefully she had.

Hugh, of course, had made it abundantly clear that
Brenda would only ever be allowed back into the house
as a scullery maid, since that was how he viewed her. But as
it had worked perfectly when she'd stood in for Prue over
her holiday weeks, why should she not go again? Brenda
most definitely had no intention of ever ending her search,

and surely someone in the Stuart family would know something. She would give the matter careful thought.

*

Prue visited the admin office once again to request an appointment with the commandant, explaining that she was still in need of an opportunity to reveal more information about Dino Belloni. Making a note of the boarding house where she was staying, the young man said he would let her know if such an appointment was ever agreed upon, his tone of voice showing not a spark of interest.

'I look forward to hearing from you,' she stoutly responded.

Waiting proved so hard. Days and weeks passed by without a word. Prue filled her time by doing a little sewing and mending for her landlady, as well as knitting socks for the internees out of scraps of wool. Sometimes she'd treat herself to a visit to the cinema, which cost sixpence, or would take a walk out into the countryside. Swimming in the sea became another pleasure. But seeing Dino each morning was what gave her the true motivation to keep going, and to call at regular intervals at the admin office to repeat her request. Not only was she determined never to stop begging for his release, but her condition was now all too evident, so time was very much of the essence.

Eventually, one morning the landlady handed her an envelope. 'This was delivered from the camp,' Mrs Pickering told her.

Prue's hand trembled as she opened it. Would this be

good news or bad? 'Oh, the camp commandant has agreed to see me again,' she cried, with joy in her heart.

'Good luck, love. Prepare your case a bit more carefully this time,' the landlady advised with a stern nod.

'Oh, I will,' Prue agreed, determined to keep her emotions under better control this time.

A few days later, dressed in her smartest suit, she perched on the edge of the chair before the commandant's desk and began to carefully explain how the Belloni family had lived in Ancoats for years. 'They have always been looked upon with great respect as a valued part of the community. Even the police who came to arrest his father, and then Dino, were exceedingly polite and apologetic. In addition, his two brothers have been regular soldiers in the British army for years.'

The commandant frowned. 'I was unaware of that fact. Why did Belloni not mention it?'

Prue gave a sad shake of her head. 'I'd say because you would have interrogated him on why he had not joined up with them.' She went on to explain about his eyesight problem. 'He was sent his call-up papers, but was rejected for that reason. It's a disability he prefers to keep private. But I assure you, he is an honest man and greatly relieved to be given the chance to work on our farm to do his bit for the war. I believe most internees have now been released, so will you please see him as a friendly Italian national who was brought up in England, which he loves, and not as an enemy? I would really appreciate your help to get him repatriated.'

Regarding her in silence for some moments, perhaps pondering on what she'd told him, the commandant then examined a file lying open on the desk before him. Was this Dino's? Prue wondered. At last he met her pleading gaze with some compassion in his own. 'I'll see what I can do.'

Prue smiled with relief and gratefully shook his hand, thanking him from the depth of her heart. She almost skipped along the promenade to look for Dino through the wire but could see no sign of him. She'd tell him tomorrow. Oh, but things did seem to be looking up.

*

It was on one of her regular morning meet-ups for their usual chat as they walked on either side of the barbed wire, that Prue noticed Dino's face was lit with a bright smile. 'I've just received a notice which says: "Informing you that the Home Office has granted your release." Can you believe it?'

Prue halted to gaze at him in stunned delight, longing to jump through the wire and hug him, a feeling she'd experienced every single day, but even more so on hearing this news. 'Oh, then you are free at last, my darling?'

'Well, it won't happen right away. Some arrangements and paperwork have to be gone through first, but yes, *cara mia*, I soon will be. I'm told Mooragh will be closing by the end of the month, but I'll not be moved some place else. I've no idea what you said to the camp commandant at this latest meeting but it clearly worked. Thank you so much for your help, Prue darling, otherwise I might have been sent on to a prison cell.'

Within a couple of weeks he'd been issued with his papers, but instead of rushing to book a sailing back to Fleetwood, Prue went to speak to her landlady and eagerly shared her news. 'I was wondering, Mrs Pickering, if you could find room for my fiancé so that he could take a little rest before returning to work. I can afford to pay whatever it costs.'

'I assume that another single room would be required, at least until you get married?' she firmly asked.

Prue blushed. 'Yes, of course. Oh, but there's no reason why we couldn't marry now, is there?'

Mrs Pickering smiled. 'I can't see why not, dear girl. My husband and I married without either of our family's permission, and enjoyed fifty happy years together before he departed for the next world. So do what's right for you. We have a very nice Methodist Church on Waterloo Road, if that's of any interest. Or if he's a Catholic, there's Our Lady, Star of the Sea and Saint Maughold, down near Queen's Promenade.'

Giving her a quick hug, Prue excitedly dashed off. The priest was more than willing to wed them, since they were both Catholics, and of an age when they needed no one's permission but their own.

The day Dino was released Prue stood at the door waiting for him, a posy of flowers in her hand. Gathering her into his arms he kissed her, which brought forth a loud chorus of cheers and whistles from every window.

'I've found a priest willing to marry us and the necessary licence has been granted, unless you've changed your mind about me, of course,' she said with a shy smile.

'Never. I shall love you forever. Are you saying we can go and wed right now?' he asked, admiring how beautiful she looked in her cream silk gown.

Prue nodded. 'And Mrs Pickering, my—our—landlady, is willing to come and act as matron of honour.'

Not only that, but the good lady had brought along a few of her friends who were already seated in the pews waiting to welcome the bride and groom. There was no one to give Prue away, but reminding herself that Hugh had refused, she resolved not to allow this to trouble her in the slightest. All that mattered was that at last she and Dino were free to be together and live their own lives. The service was beautifully done and a little confetti and rose petals were tossed upon them as they walked arm and arm out of the church. There was even a local reporter to take a picture of them.

On returning to the boarding house, Mrs Pickering provided sandwiches, cake and even a small glass of wine for everyone.

'Bless you, what a treasure you are,' Prue said, giving her a kiss on her plump cheek.

'What a wonderful day this has been,' Dino said, as later that evening they entered the double bedroom now granted to them.

'I shall carry the memory of it in my heart forever,' Prue agreed. 'We are together at last.' And as he sank upon the bed with her in his arms, she helped him to peel off her clothes, her heart swelling with happiness.

*

As always, Mrs Harding was delighted to see Brenda, listening to her latest news with compassion etched into her wrinkled face. 'Thanks to the return of the fighting men, I've lost my job,' she explained.

'Nay, that's dreadful. What a callous way to treat women.'

'It's perfectly understandable in a way, yet highly inconvenient and hard to live with. I've paid my rent on the flat for the next three months. How I'll survive after that, I really can't say. And finding work has so far proved to be impossible.'

'Tha'd be welcome to come back and work here, chuck, and bake us more cakes and puddings. Miss Prudence is still away, so we're in dire need of more help, for the garden as well as in the house. Particularly as Miss Melissa and her family generally come to stay for Christmas,' she added, rolling her eyes with displeasure.

Brenda chuckled, fully aware that Hugh's snobby sister was not well liked by any of the servants. 'That would be wonderful. This place is beginning to feel like a second home to me.' Brenda had always enjoyed working with this kind housekeeper, and since she could find no alternative employment why would she not accept this offer, despite the problems Miss Melissa would no doubt create for her?

Or else it was time to do something entirely different

with her life, not least to raise more money to help with her search? 'I was wondering if any other family member might know Adèle, and have her address.'

Mrs Harding looked blank. 'No idea, chuck. You'd need to ask Master Hugh, or even Prue.'

Brenda sighed. 'I'll keep asking.'

One afternoon, filled with thoughts of her lost son, Brenda took herself off for a walk in the woods, feeling quite alone save for dear old Kit the collie. She followed a path uphill that lay through tall grasses, clearly not well used, passing spires of purple foxgloves standing tall and proud. She smiled as a squirrel scampered up a tree to sit on a branch and sun itself. Were Tommy here, he would no doubt want to climb up after him. She too had loved climbing trees as a child. Tossing a stick for Kit to chase, in her mind's eye she could envision a small boy chasing after the old dog too. What fun they would have had together. She was facing the trauma of another birthday coming up soon, when he would turn five. It made her shiver with anguish at the thought. Brenda pictured his baby-blue eyes and fair curly hair. Would they have darkened by now? she wondered. She could ask Hugh to show her some photos of Jack as a boy, which might help in her search.

Once again tears clogged her throat. Where was dear Adèle? Did no one know?

Coming out of the woodlands, she reached the top of the hill to look out over the barren moors across the Southern Pennines. This was the land where Tommy should be living, and would one day inherit the family estate. In the distance she could see the Saddleworth war memorial marking the First World War, and steep paths circling the reservoir. They were but a few miles from the city of Manchester but it felt like a different world, and at least safe from the war she'd experienced.

Poor Emma's husband was also still missing. Such was the reality of war. But dwelling too much upon the anguish it caused did no good at all, or so Brenda had discovered. She resolutely attempted to block the pain out, still finding it difficult to speak of her traumas. She was at least still in touch with Emma and the two friends regularly exchanged letters, although they hadn't yet been able to meet up.

But what did life have to offer her now? She really had no idea. Here she was, without a job and back at Trowbridge Hall, still treated very much like a servant. Hugh was a confusing man, at first so bossy and disapproving, but sometimes when he looked at her there would be a bright sparkle of interest in his grey eyes. He clearly had his problems too, for which Brenda had every sympathy. Were it not for the anguish they were both enduring, would relations between them be better? A part of her wished that could happen.

With a sigh Brenda turned back towards the woods, her mind once again reliving her own traumas. She remembered how any family suspected of being Jewish would be arrested, the children ordered to walk away or they too would be taken. Fortunately, hundreds did manage to escape, transported by train to Holland, England and other safe countries. Would Tommy be among them? Or was he in Switzerland with Adèle?

Her mind being so occupied with the past, Brenda suddenly realised she was lost. She'd entered the wood in an entirely different place, wandering the paths without properly checking in which direction she was walking. Coming to a halt and meeting Kit's adoring gaze as he stood panting before her, she chuckled.

'Oh dear, made a mess of this, haven't I? Where are we, old lad?'

The dog looked about him, almost as if he understood her question, but made no move in any direction. And then she remembered Jack's instructions to follow the moss on the side of a tree to head north, which would be straight ahead, or go downhill to find the river. An entirely different direction.

'Which way do we go?' she asked the dog. As she struggled to make up her mind, it began to rain and within minutes found herself soaked, not having thought to bring an umbrella or coat with her. Kit shook himself, spraying water over her feet, then trotted off along a downhill path. Brenda followed him. After walking for about half an hour she found one of the cairns Jack had built, and her heart skipped with relief. So Kit did know which way to go, having been properly trained by his master. And perhaps Jack was still keeping an eye on her. She smiled to herself at the thought.

It was as she approached the house that she spotted a group of giggling children: three lovely young girls, two of them clearly twins, and a small boy. They reminded her of all the children she'd come to know when working with Emma for the OSE. That had been over a year ago, a heartrending and difficult time, but at least they had done their bit to help other children. And with no small degree of pain, she recalled all she'd learned about how they had suffered. Could Tommy be suffering too?

Eighteen

France—1942

The *Oeuvre de Secours aux Enfants* did indeed prove to be experts with regard to rescuing children, exactly as Alexis had promised. Brenda and Emma met Jeanne, the lady he'd mentioned, at a local café where she happily filled them in on the work they were doing.

'The OSE, or Children's Aid Society, as you British like to call it, gives assistance to thousands of children throughout the country. When the Nazis entered Paris in June 1940, many were sent overseas by parents desperate for their children to escape the occupation.'

'I know the feeling,' Brenda sadly remarked, and quickly told her own story, and how she'd so far failed to find her beloved son. 'I want him back so badly, and really would appreciate any help you could give me.'

'We'll do our best,' Jeanne said with a warm smile. 'Separation is deeply traumatic for both children and parents, but sadly for some it can become permanent.'

Brenda felt a tremor run through her at these words. The prospect of never seeing Tommy again was too dreadful to consider. But Jeanne was probably speaking of people who'd been sent to a far more dangerous concentration camp than the one they had suffered.

Seeing the anguish in her friend's face, Emma slipped an arm about her, speaking with her usual calm confidence. 'We're quite convinced we'll find him eventually, it's just knowing where to look.'

'We should have left Paris much earlier,' Brenda groaned, going on to tell what had happened to Jack after the occupation. 'Unfortunately we couldn't, as we were caring for my husband's sick mother. After that it was quite impossible to leave. I was trapped.'

Offering her sympathy, Jeanne did agree that things had become more difficult. 'At first people were almost encouraged to leave, as the country would be "cleansed" of Jews, and even the unwelcome British. Then the situation worsened. As a result we've had to go underground, but we continue to find rescuers willing to hide these lost children.'

'That can't be easy, considering the risks involved,' Emma said.

'I'm afraid not. Particularly as we cannot say how long they'll be obliged to care for the child. It could be a few months or years. Most people gladly share their home or farm with these lost souls. French Protestants, Catholics, including convents, schools and orphanages, are all prepared to offer accommodation. Muslim families help too. Finding enough food for the children without proper ration cards is not easy but the main problems are the searches that take place fairly frequently. Young refugees then have to hide in the loft or cellar, or even a chicken coop or garden shed.'

'Are you saying they are at risk of capture too?'

'I'm afraid many Jewish children are sent to concentration camps. If the Gestapo get wind of where they might be hiding, or if money runs out or danger threatens, they often have to move countless times.'

'That must be so painful for young ones,' Emma said. 'I remember having to change schools several times because my father moved about a lot, being in the military, which meant I kept losing the friends I'd made. It was so debilitating.'

Jeanne nodded. 'It does take time for these youngsters to recover from the loss of their parents and form a new attachment, and yet another separation means they do tend to lose trust in people, protecting themselves by rarely showing any affection towards their new foster carers.'

Recalling how she still harboured resentment over the way her own mother had abandoned her, Brenda could fully understand this emotion. Would her son ever forgive her for leaving him behind? She couldn't bear to think about that. 'They must also lose all sense of safety.'

'In order to make them truly safe, whenever possible we smuggle them over the border into Switzerland, or transport them to America or England. This can involve a dangerous journey, fake IDs, and a considerable sum of money required for train fares and possibly an escort. Thanks to the Resistance movement we do manage to save a substantial number. And Jewish children, who are expected to wear a "Star of David", must dispose of that and pose as Christians in order to stay safe and conceal their true identity. Worryingly, some of the younger ones may soon forget that they are Jewish, let alone their nationality or who their parents were.'

'That's what I fear may have happened to my child,' Brenda said. 'Even though he is not Jewish, I worry he too may have been captured or else dispatched into some unknown country. And being only a baby when I was arrested, how will he remember me or where he came from? Even when I find him I will feel like a complete stranger to him. It's a terrifying thought! Nevertheless, I shall go on searching for Tommy as we make our way back to England, so if you're looking for an escort any time, I'd be glad to help.'

Jeanne's expression brightened. 'Are you saying you'd be willing to help us in return for our making some enquiries about your son?'

'Gladly,' Brenda said. 'In any way I can.'

'Me too,' Emma agreed.

*

They happily volunteered to work for the OSE while these enquiries took place, and thankfully accepted accommodation, sharing the spare room in Jeanne's apartment. How comfortable that felt in comparison with the filthy bleakness of the camp they'd endured for so long. Life was suddenly lit with hope and a delicious sense of freedom.

'I'm delighted to help the OSE, as children should never

be put at risk of capture,' Brenda said to Emma as they settled in their beds that first night. 'What a dreadful prospect
that they could be arrested and brutalised! And the thought
that poor Tommy may not know who he is, or where he
comes from, makes me fear he too could be accused of
being a Jew, and also captured.'

'Let's think positive, honey,' Emma said, her tone of
voice again revealing her strength. 'He's surely safe with
his grandmama.'

'You're quite right. I must keep a tight hold on my
emotions and not let fear win the day,' Brenda said with a
wobble of a smile. 'In the meantime, we must do as much
as possible to help other lost children.'

They were required to go through a course of training
on how to check out a potential volunteer rescuer, and
learn how to acquire the necessary visas and forged papers.
Germans and police closely checked identity documents
in the constant searches they made, so these had to be as
perfect as possible. While involved in this training the
two friends worked at the orphanage, getting to know the
children well.

Their first task was to find a home for a ten-year-old
Polish girl. Her parents had put her on a train, telling her
she was going away on a lovely holiday to her uncle's
house in southern France, and that they'd shortly join her.
Sadly, she'd not seen them since.

'No doubt because they've been arrested and taken to
Dachau,' Brenda surmised.

'Her uncle too has apparently vanished,' Emma added.

The girl was so sweet and brave, but feeling entirely alone in the world. Fortunately, they soon found a local family prepared to take her who seemed friendly and caring, even though they were quite poor. 'Are we paid anything for this?' the woman asked.

'We're low-skilled workers and don't have much money,' her husband admitted.

'I'll make the necessary enquiries,' Brenda told him. Speaking to Jeanne, she learned that the girl's parents had stitched a large wad of notes in her pocket, so a small sum was granted to the couple.

'At least she is finally safe and being well cared for now,' Emma said.

'Which is a great relief when her entire family is in turmoil.' It filled Brenda with pride and joy that they'd managed to help the poor child. But a week or two later Jeanne informed them that the so-called rescuers had broken their promise and handed the girl over to the Gestapo in return for an additional reward.

'Oh no, that's dreadful, after all that poor child has already endured!' Brenda cried, clenching her fists in a spate of fury. 'Why did we trust these people when they asked for money?'

Jeanne gave a sad smile. 'Most rescuers are given funds to help them. Caring for children is not cheap, but trusting anyone these days is becoming something of a problem. We can only go by our instincts.'

Taking a steadying breath and rubbing her palms over her arms, Brenda felt as if she was about to burst into tears, but what good would that do? 'I doubt I shall trust mine ever again.'

'Yes you will. You were most unfortunate, but these are rare incidents. With luck, she'll be released eventually.'

'I pray that will be the case. And I shall make sure I ask far more questions in future.'

*

As Brenda slowly recovered from this anguish, as well as anxiously awaiting news of her own child, she and Emma devoted themselves to finding homes for many more youngsters of all nationalities and religions. The children came from many different countries including the Netherlands, Germany and even Siberia, and Brenda made sure they investigated would-be rescuers much more carefully. They also learned to keep a watch out for army patrols or road blocks, and any jack-boots on parade.

Brenda and Emma found that they loved working with the children, even though it was not always easy. Because of the traumas they'd suffered many would frequently fall into tantrums, or sink into silent depression. Brenda did her best to offer comfort and support, and happily taught them a little French and English. Emma taught them how to paint pictures and sew, being a very gifted lady.

But sadly, there was still no word about where Tommy might be, beyond the confirmation that the two ladies were no longer in Paris.

'Fortunately they left before Camille's apartment was bombed,' Emma pointed out. 'You may not yet know exactly where they are living, but can assume your son is still safe, alive and well. I've still received no word from my husband either.' Her lovely oval face twitched a little as she fought back tears, and a bleakness entered her hazel eyes.

'Let us pray they are both safe and well,' Brenda gently said, fear reverberating through her too about whether Tommy was still alive. There was a war on, after all. She was thankful to have at least found a purpose in life, which helped her not to dwell too much on her sense of loss. It felt good to be doing her bit for these lovely children, even if there was increasing anguish whenever something went wrong.

Strengthening their resolve, the two friends strode off together, arm in arm, to face their next challenge.

Having managed to get back in touch with her parents, Emma did eventually receive the good news that her mother was on the road to recovery, and at once began to discuss a possible return to England. 'I'm anxious to return home just in case she falls ill again,' she admitted. 'In addition, there may be ways I can help to find Paul by contacting the Foreign Office. I've heard nothing from him in over a year now. I did ask Dad to write to him, but he's received no reply either. God knows what's happened.'

'They might simply have moved him to another camp, or stopped all correspondence,' Brenda suggested.

'Or else he's died of some disease, or even been executed.'

'Don't even think such negative thoughts,' Brenda said,

giving her friend a comforting hug. 'Have faith and think positive, as you keep telling me.'

Gazing at Brenda out of tear-filled eyes, Emma struggled to smile. 'I might sound outwardly lively and optimistic, but in my heart I'm a complete wreck, while you're such a brave girl.'

'Or a feisty little madam, depending on how you view me,' Brenda said with a laugh. 'But at least we are a great support to each other. And yes, it is perhaps time we started to think about going home.'

Nineteen

1945

Melissa was enjoying a delicious lunch with her husband Gregory in the smart restaurant at Fortnum & Mason. 'At least good meals still exist,' she said, as she chose lobster.

'If at a price,' he snarled. 'Can we afford it?'

'And we'll have a bottle of claret,' she told the waiter, completely ignoring this question until Gregory too had ordered lobster and they were left alone.

'You do realise that I will have to go back north on another visit soon, darling, just to check how things are progressing with this death duty issue. I need to know whether it will affect my allowance.'

'Wait till we go for Christmas, then I'll be there too.'

'There's really no need, I could just make a quick visit now.' She was far from convinced it would be a good idea to take the entire family with her, bearing in mind what she wished to do.

'Yes there is. I wish to speak to Hugh too. The damn fool is ignoring every letter I write to him requesting information. If there really is a problem with the family business, we need to be fully informed about exactly what that is and how it can be resolved.'

'As well as the effect of this war, there is of course the death duty to deal with,' Melissa said, with a sigh. There were other issues too she needed to investigate, which she carefully never mentioned, certainly not to Gregory. She'd done her best to be a good wife to him and had no wish to argue, even if some of his demands upon her had proved difficult to fulfil. But despite her obedience to his every whim, she wasn't even certain he'd remained faithful to her. Their marriage was a little blow hot, blow cold, perhaps because they saw very little of each other, thanks to the war. So Christmas at the Hall might not be a bad idea. Melissa felt in dire need of more time with him.

'Of course, darling, if that is what you wish,' she agreed. 'A little break from the city would do you good. You've been working so hard lately. Not to mention frequent trips abroad, doing whatever it is you do there.'

'That's what my work at the Foreign Office involves, and you know I cannot discuss that,' he retorted. 'Inform Nanny Holborn of our plans and I'll see if I can arrange for a chauffeur to take us, then we don't have to fuss with trains. I may need to leave as soon as Christmas is over, but will stay long enough to tackle Hugh on this issue.'

The lobster arrived at that moment, and Melissa gave her attention to that, saying nothing more. But in her head was the happy thought that Gregory leaving early would mean she could set about dealing with these other problems.

Right now it was wonderful that he'd even found time to take her out to lunch.

'Since you've been given some time off today, perhaps we could pop back home for a little afternoon romp before you return to the office,' she teasingly suggested.

Lifting his attention from cracking open the lobster to roam his gaze over her, he gave a little shrug. 'Sorry, maybe later. I have a busy afternoon planned.'

Was that with his latest mistress? she wondered; struggling to keep a hold of her temper as she gave him a pinch of a smile. 'I shall look forward to it.'

But when her husband returned quite late that evening he did not even come to her room. As was often the case these days, he chose to sleep in his dressing room. Melissa sat up in bed in the glamorous new nightgown she'd bought that afternoon, quivering with fury. She would go home first to deal with what she needed to do, and Gregory could join her later.

*

Brenda was feeding the hens when she found herself surrounded by four giggling youngsters who clearly belonged to Melissa, the family having recently arrived. She felt deeply envious of that lady's good fortune. How different life would have been if Jack had survived, she hadn't been arrested and Tommy not lost. And she'd just gone through the anguish of yet another of his birthdays.

'Would you like to help me collect the eggs from their nesting boxes?' Brenda asked them with a smile.

Claire, the seven year old, wrinkled her nose. 'No thanks, it stinks in there.'

'Only of hens,' Brenda laughed. 'It gets cleaned out regularly.'

'I don't like eggs,' said one of the twins.

'Yes you do,' Claire told her. 'But it's not our job to collect them. Let's go and skip.' And grabbing their skipping rope, she swung on her heels and marched away, the twins running after her, giggling. How like her mother she was, Brenda thought with a sigh.

'What are you giving them to eat?' the little boy asked.

She looked down at him, feeling a sudden urge to stroke the butter-silk locks of his hair. 'Mash, but I'll give them a little grain later. Would you like to fill the hoppers with it, then fetch some fresh water?'

Giving a little nod, he carefully put the mash into the drums that hung from the roof of the hen coop, then dashed off to fetch the watering can and fill the water bowls. Happily watching the hens tuck in, he then asked, 'Are they allowed to run about anywhere?'

'Of course. They like to perch on trees, or sit and bask in the sun. They are free to do as they please.'

'I'm not,' he said with a grunt.

'Really? Why is that?'

'Mama won't let me wander too far.'

'Well, I suppose she is trying to keep you safe. At night the hens have to be carefully kept safe too, sitting on their perches in the coop, away from any foxes and out of the rain. So what is your name?'

'I'm Ross,' he announced, in almost as stern a voice as his uncle's.

Brenda put out a hand to gently shake his. 'Pleased to meet you. I'm Brenda.'

'Can I collect the eggs?'

'Of course. Your assistance would be most welcome.'

And with an excited little smile he picked up the basket and began to search each nesting box. At that moment Melissa came storming across the farmyard, her heels clicking sharply on the flags, cheeks crimson with fury. 'What are you doing, child?'

'Just helping with the hens,' he muttered, the happy expression instantly fading from his face.

'It's far too cold for you to be outside and I've already made it perfectly clear that working in the garden, or on the farm, is not your job. Now put down that basket and come inside this minute.'

Tears filled his eyes as he handed it back to Brenda. 'Sorry,' he whispered.

'Thanks for your help,' she quietly responded, but he was already scampering away indoors. Turning to Melissa, Brenda said, 'Actually, it's not terribly cold. We even have a little sunshine, and your son has been most helpful.'

'Don't you dare give him such jobs to do. Those stupid hens are your responsibility, not my son's.'

Brenda felt frustration bubble within her as she watched Melissa march away, looking so elegant in her navy jersey suit, while she felt a scrubby mess in her overalls and wellies. No wonder she was still being treated like a servant. Maybe that's exactly what she was.

To her amazement, young Ross continued to visit the hen coop quite early each morning, but Brenda took care not to encourage him to linger too long. The boy clearly had a mind of his own but she had no wish for him to get into trouble with his stern mother. Not that Melissa did much in the way of caring for her children, leaving such duties largely to Nanny Holborn. She was a stocky, solemn-faced woman, quite old, with a fleshy nose, a discontented slant to her dry lips and grey hair drawn up tightly into a knot at the back of her neck; although quite pleasant and friendly. And she clearly adored these children.

Brenda could well understand why, but becoming too attached to this child would be an extremely foolish thing for her to do.

*

Christmas was almost upon them, her husband had joined them and Melissa appeared to be very much in charge. She was constantly giving orders for what Mrs Harding, and in particular, Brenda, must do in preparation for the Festive Season. A tree had to be picked and decorated, together with wreaths of holly and mistletoe. And a seemingly end-less list of food was required to be cooked, from turkey to ham pies, Christmas cakes and puddings, mince tarts, trifle and a whole host of other delights.

'Finding the ingredients, with shortages and rationing still in force, will be a nightmare,' Mrs Harding moaned.

'We'll do our best to be inventive,' Brenda said. 'If we can't find a turkey we'll have goose. I reckon Joe could provide us with one of those. And we can use mock icing sugar for the cake, and make mock marzipan out of ground rice and almond essence. And we can put grated carrot and bread crumbs into the Christmas pudding with the mixed fruit, instead of suet and sugar, boiling it a little longer to make sure it's soft and rich in flavour. There are always alternatives.'

'What a star you are, chuck.'

Melissa would call upon Brenda to serve her breakfast in bed, fetch her coffee each morning and provide afternoon tea, on top of all the work required of her in the fruit and vegetable garden, let alone the kitchen. She'd even ring the bell to call for Brenda to fetch her coat and hat whenever she wished to go out, as if she weren't capable of finding these herself. Melissa would often demand that a certain gown be washed and ironed in time for a party or event the next day, no matter how bad the weather, which would make drying it difficult. She'd even check the dust on the furniture with her fingertips, making Brenda polish it all over again, and finding fault with pretty much everything she did.

One lunchtime Brenda served plum pudding, which she'd thought of as a treat. Melissa took one mouthful, then slammed down her spoon and complained it did not have enough sweetness to it.

'We're still short of sugar, but there's a little here if you'd like more,' Brenda politely pointed out, handing her the sugar bowl.

'No thank you, it tastes dreadful. *And* I asked for more wine,' she snapped.

'That's Carter's job, not this young lady's,' Hugh tactfully reminded her, and as the butler scuttled over to fill her glass, he took a mouthful of the pudding. 'Actually, it tastes delicious.'

'Let me try it,' Gregory said. 'Hmm, not bad at all.'

'I like it too,' young Ross said, savouring a spoonful of the spicy fruit-and-suet pastry.

'Nonsense, this girl is a rubbish cook. She should be sacked for serving such dreadful food.'

Snatching his dish up, Melissa tossed it back on to the tray, together with her own and her husband's. 'Take it away, girl, we don't want it.'

'I do,' Ross said, and began to cry.

'Stop that noise at once, you naughty boy.'

Opening his mouth wide, he wailed all the louder. 'I want my pudding,' he cried. Melissa smacked him across the back of his head, whereupon he yelled all the louder.

'I say, that's a bit harsh,' Hugh protested.

'Nonsense! Papa would have done the same, had he been here.'

'I very much doubt it. Our father never beat us. Smacking a child is not a good idea.'

Gregory snorted his disapproval. 'We all know Sir Randolph was a bossy brute of a man, as are you.'

'I believe the same could be said about you too,' Hugh stoutly responded. 'I think the girls would like to try it too, wouldn't you?' he asked. But glancing warily at their mother, they chose not to answer.

'It's none of your damn business how my wife deals with her children, let alone what she allows them to eat. Although, I will admit, this chit of a girl is not too bad a cook, and has other interesting qualities too,' Gregory said with a chuckle as his eyes fixed upon her breasts.

Feeling shocked and embarrassed, Brenda beat a hasty retreat, tray in hand.

'I want it! I want it! I want it!' the little boy yelled.

She paused at the door to watch in horror as, leaping to her feet, Melissa grabbed his arm to drag him off his chair and march the screaming child out into the hall to thrust him over to Nanny Holborn, who was hovering close by. 'Put this child to bed at once. I will not tolerate tantrums, particularly one caused by this scraggy mess of a girl.'

What a mad woman she was, Brenda thought.

Later that afternoon, having been confined to his bed for well over an hour as if he were a naughty puppy, young Ross suddenly appeared by her side when Brenda was weeding in the garden.

Shuffling his feet, he gave her a sideways glance. 'I'm hungry.'

Brenda smiled. 'Oh dear, that won't do.' She glanced around, to check they weren't being watched. 'Where's Nanny?'

'Taking her afternoon nap. Is there some of that pudding left?'

'And where is Mama?'

'Gone out shopping. *Again*! Can I have some? I won't tell,' he said, giving her a cheeky little grin.

Moments later he was sitting at the kitchen table shovelling down a dishful of plum pudding as he happily chatted with Brenda and Mrs Harding. Then he rolled about on the rug stroking and playing with Kit.

'What a grand little lad he is,' the housekeeper said.

Hearing Nanny Holborn calling for him, he gave them a cheery wave and scampered away giggling, obviously having enjoyed his treat.

'He is indeed,' Brenda said, a certain sadness in her tone. 'But his mother bullies him for no good reason.'

Mrs Harding heaved a sigh. 'That's how Miss Melissa is, an attitude inherited from her father.'

*

Brenda worked hard in the kitchen alongside Mrs Harding throughout Christmas, everything she did seeming to indicate that she really was a servant and not related to this family at all. How furious Jack would be, were he still here. But Brenda knew that the only way to deal with this problem was to accept that she was indeed inferior to that grand lady, Melissa.

Having taken her demanding sister-in-law her nightly drink of hot chocolate, Brenda was heading for the stairs along the landing, eager to go to her own bed, when the bedroom door opened yet again. Turning with a sigh, expecting to be faced with yet another complaint, she instead found herself confronted by Melissa's husband.

Gregory Fenton, dressed in a dashing tartan dressing gown, was quite tall with beady dark eyes cloaked beneath heavy eyelids. His nostrils flared and he wore a lopsided smile as he approached. Coming to stand before her, his eyes roved over her from top to toe.

'Sorry about that business earlier. Such is my wife. Don't let it bother you. Melissa has told me how you spread your favours wide throughout the war. Looking at you, I can fully understand why. You're an attractive little wench and most well endowed. I fancy a taste myself.' And gripping her chin with one hand while the other squeezed her buttocks, his mouth closed over hers, thrusting his tongue inside.

Shock reverberated through Brenda, and the memory of the night when she'd been raped at Besançon flashed into her head. Never again would she allow such a thing to happen to her. The fear she instantly experienced was quickly replaced by cold fury and, lifting up her knee, she punched him in his private parts. Letting out a yelp, he leapt away, crouched low in agony. Brenda flew quickly down the stairs. No devil would ever win her again.

Back in her room she began to shake and quiver, then fell into bed sobbing her heart out. Would nothing ever go right for her? Why did these devils pursue her? She wasn't a bit of rubbish for any man to play with. How she longed for someone to truly love her as Jack had done. And loving him in return, their intimacy had been such a joy. In future she'd need to keep well out of this monster's way, which she most carefully did over the days following.

As New Year dawned it was with great relief she learned that Gregory Fenton, together with his wife and children, was returning to London. Before she left Melissa did, of course, attempt to dismiss her. She looked quite shocked when Brenda simply laughed out loud.

'How can you sack me when I'm not actually employed by you or Hugh? I just offered to help Mrs Harding and stand in for Prue for a while, until I find myself a job. I'm a volunteer and don't even receive any wages.'

After a moment of stunned silence Melissa's lips curled with derision. 'So you'll be leaving soon?'

'I will.'

'Thank goodness for that. *I* was born into the kind of family that endears itself to society. *You* were born in the gutter, which is where you should stay. Make sure you are not still here when I return at Easter.'

How thankful Brenda was to see Melissa leave, and in particular her sly-faced brute of a husband. But with the house now empty of laughing children, Prue still away and still no sign of her son, she felt lonelier than ever.

Twenty

The land was thick with rowan, holly and bilberries, not a sound to be heard save for the whisper of willow skimming the water of the river. As Brenda sat on the bank staring at the wind-blown ripples, a kingfisher flew into the air. Like an arrow of blue light it dived into the water in search of a fish. Seconds later, having failed to find its lunch it flapped its wings in a frenzy and returned to perch upon another branch, again patiently waiting. Fortunately, Kit the collie wasn't in the least interested in birds, and paid no attention.

Giving him a soft pat as he lay beside her, Brenda gave the kingfisher a little smile of sympathy. 'Poor you. I know the feeling of failure well. I seem doomed to have everything go wrong for me too.'

She'd heard nothing from the family solicitor for some weeks and Brenda found herself struggling to raise the courage to complain, in view of the stern instructions not to call unless invited. She despised herself for such cowardice. Hadn't she dealt with far more difficult people than this solicitor and his secretary? Surely she deserved to be kept informed of the enquiries they were making, as well as any responses they were receiving? Brenda felt almost as if they were ignoring her. Why was that?

'Will I ever find darling Tommy, or has something dreadful happened to him?' Kit wagged his tail, as if assuring her that she would find him one day. 'You're quite right, I fully intend to battle on.'

Spring was approaching and she'd endured a long and difficult winter worrying over what she should do with her life. Fortunately, bossy Melissa and her dreadful husband had not returned since Christmas. Brenda had decided to spend Easter with her friend Cathie in Manchester, aware that she needed to steer well clear of them both. Leaving this house altogether might be sensible. There was really no necessity for her to remain. Was she staying on just because of her memories of Jack, or for some other reason?

Hearing the crunch of stones underfoot, she was startled to see Hugh strolling along the path towards her. She'd seen little of him since Christmas and felt her determination tighten. If he too was seeking favours then he'd find himself kicked into the river. She cringed at the thought, then laughed as Kit bounced up to excitedly welcome their visitor.

'I thought I heard someone talking, but you're all alone,' he said, giving the dog's ear a little rub.

Seeing him standing before her, his fair hair blowing in the cool breeze and an unexpected smile on his face, Brenda found herself responding with a grin. 'I was talking to the kingfisher. We've had quite a chat.'

Hugh gave a little chuckle. 'I'll admit there aren't many

people to talk with around here. I'm off for my daily walk. Would you care to join me? It would have been Jack's birthday next week and he's very much on my mind.'

Giving a sad little nod, she stepped up beside him. The anguish of yet another birthday to deal with. 'My pleasure.'

Sunlight and shadow ribbed the path as they followed it through bracken with moss underfoot. It then swooped upwards over the hill, Kit rummaging around, sniffing for rabbits as he always did, although failing to find any. Brenda carefully stepped over a tree root covered in green lichen. On the tenth of March 1946 Jack would have been twenty-eight. They'd enjoyed celebrating birthdays together, but now she could hardly bear to think of it. And come November, their lost son would turn six.

'When we were boys Mama used to take us to the circus to celebrate a birthday, although Jack never liked to see lions shut up in cages, or elephants ordered to perform, so that eventually stopped,' Hugh told her with a laugh.

'He was very picky about freedom, and loved the outdoors,' Brenda agreed. 'As do I.'

'You two had much in common. Is that why he married you?'

These words so surprised her that Brenda tripped over a tree root, and would have gone flying had he not caught her. Meeting his gaze as he held her in his arms, she felt almost mesmerised by the sparkle in his soft grey eyes. Her cheeks flushed pink at the feel of his hands upon her waist, a sense of awareness seeming to flare through her at his touch. But he did seem much more relaxed today, not at all the bad-tempered man she'd become accustomed to. Nor was he touching any part of her that he shouldn't, as that Gregory fellow seemed to think he had the right to do. Did this comment mean that he now believed her? His next words quickly flattened that hope.

'Assuming we eventually find the necessary evidence to prove what you tell me is correct,' he blithely remarked.

Frustration flared within her. What a confusing man he was, one minute all pleasant and friendly, the next back to his old sceptical self. Dusting herself off, she stepped back. 'Let's not go into that right now. Sorry I tripped, I was thinking of Jack and not concentrating. And yes, I'm pretty picky about freedom too, having been incarcerated for almost two years.'

'That must have been dreadful.' His expression became more serious and thoughtful, as if he was assessing and appraising her.

'It's not something I care to remember or speak of.'

'I can understand that.'

'Were you ever to remember some member of your family who might know Adèle and where she lives, do please let me know.'

'Sorry, she's from a part of Mama's young life we know little about.'

So returning to Trowbridge Hall had been a complete waste of time. They walked in silence for some time, the dog trotting along beside them, and on reaching the top of the hill gazed out across at Dovestone Reservoir on Saddleworth Moor, the village of Greenfield tucked to the west below it. Brenda found the view so beautiful it struck to the heart of her. How could she ever bear to leave this place?

'I feel I should apologise for my sister's arrogant attitude towards you,' he said, breaking into her thoughts. 'You worked hard for us over Christmas, which I do appreciate, and no matter what she says, you are an excellent cook.'

'Jack thought so too. He particularly adored my custard tarts, as did Camille,' she stoutly responded.

He grinned. 'I can well believe it. I'm afraid Melissa is too full of herself, a bit of a narcissist with a preoccupation for power and prestige. But she has a very demanding husband. Gregory is a bureaucrat at the Foreign Office. He's very controlling, which makes Melissa take out her resentment upon other people.'

Brenda felt the urge to comment that this seemed to be a trait in Hugh too. But biting her tongue, decided it was wiser to remain silent. Nor did she wish to mention what that fellow had attempted to do to her.

'You once expressed an interest in visiting the factory. I wondered if you'd still like to do that.'

She looked up at him in surprise. 'Oh, yes, I'd love to do that.'

'Good, we could go tomorrow if you like?'

Surprised and flattered by this change of attitude towards her, she gave a little nod. 'Thank you, that would be most interesting.'

*

The factory seemed to be packed out with machinery and workers, the air filled with the sweet smell of biscuits. There were long conveyer belts carrying hundreds of biscuits, with women in overalls seated on either side picking and packing them.

'So women do work here,' she said with a wry smile.

'They don't have any say in the running of the business,' Hugh casually responded.

'Tut, tut! As if you would allow such an outrageous thing. Do you enjoy working here?' Brenda asked one of the ladies. But glancing anxiously up at a rather solid-looking lady hovering close by, she said not a word.

Hugh, staring at Brenda through narrowed eyes, seemed to be struggling to find a suitable response. 'This is Edith. She has worked here for years and trains the new girls, which she does very well.'

Brenda shook the forewoman's hand. 'Do they need any special qualifications?'

'None at all, only the ability to work hard.'

'Right, I might come looking for a job then,' Brenda said with a grin.

Hugh instantly stepped forward to lead her away, almost as if he feared Edith might offer her one there and then. They passed through various rooms dealing with the different ingredients needed for biscuit making, including the making of chocolate, cream, coconut and custard. Finally he took her into the bake-house.

'This is where the hardest work is done. You have to be

careful when you pick up the trays as they are piping hot so you could easily burn yourself.'

The dangers were fairly obvious as Brenda took in the sight of several huge ovens churning out heat and smoke. Two men appeared to be in charge, and several women were carefully stacking trays of biscuits into racks. Others were busily rolling out dough, adding chocolate or raisins, then cutting them up.

'Do you enjoy the work?' she asked, trying again with one of the younger girls.

'I do, miss,' she said with a nod, although the expression on her face told quite a different story.

'You don't find it boring?'

''Course not. We do sweat a lot in here though, and need to drink a lot of water, whenever we get the chance.'

'I'm sure you do. But it all looks very efficient,' Brenda said. Then turning to Hugh asked, 'Do you make crackers and water biscuits too?'

'Of course, and cheese biscuits, wafers, garibaldi, oat, ginger. Every variety you can think of.'

'And cakes?'

He shook his head. 'We'd probably need another kitchen in order to do that.'

'These shortbread biscuits look absolutely delicious. Am I allowed to taste one?'

'You can choose a packet on your way out,' he said, at last looking relaxed enough to offer her a small gift, as well as a small smile to go with it. 'But not one of these, as they're still warm.'

Giving a little chuckle, she picked one up. 'I don't mind that. Ooh, they're very tasty,' she said with relish. 'It's so sad that the business has suffered from the war. I have an idea I'm hoping might appeal to you, as I'd love to help.'

Hugh's eyes widened. 'What makes you think I need *your* help? You seem to be assuming there are problems I cannot personally resolve, which is most definitely not the case.'

'I feel I've nothing to lose by talking to you and everything to gain. Whether or not you're prepared to admit it, I'm fully aware that the factory's profits are going downhill fast.'

Hugh grabbed her by the elbow and marched her into his office, slamming shut the door. His face was flushed crimson as he turned to her, a white line of anger curled around his lips. Yet strangely, Brenda felt a sudden urge to kiss his tight mouth, as if needing to revisit the feelings she'd experienced yesterday when his attitude towards her had been much more appealing. Or else she simply felt the need to curb his temper.

With a huge effort of will, he seemed to bring himself under control. 'I fully accept that you're a lively and courageous girl, but what makes you imagine you can resolve serious business problems?'

Brenda took a deep breath. She'd been doing quite a bit of thinking lately, before Christmas when she'd been out and about seeking work, and in the weeks since when she was treated as a servant by Melissa just because she'd offered to help in return for accommodation. All of this anguish and worry had made her take note of her own skills. And needing to seriously consider her future, she'd decided that one thing she was good at, was baking.

'You've readily accepted that I'm a good cook, so I wondered why you wouldn't be prepared to offer me a job?'

'Why should I?'

'Because I'm young and a hard worker. Ask Mrs Harding, if you don't believe me. I thought I'd offer to bake cakes and tarts for you. You could sell them to Kendal Milnes, Selfridges and other department stores. They are the ones with power. And as the war is over, you need to expand. Right now this business feels in the doldrums, and you seem to be turning into something of a stick-in-the-mud, as I believe your father was.'

Hugh growled. Nobody had ever said such things to him before, or stood up to him in so bold a fashion. Who did this little madam think she was? He gave a snort of disbelief, bending his head so close she could smell the intoxicating scent of his male skin, and the soap and aftershave he'd used, so like Jack's. 'What makes you imagine you have the right to become involved in the family business?'

'As Jack's widow, why shouldn't I work here?' she tartly responded. 'I'm prepared to put some effort into helping to improve things because I'm in dire need of a job and a good future.'

'Yet you know nothing about running a business. Few women do.'

'Absolutely not true. The war has taught us women a great deal: how to be strong and independent, brave and skilled. You're living in the past if you refuse to accept that, a view that is completely out of date.'

'You're also an imposter, so why would I be stupid enough to accept such an offer?'

Brenda glared at him, deeply hurt to the core of her that he could make such a callous comment, particularly after they'd got on so well this last day or two. 'An imposter? Is that how you still see me? A fraud and a liar. So what will you charge me with next? Like it or not, I *was* married to your brother, and will prove that very soon. Lord, you really are a nasty piece of work. Just like your bloody father.'

Having heard enough, he marched to the door and flung it open. 'Get out! I'm not standing here to be preached at by some greedy little brat.'

Brenda left without another word, the crush of defeat almost too much to bear. It had been naïve of her to make this suggestion, but she'd so looked forward to a future working with this man. Now all hope and optimism was drained out of her. Of course, it might have helped if she'd kept a better hold upon her own temper.

*

It was a great relief when a few days later she received the letter she'd longed for from the solicitor's secretary, asking her to call. She gladly caught the next train to Castlefield, very much feeling the need to escape. This time the secretary looked flustered, and kept glancing over her shoulder as if she knew the solicitor was listening so had to be careful what she said.

'I'm afraid we have not managed to get the necessary paperwork to prove your marriage, *Mrs* Stuart, or are ever likely to do so. It has proved to be entirely impossible, since buildings and archives have been bombed and documents destroyed. Nor have we any word of your son. There's nothing more we can do to find him, and have discovered no evidence about where Camille's cousin might now be living. She too has disappeared. Our investigation has come to an end.'

Bleakness grew within her as Brenda listened to this dreadful news. So after all the searching she had gone through over the years, and the questions these lawyers had asked, this was the end of the road. Her heart plummeted. Her future seemed to be completely blank and without hope. And following the row that had taken place between herself and Hugh, she had no desire to return to Trowbridge Hall, much as she loved Saddleworth. Prue was still away and Melissa and that stupid husband of hers were currently in residence. Nothing would induce her to be yet again treated as a servant, or be pawed by that dreadful man. What a family they were! All the lovely kind members of it now gone.

Returning to her flat, she locked the door and sat at the kitchen table with her head in her hands, quietly sobbing in despair. It felt as if her life was over, and she had no reason to go on. Loneliness and despair overwhelmed her. Valiantly pulling herself out of this sorrowful depression, Brenda wrote to Emma to explain what she'd been told. How she wished her friend was here with her, as only

Emma could properly understand what she was going through.

Days later, Cathie suddenly called in with the news that she'd found a job at the Christmas card factory. Brenda blinked at her in shock. Could this be the answer? What did she have to lose by giving it a go? Grabbing her coat from the hook behind the door, she ran round right away. Her aim now must surely be to work hard and keep busy, if only to get her through each day.

'I'll come with you while you go in and ask,' Cathie told her, waiting outside with little Heather, her niece.

Brenda was thrilled to be offered a job, and the two old friends did a little jig on the pavement. Perhaps life would start to look up a little, at last. This new job would at least pay the rent, and might give her the energy she needed to make more long-term, tough decisions about her life.

She returned at once to Trowbridge Hall to collect her possessions and inform Hugh that she would be leaving for good, thanks to her friend Cathie having found her a job in the Christmas card factory. The dismay on his handsome face was electrifying.

'I'm aware that we had a disagreement, but there's really no need for you to go forever,' he said. 'You are most welcome to stay here as long as you wish, or come and go as you please.'

Brenda could smell the exquisite scent of bluebells. The hens were pecking about in the grass, cows mooing in a nearby field, and a part of her longed to stay. But to do what? More washing and cleaning, and waiting hand and foot upon Melissa whenever she appeared? Not to mention fighting off her bastard of a husband.

'Sorry, but it's too good an opportunity to miss. I need the money.' Not least to continue her search for Tommy. 'Prue has written to say she'll be returning soon. Until then, I'm afraid you'll have to find someone else to work in the house and garden.'

Giving him a polite little smile, she turned to head to her room and pack. Later, she wondered if she really had heard correctly when he quietly remarked, 'I'll miss you.'

Twenty-One

Prue felt so happy now that they were married. They had spent the winter in Ramsey, Dino working with the fishermen. In February she gave birth to a beautiful baby girl. They called her Flora, her full name Floriana in Italian, which seemed quite appropriate as they were both garden-loving people. How thrilling it was to have a family of her own at last, and to have succeeded in helping the man she loved to be released. When Flora was three months old the time seemed to have come for them to return home, not least because Prue was feeling homesick. Dino was also eager to visit his own family, which he did, taking his new wife with him.

What a delight it was to see his mother's tears of joy as she embraced her son and new grandchild, a shining light of pride in his father's eyes.

'Are you sure you want to come back to Trowbridge Hall, or would you prefer to stay here in Ancoats?' Prue asked him as his parents bustled about preparing a meal for them.

He shook his head. 'No, *cara mia*. I have no wish to live in a city ever again. I need the open air. Besides, according to my father, the number of Italians now living in Ancoats is about half what it used to be. Most of the people I knew have left. Even my parents are retiring to the suburbs. The community is attempting to re-establish itself and businesses are rebuilding, but it's not an easy task as people are nervous of being attacked. The anti-Italian attitude is still strong in some areas. They didn't even dare to carry out the Italian Whit-Walk procession, and that was always so popular. We too may suffer problems, of course,' he gently warned her.

'Despite the ban on fraternisation having been lifted before Christmas?'

'People have their own opinions on what is right and proper. They don't always listen to politicians, lawyers, or even the Church.'

'Then whatever prejudice we are faced with, we will cope with it together, darling, and with great tolerance. I'm sure we'll win people round eventually.'

'I agree. And we'll never allow ourselves to be parted ever again.'

'Never!' she said, falling into his arms as she so loved to do, and they began making plans.

Dino was proved to be right when a few days later a stone came flying through the window of the cottage, scattering pieces of glass everywhere, causing them to jump up from their cosy clinch on the sofa. He ran outside to find the culprit but could see no one.

'I'm sure things will calm down,' she assured him as they locked all doors and boarded up the broken window.

'Although it might take a while. I shall speak to Hugh about our future, which I admit won't necessarily be easy.'

'I'll come with you,' Dino said.

'Perhaps it would be better if I talked to him first, sister to brother.'

'You may need some support.'

She agreed that her brother was in many respects a solemn, taciturn man. 'He is a bit strung up with problems of his own, although thankfully not as bad as our father was. At heart he is a kind and caring man. Once he's been won over,' she added with a wry smile. 'I will carefully explain how we battled for your release and finally managed to get married.'

Dino looked unconvinced. 'He might be angry because you stayed away so long, and married without his knowledge or permission.'

'Why should I ask his permission? I'm over twenty-one, and a modern woman. I don't need looking after or to be dictated to by him. He is not my father.'

'You know why, because of his prejudice against enemy aliens. You also robbed your charming sister of the pleasure of being able to buy a new hat to show herself off in church,' he said with a grin.

Prue giggled. Put like that, it did sound a bit funny. 'I suppose I should apologise to them for being terribly selfish and getting married far away from home. On top of all the other disappointments he's suffered, Hugh may be quite cross that he didn't get to come. Not that he expressed any interest in giving me away,' she admitted.

'All that matters is *us*,' Dino told her, giving her a kiss. 'We are happy, and it's our life, not Hugh's.'

'Quite right, darling, and I love you so much. I just feel the need to apologise for his unwelcoming attitude towards you.'

'That is not your responsibility. Besides, being in love means you don't have to keep saying you're sorry,' he told her with a smile.

'What a lovely thought,' she said, sinking into bed with him to make love. Prue made a promise to attempt to put things on a much better footing by describing to her brother the wonderful time she'd had in the Isle of Man, and what a lovely man Dino was.

*

'So you've wed the fellow, after all,' Hugh grumpily remarked when she went to speak to him in his study first thing the next morning.

'I'm delighted to say that Dino married me the moment he was released, and yes, we're so happy. Isn't that wonderful? And here is your lovely little niece,' she said, placing the baby in his arms.

Hugh looked so startled, his shoulders became quite stiff and rigid. 'Oh, my goodness, not sure I know how to hold a baby,' he said, lifting the child awkwardly in his outstretched hands. But looking down at the curl of her eyelashes and her blue eyes gazing up at him, he seemed to melt and relax, tucking her closer and cooing softly to her. 'Oh, she looks so sweet.'

'She's a love. Say hello to little Flora.'

'Hello, little Flora. She's beautiful.'

Relieving him of the baby before he did something fool-ish like drop her, Prue tucked her back into the pram and then addressed the problem that was occupying her mind. 'As you will appreciate, it's quite common for PoWs not to want to stay indoors or in confined spaces, so Dino has no wish to return to the city. He feels much happier working out in the open, and spending his free time walking over the hills. You should be able to sympathise with that, since you love that sort of lifestyle too. I was wondering if you would agree to our renting one of the farms belonging to the estate. Are there any available?'

'Not that I'm aware of,' he said, looking slightly taken aback by this request.

'Then could we perhaps take charge of this one?'

'Why on earth would I allow you to do that?' he scorn-fully remarked.

'Because I'm your sister, and you love me, yes?'

He flushed crimson. 'Of course I do, but the trust set up by our father leaves the farm and business to his eldest son, and with Jack gone that means me.'

'I'm perfectly aware that Papa always ignored we girls, and his wife, but I was hoping you would be more generous-hearted. Besides, you surely have enough to do running the biscuit factory. And old Joe can't cope on his own forever. Both Dino and I love farm and garden work. So what is your problem?'

'I'll think about it and let you know,' he mumbled, looking slightly confused.

'Dino would very much like to speak to you on the subject, and to discuss his thoughts and plans for the farm. May he come round later?'

'Not until I've had time to consider all the implications and gone over the finances of the estate.'

*

'I could have smacked his face,' Prue told Brenda when her friend came on a visit the next weekend to welcome her home. It felt so good to see her again, and she seemed to find this remark so amusing she burst out laughing.

'Your brother is a confusing sort of chap. One minute very friendly, the next immensely domineering, and so slow to make a decision.'

'I know, not at all the relaxed person he used to be.'

'Perhaps because he doesn't think through what he's saying carefully enough,' Brenda suggested. 'No doubt caused by the anxiety he's suffering over business problems, which he insists on keeping to himself. Or else the rules made by your father live on in his head.'

Prue gave a resigned sigh. 'That wouldn't surprise me. But I can't bear the thought of giving up this land, which I love. Why would I wish to? Were Jack, who should have inherited the estate, still here, I'm sure he'd have no objection to Dino and I staying on and sharing the work with him. It would matter to him greatly that we were in a position to build ourselves a good future together.'

'I'm quite certain he would do everything he could to help,' Brenda softly agreed. 'Sadly, brave Jack is no longer with us to put forward his point of view. But hopefully, Hugh will come round to seeing the logic and fairness of your request. I too am concerned for my own future. According to the lawyers, I may never find the necessary papers to prove that my marriage to Jack did exist and was entirely legal. They've called an end to their enquiries.'

'Oh dear, I didn't know that. Can't you ask them to keep on trying?'

Brenda shook her head. 'I've already tried that. They've closed the case, claiming there's nothing more to be done. As a consequence I'm fully aware I won't be granted a penny from Jack's share in the estate, despite the will he made. But with the war over and apparently no hope of finding my son either, I really need to think through my future most carefully.'

'I see. You have my deepest sympathy. We're doing the same.'

'The fact is, I'm a bit bored with working at the Christmas card factory. It isn't a permanent occupation, more of a summer job, but I was thankful to my dear friend Cathie for finding it. She has always been very supportive, as I have been of her. She lost her sister and loving her niece as she does, wanted to keep her, even though her fiancé did not agree, so she was badly in need of employment too.'

Brenda used to be more than happy to baby-sit for Cathie. Now she found herself avoiding little Heather whenever possible. She kept experiencing a great desire to pick the little girl up in her arms and run off with her, which wouldn't at all be the right thing to do. She also felt the need to avoid Melissa's son whenever the family was visiting, although he would constantly come looking for her, and the hens, of course. This feeling must have something to do with the fact that all hope of finding her own child had gone completely.

And she felt wickedly jealous of the new relationship Cathie had achieved, and of Prue too. Why couldn't she find the love that she so longed for? Not that any relationship with Hugh would be sensible, she warned herself, even if she did find him attractive. He was her brother-in-law and not an easy man to get on with. So as all hope of love was now gone, creating a new life for herself was absolutely essential.

'I'm sure Cathie and I will remain friends, even if I leave the card factory. I feel the need to do something different and more positive. Remember how we once made a pact to help each other rebuild our lives?' she reminded Prue. 'Well, a new beginning feels even more important now.'

'To me too.'

'An idea has popped into my head in recent weeks, which I shared with Hugh,' Brenda said, and went on to quickly explain how she'd offered to widen the market of the biscuit factory to help improve its profits. 'Unfortunately, he wasn't interested. However, I'm still keen on the idea so I've decided to start my own baking business instead. I'll need to speak to the bank manager about a loan, but hopefully that will be possible. What would you say to joining me on the project? Not necessarily with the baking, although you'd be most welcome to do that if you wished. Otherwise, you could supply me with some of the essential ingredients: milk, eggs, fruit and vegetables, whatever you can.'

'I'd love to. It's a deal,' Prue said, eagerly shaking Brenda's hand.

*

Hugh was driving across the open countryside, which always felt like a wonderful release. Summer was passing but the wild roses were still in bloom. He could hear the melodious chatter of fieldfares, thanks to the mild weather. He gazed across at Pots and Pans hill with its obelisk, a war memorial built in the twenties to commemorate the First World War. Yet more soldiers' names would no doubt be added to it soon, including Jack's. He intended to park up and take a much-needed walk across the moors, and perhaps around Dovestone reservoir. There was so much going on in his mind that he badly felt in need of some fresh air and escape. So perhaps that Dino chap deserved some sympathy for feeling the same.

A part of Hugh was beginning to think it would be a good idea for his sister, and this new husband of hers, to take over the farm. Farming had not come naturally to him, despite being forced into it by his father, so why had he been reluctant to agree? He'd sold several pieces of land, which had largely resolved the death duty issue. It had of course resulted in a reduction in the income they received from tenants.

The farm was much improved. Farmers had always been willing to accept a certain degree of government intervention in return for an improvement in their income. Save for his father, of course, who had very much insisted upon being in control and doing things his way.

Once Sir Randolph had passed away, old Joe's management had proved to be much better. He could no doubt remember the time of the 1930s depression when thousands of acres had been left desolate and unfarmed. Rural life had been pretty well ruined as a result. But as a consequence of war, derelict land had been reclaimed, numerous livestock slaughtered in order to save on feed and plough up more land, and the use of tractors became a requirement. Things might change a little now the war was over, but the days when farms were ruled by the Big House were long gone. And the government was still determined to ensure that sufficient food was produced. Thanks to the drop in imports and guaranteed pricing, farm profits had risen surprisingly well, so why not build upon that? This Dino chap sounded quite keen to do so. Hugh decided he would speak to him on the subject, and see what his plans were.

But as he walked he still felt oddly unsettled and undecided on what he should do about the factory. Had he been too quick to dismiss Brenda's suggestion too? Or was he simply regretting that decision because he was missing her?

*

A day or two later, Brenda was delighted to receive one of her regular letters from Emma:

'Dear Brenda

I was wondering if you're any nearer to finding Tommy. I've had to stop looking for Paul, my lovely hubbie, as I'm afraid he's gone from this life. But you might be interested to hear that I've involved myself again with OSE, helping to connect families with lost children. It's proving to be quite difficult and painful, taking months, so you do have my sympathy. Some parents resort to placing notices in newspapers. Have you thought to try that? Many people search convents and orphanages, as well as foster families. Even if we are fortunate enough to find them, some of the younger children have no memory of their true parents or any knowledge of their Jewish origins, as we were warned could happen. So sad, and quite upsetting for them. They think of their rescuers as the only family they know and love, and are often quite reluctant to leave them. Some foster parents move or hide the children again as they have no wish to part with them either. At other times, the search can end in tragedy, the parents discovering that their child has been killed or vanished completely. As Tommy isn't Jewish, let's hope he's been more fortunate than these poor souls. I'm sure he must still be safe and well somewhere. If only we knew where. I could speak to the OSE about him, if you wish. Don't ever give up looking.

All my love,

Emma'

Brenda found this news utterly heartrending. She worried all the time that poor Tommy might have been packed off to a concentration camp where he could have died of neglect or disease, as she knew from experience. It was a prospect that really didn't bear thinking about.

She remembered how, when working for the OSE, she'd learned how children and parents would each bear the grief of separation in silence, anxious not to jeopardise the safety of the other and terrified it could become permanent. Even those families who did get together again often suffered from dreadful problems, their relationships having been seriously damaged.

She remembered once helping to reunite a father and son. The man had managed to escape after having been confined for months. His head had been shaved, his face turned into a wrinkled mess and his body a thin shabby wreck. Sadly, he was also no longer the loving and patient father his son remembered, being filled with anger and wracked with nerves. And having lost his mother who'd died of dysentery, the boy was not in a good state of mind either. The pair did not seem close, both being psychologically damaged and torn apart.

'The boy probably feels like a small bird who has been tossed out of the nest and has resolved to remain independent and take care of himself,' Emma had said, as they'd watched them walk away, yards apart. 'We can but hope things will improve for them in time.'

Having seen how these parents and children suffered, Brenda feared that even if she did find Tommy again, would he even want her? She would be a complete stranger to him. Striving to block out these negative thoughts, she read the letter again.

Emma had made some suggestions worth trying, and Brenda decided that she would indeed put a notice in various newspapers, asking for anyone who might have information about Adèle Rouanet, as well as her son, to contact her. Pulling out a sheet of paper she began to reply to her friend's letter, saying she'd give this a go, and would Emma please speak to the OSE about Adèle.

*

'*Any help you can offer would be greatly appreciated, and I'm so glad to hear you are still helping those poor Jewish children. I loved doing that too.*'

Twenty-Two

France, 1943

Towards the end of 1943, Emma was still happily working in the local orphanage. Brenda's latest challenge was to find accommodation for two young brothers from Nuremberg, who spoke barely a word of French.

'This would only be until we can get them a visa to go to England, although that could take a while,' Jeanne explained. 'A local farmer and his wife have volunteered to take the boys. You'll need to check them out carefully.'

'Happy to do that,' Brenda agreed, and went to meet the two brothers: Kurt who was nine, and Walter aged eight. She spent the next week helping them to recover from their journey and teaching them some French. They taught her a little German too, which was useful and even fun. Little by little they shared their story.

'I believe our father was executed,' the elder boy told her. 'Then our *mutter* too was arrested by the Gestapo and sent to Auschwitz concentration camp just for owning a radio and listening to the BBC. We pray she will survive.'

'I'm sure she'll be pleased that you two boys remained safe,' Brenda softly said.

Walter nodded. '*Mutter* instructed us to hide behind some wood panelling when anyone called, which we did.'

'After she was arrested, one of our uncles took us through Luxembourg and sent us by train to Paris. We hoped to then find one to take us to the coast where we could catch a boat to England. We have an aunt who lives there,' Kurt explained. 'Unfortunately there were no trains to be found, so we walked for many kilometres.'

'We managed to grab a few lifts in tractors and trucks,' Walter put in with a grin.

'Good for you,' Brenda said. 'I'll do my best to find you somewhere safe to stay, then organise the necessary visas for you to get to England.'

*

'You do appreciate the risks you will be taking by harbouring Jewish children?' she informed their potential carers. Finding herself visiting this small farm reminded her of her time at Trowbridge Hall, although that was a much grander house. How she missed it, and still agonised over how she would ever manage to return. But right now protecting these two young lads was more urgent.

'We do appreciate the dangers involved, yes. We have a daughter, but need some help on the farm to grow vegetables so we decided it was worth it,' the man said.

'And we do, of course, feel sorry for them,' his wife quickly added.

Knowing they would be granted a small sum of money for the care they were offering, Brenda felt quite cautious, remembering how it could all go wrong. 'I'm sure the boys will be willing to help a little on the farm. But mainly they must be kept indoors, certainly when any German soldiers are around. And wherever they are hidden, they must keep absolutely silent. No giggling, singing, chatter, or playing around as youngsters love to do, as this could arouse suspicion among neighbours.'

'We don't have any neighbours out here in the country-side, miles from anywhere.'

'Then just be wary of any passers-by who might alert the police or military if they see or hear something suspicious. Neither are Jewish children allowed to seek safety in an air-raid shelter should there be any bombing, which can happen even in the middle of nowhere. Also, as these boys are of German origin they must speak only French. They do not speak the language well, so remaining silent and hidden is the best option. Any mistake they make in language or behaviour could reveal their true identity. For that reason they cannot attend school. Nor can your daughter bring friends home. Even you should try to avoid having visitors.'

'Or that will put us in more danger, I suppose,' the farmer said.

'Exactly. No one must know they are here,' Brenda firmly stated. 'Are you still happy to take them?'

'Of course,' his wife said, and the farmer nodded in agreement.

Brenda could well understand the stress, anguish and

fear these people must feel for their own safety, which could give them some doubts. Children too suffered from fear, loneliness and trauma, and she gently pointed this out when she brought the two boys the following evening.

'I'll call back in a few days to see how things are going,' she promised them. Brenda fully intended to make sure they remained safe and were properly cared for.

To her great relief, Kurt and Walter settled in well, and were happy to help dig vegetables. She called several more times over the coming weeks to check they were still secure, but on her next visit Brenda was shocked to find that the barn had burned down and they were nowhere around.

'Thank goodness you came again,' the farmer said, rushing to meet her at the gate. 'We were about to come and ask you to save these boys. Someone must have realised they were here and this is what we've suffered as a result.'

'Oh, my goodness, where are they?'

'I've no idea. They just vanished.'

Devastation struck her. 'Dear lord, don't tell me they were arrested.'

'No, no,' the farmer's wife said. 'They ran quickly away. I think they're hiding in the forest. We could go and look.'

Hours later they found the two of them nestled together under a tall pine tree. It was such a relief to find these young boys safe, and not captured by the Nazis, Brenda gave them each of them a warm hug. 'Right, lads, the good news is that I now have your visas, so you can come with us to England.'

*

Emma and Brenda made fond farewells to Jeanne, thanking her for her efforts to find Tommy, even though she had not been successful. They were taken in a horse-drawn cart by a member of the Resistance movement to catch a train at Saint-Pierre-des-Corps for Biarritz. Buried beneath bags of straw, the two young brothers were, as always, instructed not to make a sound.

'Definitely no coughing or sneezing,' Brenda warned them.

Bursting into giggles, they slapped their hands to their mouths and silently nodded, their small eyes alight with excitement.

Jeanne had bribed a railway official so that they could occupy a compartment generally reserved for German officers. Brenda felt deeply grateful for this help, as so many people had been obliged to escape France by crossing the Pyrenees, which was a long and dangerous walk.

As they climbed on board the train, she saw a likely member of the Gestapo standing in the corridor. When he later opened the door of their compartment to ask to see their papers, he said something to her in German that she did not understand. Brenda cast Kurt and Walter a quick warning glance, in case they felt the need to translate, then smilingly chatted to him in French, telling him they were on their way to see her sick grandmama in Toulouse. A complete lie, but she believed she needed to say something. He handed the documents back to her and left them in peace.

'Thank goodness for that,' she said with a sigh.

'He did say something rude,' Kurt said, as his younger brother giggled.

'Oh, what was that?'

'He said you should learn to keep your stupid mouth shut, you silly bitch.' And they all fell about laughing.

The journey took several hours but Jeanne had packed them plenty of food so they didn't go hungry. Brenda and Emma took it in turns to sleep while keeping a close watch on the two brothers. They'd contacted their aunt in England, although they would need to do that again once they knew the date of their arrival. Brenda was determined to keep these young boys safe, as if by doing so it would help her to believe that some stranger would do the same for her own son.

On arrival at Biarritz station there was a strong military presence at all the barriers, demanding to see credentials. Anxious to avoid being examined, they chose a moment when the guard at their barrier was busily saluting an officer with *Heil*! They slipped through along with a crowd of local school children and their teachers.

'Success!' Emma whispered, and they all chuckled with joy.

They hurried across the road only to find themselves confronted by another German officer. Terror escalated through her as Brenda realised this time it was clearly a member of the Gestapo. Fearful of the secret police, the boys quickly spirited themselves away, as they had learned to do. The officer hustled the two women into the admin office, where he ordered them to strip off.

Glancing at each other in horror they realised they had

no choice but to do as they were told. Heart pounding, Brenda began to unfasten the buttons on her blouse with trembling hands. Was she about to be raped yet again? Dear lord, she hoped not. For some considerable time she'd lived in fear that she'd been made pregnant, but fortunately hadn't. Were it to happen a second time, and being a little healthier, she might not be so lucky.

Standing naked before him, the two women covered themselves with their arms and hands, but were then ordered to put them up. The officer searched each of them by groping and fondling their breasts and private parts while he smirked with pleasure. Brenda gritted her teeth, desperately blanking out her mind. Unfortunately, Emma was less tolerant.

'How dare you!' she cried in her haughty tones, only to get her face slapped. Then opening their bags in retaliation, he tossed all their possessions out on to the wet road. To Brenda's huge relief they were then allowed to dress and leave.

'Was he looking for secret coded messages to prove we're spies?' she muttered to Emma as they scrabbled to gather up their belongings.

'No, he just fancied a grope, the bastard!'

'We got off lightly, then.'

'We certainly did, and it wasn't as much fun as I'd once hoped,' Emma said with a giggle.

Kurt and Walter were hiding in a shop doorway, anxiously waiting for them, but the two women made no mention of what had happened.

'Just a few questions we had to answer. Now all we have to do is find a ship home,' Brenda said, giving them both a hug.

None were available in Biarritz. They managed to take a train to Saint-Jean-de-Luz but as there were no ships heading for England there either, and no trains going anywhere else, they were told by a friendly Spaniard they'd need to walk to Bilbao. It was well over a hundred kilometres, and the long journey deeply worried Brenda. Did these young boys have the energy to walk so far? And did she and Emma? The years they'd spent in the internment camp had greatly depleted their health and stamina. Nevertheless, they had no choice but to try. As night fell they bravely set out across the Basque country with steely courage and determination.

'Are you all right, lads?' she asked time and time again as they walked, and they would nod in silence. These two boys were not at all chatty, being quiet and withdrawn, probably as a result of all they'd suffered with the loss of their parents. How sad that was.

'I know this journey won't be easy, but there's no rush and I have every faith you can do it,' Brenda told them, giving the brothers an encouraging smile. They returned it with a small flicker of gratitude.

'We just need a bit of good luck,' Emma agreed, sharing an anxious glance with Brenda.

Carefully avoiding frontier posts, and keeping as close to the coast as they could so as not to get lost, they climbed a high mountain that seemed to go on forever, finally emerging out of the mist at dawn to stare across a magnificent bay lit by a bright, pink sky. After taking a rest they then walked down the steepest slope imaginable, crossed through pine woods and even swam through a cold dark river. The journey took days. They'd stop to sleep under hedges or trees, or sometimes in barns. On occasions they would find themselves booted out, at other times they'd be offered soup or bread and cheese, for which they were deeply grateful, as the food Jeanne had given them was all gone now.

Arriving in Bilbao feeling pretty exhausted but elated by the success of their journey, Brenda went straight to the harbour to make enquiries about transport to England. Eventually, using all her charm, Emma managed to find them accommodation on a troop ship.

The boys beamed with delight. 'Thank you so much for saving us.'

'You're welcome,' Brenda said, giving each of them a hug. 'Now we must send a telegram to your aunt, then home we go.'

*

It took the better part of two days to make the crossing. The sea was fairly bumpy as the ship sailed through the Bay of Biscay, and the two boys were seasick as a result. Thankfully, their aunt was waiting for them when they arrived at Portsmouth docks. What a thrill it was to see them fall into her arms with such joy, at last safe with a member of their family.

'Thank you so much for bringing them home safe,' the lady said, vigorously shaking Brenda and Emma's hands, then giving them a kiss on each cheek. 'You wouldn't believe what a relief it is to see them again.'

'We understand completely,' Brenda said with a soft smile, then went to give the boys a farewell shake of the hand. 'Take care and enjoy life, as your parents would wish you to do.'

They met her gaze with great affection and gratitude, then wrapped their arms about Brenda to give her a hug, and did the same with Emma. 'We will, and thank you.'

Emma's parents too were there waiting for her, and she hugged them with relief and tears in her eyes. 'Any news?' she asked, and they sadly shook their heads.

Bravely, she tightened her trembling lips and turned to Brenda. 'I shall hold fast to my faith that when this war is finally over, Paul will eventually return.'

'I pray that we will both find our missing loved ones,' Brenda said.

The moment had come to say goodbye, which felt utterly heartrending considering they'd lived as close as sisters, enduring years of trauma together. Emma lived in Devon while Brenda would be taking a train north to Manchester, then probably a bus on to the Pennines.

'I can hardly imagine life without you,' she said, tears rolling down her cheeks.

'I'm sure we'll meet up again one day,' Emma assured her with tears in her own eyes as they again hugged each other tight.

'Of course we will,' Brenda firmly responded, even as her stomach pulsed with that all-too-familiar sense of loneliness.

Moments later they were waving goodbye and she watched them all walk away. The boys' aunt had an arm around each of them, and Emma walked arm in arm with her parents. How Brenda wished she could savour the same experience, but she had no family at all. Never had, in fact. And having started to build one of her own, that too was now gone. There wasn't a single person waiting to welcome her home.

Standing on the platform as they disappeared from view she felt totally alone in the world.

Twenty-Three

1946

Hugh went to speak to Dino, hearing how he planned to increase the flock of sheep, build more greenhouses for food production and improve mechanisation even further.

'The state of the country being what it is, food rationing isn't going to end any time soon,' he said. 'And hopefully pricing guarantees will continue for a while longer too.'

Shaking his hand, Hugh agreed that he'd be welcome to take charge of the farm. 'No rent needed. The work and investment you'll be offering is more than enough. We're in a new world now and must learn to work together as a team, particularly now that you are part of the family. If I was a little doubtful about you at first, it was probably as a consequence of my own losses. And also because Prue had made a hasty decision over her first marriage when she was young and foolish, which turned out to be a bad mistake. I was fearful that her impulsive, rebellious nature might again be leading her into trouble. But clearly that is not the case. Thank you for making my sister happy.'

'She's also made me the happiest man alive,' Dino said with a smile.

'Then you are most fortunate.'

With tears in her eyes, Prue gave her brother a hug. 'Thank you for welcoming Dino into the family. I do hope one day you will find happiness too.'

'I'm slowly getting the message that we need to move forward,' Hugh agreed, 'and will be making new plans of my own.' Then giving her cheek a quick kiss and calling Kit to heel, he walked proudly away. Prue did not fail to notice the sunlight flashing on a slight wash of tears in his grey eyes, making them shine like velvet.

'Something is still troubling him,' she said, giving a little sigh. 'But I can't quite make out what it is. Ah well, come on, let's look over the farm.'

'I am quite familiar with it,' he laughed.

'I know, but we need to make some decisions.'

They explored the great stone barns filled with the sweet scent of hay, the milking parlour and the tractor shed, giggling like children as they examined gear-sticks and steering wheels with their probing fingers. Then they moved on to the sheep-folds, and the lush green intake land close to the cottage where the flock was wintered.

'Yet more walls are crumbling,' Dino said, examining the dips and holes in the drystone wall that circled the field.

Prue laughed. 'Wall building was a job my father hated. He always said he'd get round to it tomorrow. But tomorrow never came, and poor old Joe never has enough time to do everything. You did the best job but next time you repair a wall, you will not be arrested, my darling.'

At that moment old Joe ambled over from the sheep pen where he was in the process of inspecting and trimming hooves. Crook in hand as he stood before them, he gave a toothless grin. 'Eeh, lad, it's good to see thee back. I'm busy removing mud, manure and small stones to stop foot rot. Asta come to help wi' the sheep?'

'I have, Joe. Every day from now and forever. Good to see you too.'

'That's gradely! Let's get cracking, then.'

As Dino went off to assist with this back-breaking task, Prue beamed at them both with joy and pride. While Dino and Joe were looking after the animals, she would grow food. This was to be their new future together. Next, she must speak to Brenda to see what decisions she had made for her own.

*

Brenda was delighted to learn that Hugh had agreed to hand over the running of the farm to Prue and Dino. If only he'd welcomed her into the family too. As if the anguish of living without her husband and son wasn't enough for her to contend with, he'd accused her of lying and being an imposter, possibly because he was influenced by Melissa. In addition, he had arrogantly dismissed the idea she'd put to him, absolutely refusing to allow her to join the family business. Irritating as this attitude was, to her amazement she found herself missing him more than the job. Why was that, when he'd been most obnoxious towards her?

Having made up her mind to satisfy her passion for baking by starting a business of her own, Brenda found a possible shop to rent in nearby Greenfield. She'd certainly learned a good deal over the years, and from Mrs Harding too in recent weeks. Prue happily agreed to supply her with fruit, vegetables, milk and eggs.

'Whatever I can provide,' she said as they looked over the premises together. 'If you're sure this is what you want to do.'

'It certainly is.' The excitement of developing her own business thrilled and engrossed Brenda far more than she would ever have thought possible. 'My funds are limited, of course, and rationing means the shop could only open for three days a week. But I believe it will do well. I'll need ovens, cake tins, trays, racks, mixing equipment, loads of stuff for the kitchen, as well as shelving to store the finished products in the shop itself.' She'd already visited a local warehouse to take advice on what was needed by way of equipment, carefully making the point that she must keep things to a minimum and not overspend.

'Plus you'll need to do lots of advertising to prove that your cakes and puddings are made from local products,' Prue said. 'But how are you going to find the necessary money for all of these requirements? Have you spoken to the bank manager yet?'

'I have, yes, and he was most accommodating. After various questions to check my skills and abilities, including what I can afford, he has agreed to make me a small loan. I'm going to see him tomorrow to sign the necessary paperwork, once I've made up my mind to take this shop on. What do you think of it?'

Prue frowned. 'It's a bit shabby and would need a good clean, although I'm sure that's possible. There's also a crack in the window and the door seems warped, as it's difficult to close. Will the landlord fix those problems? And where would you live?'

'There are a couple of rooms above the shop. They too would need quite a bit of attention, let alone buying a bed and a few pieces of furniture, perhaps from the local pawn shop,' she said with a giggle.

Going upstairs to inspect this possibility, Prue looked unimpressed. 'It would be quite a task. But that's not the main problem. I just wish you didn't have to take the risk of borrowing so much money, particularly when Jack left you well provided for. It must be so annoying for you.'

'I prefer not to think about that any more. I'm concentrating on building a new life. Wish me luck.'

After Prue had gone, Brenda sat for some time mulling things over. She couldn't deny that she too was anxious about the risk involved, but knew in her heart that it was one she must take, if only for the sake of her son. She'd decided to widen her search for Tommy, privately vowing never to stop looking for him. And if and when she finally found him, he would need to be provided for. Should she never succeed in doing that, then at least she would have given herself a reason to get up each day and go on with life. Reinstating her courage and determination by working hard, as well as thinking positively, was surely the best way to block off the sadness and depression that kept overwhelming her.

Locking the shop up and returning the key, Brenda went back to her flat in Castlefield, where she spent a sleepless night struggling to reach a decision. The following morning she returned to the shop, standing in the village street staring at it with fresh hope in her heart. She was about to go and see the owner to sign the rental agreement when she heard the soft tones of an all-too-familiar voice. 'We need to talk.'

*

Nature had cloaked the hills with the bronze of autumn bracken. There were flags of gold on every tree, a landscape enhanced by the emerald delights of sloping pastures and wooded banks. How she loved the Saddleworth villages of Greenfield, Uppermill, Delph and many more with their grey stone cottages, cobbled streets and the canal that ran from Ashton-under-Lyne all the way through to Huddersfield. No boats carrying goods were cruising along it today as they walked on the towpath, the scene one of peaceful tranquillity. It felt as if once again they were celebrating the end of the war. But the pounding in her heart was not at all peaceful, being filled with tension.

'How can you possibly hope to survive?' Hugh quietly asked, Kit the collie trotting along beside him as usual.

Brenda stifled a sigh. 'Why would I not? Prue and I

work well together. She will supply most of the essential ingredients and I see no reason why I can't make a perfectly good living from baking, which as you know, I love doing.'

'I agree that you are an excellent cook, and have been most helpful to Mrs Harding—to all of us, in fact.'

'Very kind of you to say so, even though Melissa does not agree.'

'I'm fully aware that you are no longer a servant,' he added with a wry smile, which almost made her want to giggle. 'And I'm sorry my sister insists upon treating you as such.'

'She'll have to accept the truth eventually.' Brenda almost added: as will you too. But she couldn't quite pluck up the courage to say that.

'I'm just wondering why you would take such a risk. Prue has told me about this loan you've been offered, and in my opinion the rent sounds a bit high. Why do that? I doubt Jack would approve.'

'What alternative do I have, since I am not to be allowed a penny from the will he made to protect my future?'

Silence followed this remark for some time. They were approaching the Standedge Tunnel, begun back in the eighteenth century and completed by Thomas Telford in 1811. Brenda knew that the engineers had suffered enormous problems building it. But through hard work and effort, had finally succeeded in creating a tunnel that ran for more than three miles under the Pennines, which had greatly helped industry at the time. So why shouldn't she work hard to achieve success too, and feel free to do whatever she thought right for her own future?

'He must have loved you very much,' Hugh softly commented, ending the silence between them.

His words touched her deeply, not at all the response she'd expected. And the smile they exchanged this time skittered her senses all the more. 'I believe I've told you on numerous occasions that Jack and I were very much in love, which is why we married.'

'Yet you don't even have a ring to prove it.'

A shiver ran down her spine as Brenda recalled the day of her arrest. 'I gave it to Camille to look after for me, when I was taken away to be interned. Sadly, my wedding ring is now lost along with my husband and son. And the solicitor's clerk has informed me the case is closed, since all documentation has been destroyed by the bombing. Such is the effect of war. But I hope you will eventually come round to accepting the truth, if only out of love for your late brother,' she said, meeting his curious gaze with a stern one of her own.

'Jack and I were very close,' he quietly admitted. 'I miss him greatly.'

'Me too.'

Spotting a line of ants parading along beside her, Brenda stepped to one side and he accidentally bumped into her. 'Sorry,' he said.

She mumbled something about it being her fault, his smile setting her head spinning as it had done that time when she'd tripped over a tree root and fallen into his arms. He smelled of the woodland, Lifebuoy toilet soap and Brylcreem, and Brenda felt a sudden desire to touch his lips with her own; to offer him all the love he seemed in need of that lay unused within her. Loneliness must be making her go mad, she thought, quickly tossing a stick for Kit to chase in order to distract herself. Loving a dog was surely much safer.

Hugh cleared his throat, almost as if he was attempting to control his own emotions, or a sense of guilt. 'I should apologise for my behaviour when first you arrived.'

A wave of pity washed over her as she saw how his eyes looked suddenly bleak. 'Don't worry about that. I'm perfectly well aware you were going through a difficult patch at the time, as was I. Let's put all of that behind us and move on.'

'Then can I say that I've changed my mind about the idea you put to me. You are perfectly at liberty to join the family firm, Brenda, if you still wish to do so,' he gently told her.

She stared at him in stunned disbelief. 'Goodness, you made it very clear you'd no desire for me to become involved. What has changed your mind?'

'Despite being unable to provide the necessary paper-work to prove your marriage, I understand from Fairhurst that Jack did leave you shares in the business. My brother would be furious with me if I stood by and did nothing while you took such risks. Besides which, I've been thinking about those suggestions you made for expanding our biscuit trade, and have decided they are quite sound.

Adding small cakes and individual puddings to our list might well be a good idea. And Prue could be responsible for supplying all the necessary ingredients she can manage to produce. We would need to hire a new team of women to do the baking, and I am prepared to put you in charge.'

Having stopped walking to gaze at him now with joy in her heart, the longing to fling herself into his arms was almost overwhelming. It was only later that Brenda recalled that was exactly what she did. Or rather Hugh gathered her in his arms and kissed her, first upon each cheek to celebrate their decision and then as their gazes locked, full upon her mouth.

*

Melissa arrived a few days later with her children in tow. Her husband too was with her and Brenda made a point of keeping well out of his sight, determined never to find herself alone with that brute ever again. But it was lovely to see the children. She sat in the summer house working on her plans for the new business, watching with amusement as the girls played with their dolls, treating little Ross as if he was one too. They even put a bonnet on him and attempted to sit him in a doll's pram. He fiercely resisted, stomping off in a temper. Brenda put a hand to her mouth to silence her giggles, but he'd already heard her and came running over.

'Hello, I didn't know you were here, Bren,' he said, beaming as he plonked himself down beside her on the bench.

It quite touched her heart how pleased he was to see her, and that he now called her by this pet name. 'Are you a bit bored with all those girly games?' she asked, and pulling a face, he briskly nodded. 'There's a bike in the shed. Do you know how to cycle?'

He shook his head, his eyes alight with interest. 'Can you show me how?'

'I can,' Brenda said. 'I'm keen on cycling myself. Shall we have a go?'

'Yes please.'

She tidied away her notebook then paused, a thought crossing her mind. Hadn't she promised herself not to become attached to this child? And even though she wasn't asking him to do any jobs like seeing to the hens, Melissa might not approve. 'Perhaps we should ask your mummy's permission first?'

'She's out shopping,' he said. '*Again*! And Nanny is taking her afternoon nap. Can we go now?'

Tucked into the back of the garden shed were several ancient bicycles, including one she tended to use herself whenever necessary. Several of the others must have belonged to the Stuart children at various stages in their lives. 'I think there is one somewhere that might be the right size for you,' Brenda said, rummaging through them, and moving piles of boxes to search further. 'Ah, here it is. This might do the trick.'

Lifting it out, she checked it carefully to make sure the brake worked, the tyres were pumped up, and she gave it a good clean. Then taking it outside she helped Ross to sit upon it, and set his feet on the pedals. 'I'll push you along and you turn the pedals around with your feet, all right? I'll keep hold of the saddle and I promise I won't let you fall.'

She wheeled him to and fro up and down the farmyard, keeping a tight hold to keep him safe. It took no time at all for the little boy to get the right degree of balance, his face a picture of happiness. She was soon able to let go and stand back to watch him cycle round on his own.

'Hey, what's going on here?' Hugh asked, coming over to stand grinning with his arms folded and watch his nephew proudly showing off his new skill. 'Clever boy, you're doing well.' He turned to Brenda with curiosity in his gaze. 'Have you taught him how to cycle?'

'I have indeed, because he was bored with being treated as a doll, so why not?'

Hugh laughed out loud, and clapped and cheered as Ross came pedalling towards him with a big grin on his face, then sensibly slowed down and pulled to a halt with only a slight wobble. 'Well done, lad,' Hugh said, giving him a pat on the head. 'You'll make an excellent cyclist. Have you thanked Brenda for kindly teaching you?'

Jumping off the cycle to lay it carefully down, he ran to give her a big hug. 'Thank you so much, Bren.' The feel of the child in her arms made her heart turn over.

'What a lovely lady you are,' Hugh said, stroking her tumble of hair away from her flushed cheek. 'I think we'll enjoy working together.'

Twenty-Four

Hugh faced Melissa with stubborn resolve. 'Taking into account the effect of this war, I believe we should be a little more open-minded and accept that what Brenda has to say could well be true.'

'I can't understand *why* you are allowing her to win you over. You've been against that chit of a girl from the moment she arrived, an absolutely correct reaction.'

'Finding the necessary physical evidence in these times is not always possible. But bearing in mind all she has done for us, not least standing in for Prue and working hard in the kitchen, why would I not begin to believe she could be genuine? She also taught your son to cycle, when he grew bored with being treated as a doll by his sisters. She's a lovely, kind lady.'

Melissa's grey-green eyes widened with shock. 'She has no right to teach him anything, or interfere at all in my children's lives.'

'I think it's time you developed a little more tolerance towards her.'

'How dare you suggest such a thing? She's a fraudster and a charlatan.'

Coping with his sister's self-obsessed arrogance was never easy. Melissa did tend to look down on those she considered beneath her, and treat them with total condescension. He may not always be able to control her temper, but Hugh felt determined to be in full command of his own. A bad reaction simply created high levels of stress and tension, which did him no good at all. He did, however, seem to be on the road to improvement.

'I'm beginning to think that my first reaction to her was entirely wrong,' he said. 'Probably because I was in a bad state of mind at the time. She's proved to be a most caring, lively person and a good friend and companion to Prue. In addition, she's a hard worker and has come up with some interesting suggestions on how to improve sales at the factory. As a consequence I've made an offer for her to join the family business.'

'Absolutely not! I will never agree to allow that.'

'I'm afraid it's not your decision.'

Snorting with fury through her beautiful aquiline nose, she marched over to the sideboard to pour herself a glass of gin and It. 'That madam is nothing more than a piece of baggage; completely without morals. No doubt she's offered to hand you favours in return, as she did in the German brothel. That harlot should be sent packing and banished from this house forever.'

Hugh's eyes darkened. 'She has offered no such thing, nor have we any proof she did spread her favours in the past. I think you have completely misunderstood what Mama was telling you in that letter. And may I tactfully remind you that this is no longer your home, Melissa. You now live in London with your husband, so it is no business of yours who lives here, let alone what I do in the factory. That is *my* decision, and despite your accusations, I *am* coming round to the idea that she could indeed be Jack's widow.'

Melissa bristled. 'Are you saying that you prefer to trust that messy little tart rather than me, your own *sister*?'

'Let's say I'm prepared to take the risk.'

'Damn you, you'll live to regret it,' she snarled, and snatching up a vase, smashed it to the floor before marching off.

*

Brenda could hardly believe her good fortune at being invited to occupy Jack's bedroom, instead of the servant's quarters in the attic. Unbelievable, although she very much doubted Melissa would approve. It was a lovely blue room on the first floor, quite dark and manly with a mahogany four-poster bed, blue velvet curtains and a beautiful slate fireplace. She felt in her heart that she was honouring his memory by being here. Some of Jack's suits still hung in the wardrobe, bringing tears to her eyes as she buried her face in the cloth to pick up the faint scent of him. Determined not to dwell upon the fact that he was no longer present in her life, if forever in her heart, Brenda took them out and folded them into a pile for Carter to collect and perhaps give to those young men in need of clothes after this dreadful war. She then unpacked her own few belongings.

His comb and razor still rested on the shelf in the small bathroom next door. Slipping them into a drawer for safe keeping, she stared at herself in the mirror, remembering cleaning this room for him every morning as a servant. Now she had been given the right to occupy it. Wouldn't this be what Jack would have wanted for her?

Sitting at the desk in the window, she let her gaze wander over the meadows and woodlands surrounding the manor, feeling a tremor of happiness stir within her. Life was improving, and it was vital she keep up her spirits. Finding a stack of paper in the drawer, Brenda wrote a quick letter to Emma, feeling eager to share her good news.

It had been so long since she'd seen her friend, but loved to keep her informed of how things were going, as well as receiving Emma's own news, if a bit worrying at times. In this letter Brenda explained how the solicitor had refused to make any further enquiries, and that there was no longer any hope of finding the correct paperwork, let alone her son.

'But I want you to know that things are improving. Having been granted the right to join the family business, which I'm delighted about, I'm working hard to bring about good sales. I do love baking. And I confess I'm beginning to feel more at ease with Hugh now that he's much more relaxed and friendly towards me. Would you believe he actually kissed me, to celebrate this decision? Unbelievable, and oddly enough, it felt so like Jack. However, my darling

husband will always be in my heart, and I'll never stop searching for dear little Tommy. I just wish I could find out where Adèle is, as she might have the answer. I do hope she is still alive and well. But if so, why haven't I heard from her? If you can think of any way to find her, do let me know. I'm open to suggestions. I do love receiving your letters and you are such a wise and helpful friend. What's your latest news from OSE? Hope you are finding some degree of happiness too. I still live in hope.

All my love, Brenda.'

When the letter was written and the tears were wiped from her eyes, Brenda began to make a list of the recipes she intended to try first. And when tiredness overcame her she slipped into Jack's bed, her heart aching that he wasn't there beside her. But resolving not to cry, she began to count sheep in her head and soon fell asleep.

She found herself jerked awake by the sound of the bedroom door opening, a flash of fear running through her. It felt as if she were back in Besançon and a guard had entered to drag the women from their palliasses to bully and beat them. Remembering where she actually was, safe in Jack's bedroom, she flicked on her bedside lamp to stare in shock at Gregory's slyly grinning face.

Within seconds she'd leapt out of bed, opposite to where he was standing, and grabbing the poker from its stand by the fireplace held it firmly with both hands. 'Get out! If you lay so much as a finger on me, I'll call the police.'

Laughing, he came slowly around the foot of the bed to stand before her. 'You wouldn't dare. We all know how you spread your favours wide and what a little liar you are, so why would they believe a word you say? The police can be very dismissive of whores.'

Brenda ground her teeth, heart pounding. 'Not nearly as bad as the Gestapo. Come one step closer and you'll feel the full weight of this poker, and the courage they created in me.'

She saw doubt creep into his eyes. 'So you don't fancy a bit of a frolic?'

'Never! Certainly not with a bastard like you. Leave *now*, or I'll tell Melissa all about what you are suggesting.'

His smile turned into a sneer as he glared at her through narrowed dark eyes. 'Melissa does as I tell her, as will you one day.' Then to her great relief he left. Grabbing a chair, she jammed it under the door handle to lock it. Tomorrow she'd ask old Joe to put a bolt on it for her.

*

'Where have you been?' Melissa demanded of her husband when he returned to their room.

'Nowhere of importance,' he told her, as he climbed into bed beside her.

Not for a moment did she believe him. Had he approached that chit of a girl again, or perhaps the new maid who'd been taken on to help Mrs Harding? Not daring to ask, she stroked his face and kissed him. 'How lovely to have you here with me and be sharing a bed again,' she murmured, then slid her hand down to rub a lower part of him.

'Not tonight, dear. I'm too tired,' he said, and turning his back to her, mumbled goodnight.

Fury and despair ricocheted through her. No doubt he had just had his way with that harlot. Damnation, why would Gregory not show more interest in her, his own wife? As for that that greedy little madam, she was creating utter mayhem. Not only had Hugh allowed her to join the family business, Melissa had the sneaking feeling that a relationship was growing between them, which really didn't bear thinking about. In addition, he was now allowing her to live here at Trowbridge Hall, occupying Jack's room. How dare he do that? Would he next be offering her a share of the family money?

Melissa remembered all too well how she'd greatly resented the fact that Jack had been granted the largest share of her father's inheritance, simply because he was the eldest and a *man*. Hugh had been next in line, of course, which was why he was now in charge. But it was entirely unfair the way their father had treated the women of his family. Although she and Prue had been left a fair sum of money each, they were granted no share in the business and certainly not ownership of the house or land. Melissa definitely had no intention of agreeing to that cunning little fraudster taking a share of their inheritance, which could deprive her own children, in particular her lovely

daughters, of theirs. Girls had as much right to an inheritance as did boys.

Why didn't Hugh realise she was playing him along?

How stupid men were. Even her own husband was
entirely neglectful, and so dictatorial. Forever expressing
anger with her if she didn't do as he ordered, he rarely
stayed home long enough to keep their marriage strong,
let alone build a proper relationship with his children. He
would constantly go off to some foreign land, staying away
for months on end. His family never seemed to register
in his mind as being of any great importance. He looked
upon them more as a requirement to add to his status, as
well as his financial assets. His role as a diplomat was all
that truly mattered to him.

And whether he even remained faithful to her on those
long trips abroad, Melissa really didn't care to consider.
He could have a mistress in every port, for all she knew.

Life had been so much easier when that chit of a girl
had occupied her proper status, working as a servant. She'd
interfered far too much in family matters already, and the
last thing Melissa needed was for her to become more
involved, let alone engage in an affair with her husband.

But how to be rid of her? That was the question.

*

Brenda spent days in the kitchen baking samples of her
favourite recipes. She found that she loved rising early,
rolling out pastry and beating dough, despite the endless
washing up of dirty dishes, long days and short nights,

and swollen hands and feet. 'We'll start with these classic cakes, and a small Christmas pudding, since the festive season is approaching. If they prove to be successful, then we can increase the range and try one or two more,' she suggested to Hugh. He readily agreed.

'Now we need to set about finding a market,' she eventually announced. And taking her box of samples, went first to Kendal Milne in Manchester.

'Christmas is coming. How about some Christmas puddings? Do try a taste,' she said to the buyer, keeping her tone light in a valiant effort not to reveal her desperate need for an order.

'Hmm, delicious. I'll take a dozen. See how they go,' came the reply.

'Buy two dozen and I'll give you an extra ten per cent discount.'

'Right, you're on.'

She wrote the order in the book, trying not to let her customer see that his was the first. With her confidence boosted, Brenda went on to sell him mince tarts, sponge parkin, Yorkshire spice cake, flapjacks and Eccles cakes. 'If these prove to be popular, I could bring you more varieties next time,' she told him.

After that, she went from town to town: Bolton, Blackburn, Burnley, Stockport, and many more all over Lancashire. She even took the train as far as Liverpool, Chester and parts of Yorkshire, paying calls upon Selfridges, Browns and any other likely department store she could find, plus many small cafes and grocer's shops. She tried every means of persuasion she could think of to win orders: offering samples, giving discounts for bulk purchase, and agreeing to whatever delivery date was required.

Gradually the order book filled up, the ones for Christmas being more important. Her small team settled down to end-less baking, and over the first few weeks excellent sales were achieved, particularly for the Christmas puddings and mince tarts.

'It's going to work!' she squealed in delight when she showed Hugh the results.

'Well done,' he said. 'I think we should go out for a meal to celebrate this new phase in the business.'

A wave of delight ran through her. 'That would be lovely.' The glint of his white teeth as he smiled with pleasure brought a flush of longing within her. How she longed to trace the outline of his mouth and have him kiss her again, only this time more intensely. Stifling this unexpected reaction to his invitation, she politely agreed a time for them to meet up that evening.

The future was looking rosy at last. Then as she walked through the hall on the way to her room, Brenda found another letter waiting for her from Emma, one that stunned her completely.

*

By early afternoon when the day's baking was done, having been up from five o'clock working hard, Brenda went to see Prue to discuss what she should wear for this meal out.

'My clothes are entirely rubbish and I've never got around to improving them, due to lack of time and funds,' she admitted. 'What do you suggest I do?'

'Well, I am definitely not short of dresses,' Prue said, 'having been blessed with the kind of father who had plenty of money and always expected his daughters to look their best. Let's explore my wardrobe.'

They spent the next hour doing exactly that, Brenda trying on various frocks, skirts and fancy tops, laughing hilariously when something didn't suit her. A pile slowly mounted of the garments Prue was happily handing over.

'You don't need to actually give them to me,' Brenda protested. 'I could just borrow something.'

'These are clothes I've rarely worn in years and no longer need, so why would I not give them to you? You're my best friend and you've helped me, so now it's my turn to help you. I think you should wear this rose-coloured silk skirt and jacket this evening, as the colour really suits you, and it fits so neatly round your waist. Have a lovely time, darling,' she said, giving her a warm hug.

'I do have mixed feelings about it,' Brenda confessed. 'As if it's quite wrong of me to be going out with my brother-in-law. I certainly must not think of it as a date.'

'Why would you not? It's good to see a friendship developing between you two at last.'

'Yes, but I'm his brother's widow, so is it wrong of me to find him quite attractive?'

Prue smiled. 'Not at all. I think he's growing rather attracted to you too.'

'I very much doubt it.' Brenda felt her heart skitter at the thought.

When Hugh saw her waiting for him in the hall, he let out a low whistle. 'My word, you look lovely. Absolutely gorgeous and most stylish.'

Brenda flushed with surprise and happiness, pulling a wry face. 'Thanks to your generous sister.' Knowing she needed to look her best, she'd pinned her hair up into a French pleat, letting tendrils curl free on to her forehead. Examining herself in the mirror Brenda had felt quite pleased that her skin still held a certain golden quality to it, as if kissed by the sun. But it was other types of kisses that were occupying her mind far too much at the moment. 'I own little more than the odd scruffy frock and several pairs of overalls, so I really appreciate her help.'

'As she does yours,' he said.

His expression was as mysterious as ever, made more so by the narrowing of his grey eyes as he gazed upon her. Sometimes his silences gave her a prickle of disquiet, although that was not what she was feeling right now. But then he could be puzzling, letting loose his emotions but keeping his thoughts very private. As he came a step closer Brenda held her breath: expectant, happy, and smiling up at him. Was this the moment he would kiss her? She could almost sense it, and swayed slightly towards him in anticipation. Life seemed to be improving at last. If she could but persuade him to kiss her again, it would be even better. Bending his arm for her to take, he said, 'The car is waiting outside with Carson at the wheel. Shall we go?'

A shadow flickered briefly across his face and her heart clenched. Perhaps she was wrong. Would that happen this evening, or not?

Twenty-Five

They spent a lovely evening together, talking and becoming quite close as they enjoyed a delicious dinner of tomato soup followed by roast chicken.

'Would you like a dessert?' he asked with a smile.

'That was a lovely meal, but no thank you. I test and taste far more cakes and puddings than I should,' she said, giving a little chuckle. 'I'm so appreciative of your trust in my baking, Hugh. So good of you to agree to my suggestion.'

Taking her hand, he stroked her knuckles with his thumb. 'Even if you can't find the necessary paperwork, I felt I owed it to you, and to Jack. Winning round Melissa, however, might take a little longer.'

A bubble of laughter erupted from her. 'That doesn't exactly surprise me. You often seem very stern and ponderous too. Is it a family trait?'

He was grinning at her now, and joining in her laughter. 'Could be, but I'm working on it. I promise I'll be much more agreeable and tolerant in future.'

'That's good to know.' Their eyes met in a compelling gaze, one that lurched her heart.

'I admit our father could be very controlling, very much lord of the manor. Jack hated that attitude but I was still very fond of him, eager to please him and make him proud, which didn't always work. His condescending attitude tended to diminish my faith in myself. But now it's time to focus upon the present, instead of reliving the past.'

'I do agree, although it is easier said than done,' Brenda conceded. 'Loss of a loved one is so hard to live with. It's like having a big black hole in your life, into which you keep falling. I know we've both suffered anguish, as have thousands of other people. I'd like to show you something. It's a letter I've received recently from my good friend Emma, with whom I was incarcerated. We still keep in touch and she is very supportive. It concerns lost children, mainly Jewish, but I can entirely empathise with their loss as I worked with them for a time during the war. Around a million have been killed and hundreds more are missing.'

'So I have heard.' Giving a sad little nod, he took the letter from her and began to read.

'Dear Brenda,

I was so sorry to hear you are still having problems finding Tommy. Don't believe for a moment that all hope is lost. I can imagine you must be in deep anguish. Do battle on, despite the difficulties. I may have some news for you but let me start by saying that people are now often taking foster parents to court, facing a long and complicated legal battle over custody. Even then the rescuers sometimes defy the court's ruling and disappear off the face of the earth, which is heartrending even if this time it is out of love and not money. Do you remember how we suffered similar issues back in France when they'd take the money, then hand the child over to the Nazis? What selfish brutes some folk can be. And there are still so many lost children.

As you know, I'm back in France helping the OSE and have found a small boy called Thomas, currently in an orphanage here, whose parents I cannot locate. I wonder if he could be your son. I've enclosed a small snap of him so you can decide whether he bears any resemblance to your darling Jack.

At least the traumas I have to deal with are giving me a new purpose in life, doing what I can to help others. You must feel yours has entirely collapsed. I do hope the new job helps you to rebuild it. As far as Adèle is concerned, I've put out notices in various places, hoping someone might know her. Fingers crossed. I'll be in touch if I hear anything. And do let me know if you wish to meet this boy.

Love, Emma.'

Hugh looked at her with sympathy in his eyes. 'Good lord, I never fully appreciated how much these children suffered. Do you think this boy could be your son?'

Handing him the photo, Brenda gave a bleak smile.

'This news did come as something of a shock, and since Tommy was a tiny baby when last I saw him, how can I know? But as you must remember Jack as a child, do tell me what you think.'

He gazed upon the picture for some time before finally shaking his head. 'I'm not convinced. This child's hair is too dark, as are his eyes, and he doesn't have our nose.'

Brenda gave a resigned sigh as she slipped the photo back into the envelope. 'That's what I thought.'

'You two ladies must have been through a great deal together, yet how brave she must be to still be determined to help these families. But then you too are extremely courageous, lively and good humoured, despite all you have been through. I can see exactly why Jack loved you.'

Her eyes glazed over as yet again she revisited the past. 'We spent a wonderful few months in Paris; the sun shining, flowers blooming everywhere. We'd walk around the narrow cobblestoned streets and gardens in Montmartre, or sit drinking coffee, so relaxed and happily enjoying ourselves.

'Then war was declared and it was one night when we were at the cinema, watching a Maurice Chevalier movie, when we heard the first explosions. We cuddled up close and didn't let it bother us. But when we came out we found the streets deserted and the sky filled with streamers of light. A man came running over to tell us there was an air raid going on and that we should get into a shelter. We ran for cover, oddly enough giggling as if it were some sort of joke. Only later, when we walked home and found a house bombed and some people injured, did reality dawn. It was then that he asked me to marry him. "We might not have much time left, my darling, so we'd best stop worrying about not having any money and get married right away," he said. And so we did.'

Brenda went on to talk about their wedding; how his mother had loaned her a beautiful tiered gown of cream silk. 'The most beautiful garment I've ever worn in my life. After the service the three of us enjoyed a wonderful meal together at the Hôtel Ritz, again at Camille's expense. She was so sweet and generous. Once the Germans occupied Paris that building was taken over by the Luftwaffe, of course. By then we'd been married for over six months. We'd had no honeymoon but spent every possible moment we could together, until Jack joined the Resistance. After his death I gave birth to Tommy in November 1940, again with your mother's help.'

He listened to her tale enraptured, giving a sympathetic little smile. 'I hope you eventually do find your son.'

Folding the letter up, Brenda stuffed it into her bag. 'As you said, Hugh, we need to focus upon the present and put the past behind us. The war is over and we must live with the consequences of it. It's time we changed the subject. Let's talk business instead.'

She felt deeply grateful that he'd at last been willing to listen to her story, even if there were still some facts about her internment she hadn't yet told him. Now they happily discussed details of sales over coffee, agreeing on which cakes were proving to be the best sellers and others which could be added in due course to the company's list. 'No meringues or cream cakes,' she said. 'Not yet. But the Lancashire Parkin, Eccles cakes and others I've listed here have sold well, as have the individual Christmas puddings.'

'The list will obviously change from season to season, but I think this one will work well for the winter,' he agreed.

'And I would like to do a bit of rearrangement of working hours and conditions,' she said. 'Do you trust me enough to allow me to do that?' She met his grey-eyed gaze, her heart pumping with excitement as she saw how his mouth curled into a bewitching smile.

'I think women are much better at organising such routines than men are. So yes, set out your plan and we'll talk it through.'

They drove back largely in silence, as with Carson at the wheel they were cautious about what they said or did. Sitting beside Hugh on the back seat Brenda was all too aware of the warmth of his closeness, and felt his hand slide over to capture hers. As they stepped out of the car, he waited until Carson had driven off. Then pulling her into his arms he kissed her, this time with more passion, his heart vibrating against her rib-cage. Brenda's heart soared with joy, the sweetness of him running through her like fire, making her respond with eager desire. Something strange and wonderful had happened to them today and she so wanted it to go on.

When the kiss ended he opened the door to lead her into the hall. 'Goodnight,' he softly murmured. 'Sleep well.'

Flushed from his kissing, she slanted a teasing glance

up at him. 'I might not manage to sleep a wink after that. But thank you, it's been a wonderful evening. See you tomorrow.'

That night she suffered no nightmares, only dreams of love, feeling a surge of relief that in spite of all the assaults she'd suffered in the past from men, she still felt the need for love. But the man who was kissing her in the dream was not Jack.

*

The next day Brenda began to make a list of necessary improvements to the daily routine of the women bakers, for whom she was now largely responsible. Their first task each morning was to check the orders required to be baked that day, then weigh out the necessary ingredients. After that they would prepare the dough and mix the ingredients for the buns, cakes or puddings. By early afternoon they would clean the kitchen area, as hygiene was of vital importance. All dishes, cake trays and utensils also had to be scrubbed and cleaned. Finally they would need to check that the right ingredients were available for the next day. Once that was done, in theory they were allowed to leave by three o'clock. More often than not they were late finishing, which irritated them enormously. Perfectly understandable, when these women had been working since six or seven o'clock.

And there appeared to be other problems. She could see it in their faces as they worked. Yet it was vital that these women be content with the work and how the system operated. Brenda decided she needed to investigate, and during one dinner hour began to ask them how they were finding things, and if anything needed adjusting. When the question was met by silence she turned to the young woman she'd met in the main kitchen on her first visit to the factory.

'I remember you saying that it was so hot working in the kitchen that you needed to drink a lot of water, whenever you got the chance,' Brenda asked. 'Are you saying water is not always available?'

Glancing across at the man seated at the next table who was in charge of the kitchen, she gave a little shrug. 'We sometimes get one eventually, if we ask often enough. Although one lady didn't and fainted, banging her head on the side of a table.'

'Goodness, that doesn't sound right,' Brenda said, giving a slight frown. 'Surely water should be there for whenever you need it. I'll look into that,' and she made a note on her pad. 'Are there any other problems?'

A woman edged nearer to join in the conversation. 'This factory being so large, we have to walk up and down those bloody stairs to the stock room endless times every day just to collect the necessary ingredients. Wears us out.'

'I'd noticed that,' Brenda admitted.

'Aye, and a friend of mine fell down the stairs as she struggled to carry a bag of one hundred weight of flour. Even the equipment is too big and heavy for us women to lift. The mixing bowls are huge, and the tables upon which we work are far too high, so it's not easy to roll out the dough comfortably. This place was set up for men, not women.'

'Aye, that's right,' another woman said. 'Having stuff stacked on a handy shelf would make our lives a lot easier.'

The list was growing. Even time off for lunch or a visit to the lavatory didn't seem too good either, being somewhat restricted. The washing facilities were very male orientated, and there was a shortage of toilets. In view of Brenda's memories of the internment camp, she was most sympathetic about such complaints.

Speaking to Hugh later in his office, she pointed these problems out to him.

His response was slightly derisory. 'Women always like to grumble.'

'That's not quite fair. All of this baking should be carried out in a room specially converted into a brand-new baking kitchen, with all the right equipment and special ovens for the task.'

'Unfortunately, that is not possible.'

'I perfectly understand your reluctance to take out a loan when you're already in debt, but the production schedule is something of a problem since we have to share the main ovens. Cakes, parkin and fruit loaves are kept waiting for hours because the ovens are full of biscuits. That does them no good at all. I agree that items which are quick to bake should be done early in the day, but fitting everything in is becoming well nigh impossible. I cannot persuade the chaps in charge to agree to accommodate us. So, ideally we do need our own kitchen.'

'I'm afraid we don't have the necessary funds to do such a thing, so the ladies will just have to put up with reality. It's profits that count at the end of the day, otherwise they'd all be out of a job.'

'How can we achieve the necessary profits if production is not working properly? You should look upon it as an investment in the future of the business. These women also have to be quite tough. The equipment they use is far too heavy,' she reminded him.

'They all seem pretty fit and strong to me. As for you…'

Her eyes focused upon his chiselled chin and the way his mouth lifted into an impish grin, but she kept firmly to her point. 'Bakery life is hard. Are you deliberately being difficult?' she challenged him, hands upon her hips. 'Workers' requirements should be listened to and their needs taken into account.'

Giving a burst of laughter, he put his arms around her to pull her close. 'I love engaging in conversation with you when you're in one of your feisty moods. It's such fun.' His grey eyes darkened as he lowered his head to capture her mouth with his. A tremor of excitement flowed through her, her skin seeming to flare with desire at his touch.

'Behave! There might be somebody watching,' she said, quickly freeing herself, cheeks flushed. 'Can we concentrate on what I'm saying, please?'

'Of course, I beg your pardon. I'm just finding you completely irresistible.'

She looked up at him, finding his dazzling smile equally entrancing. Something was most definitely happening between them, an emotion she found difficult to justify. Was her attraction to Jack's brother a good thing or entirely wrong?

'I'm fully aware of the lack of satisfaction within the ranks, having suffered from a recent strike,' he said. 'Do whatever you feel is necessary to make life more comfortable for our workers, particularly the women, as you understand their situation and requirements much better than I, a mere male, could ever do. And I will look into the question of converting one of the old work-rooms into a new kitchen, and provide a more accessible stock room.'

Meeting his gaze with a relieved smile, she nodded. 'That would be wonderful, and most generous of you, Hugh. It's good to see that at heart you are indeed a kind man after all.'

'Just as you are a delightful, hard-working lady, happy to put the needs of others before your own, and honest to the core. I think we're coming a little closer to understanding each other, don't you?' He kissed the tip of her nose, then chuckled as she walked staunchly away, notepad in hand.

Twenty-Six

Melissa sat in the solicitor's office and demanded he support her decision not to allow this cheat of a woman to become involved in the family business, explaining how it could damage her children's inheritance. She felt desperate to rid herself of this harlot, so surely this fellow could help. There were other issues besides money, but as some family matters needed to be kept private, she didn't say a word about them to Fairhurst.

'Since she has no satisfactory proof of her identity or whether she really was married to my brother, why would I agree to that?' she haughtily remarked. 'She's just a piece of baggage looking for a pot of cash.'

Clearing his throat, Mr Fairhurst took off his glasses to give them a brisk polish. Then slipping them back on again, blinked at her with his faded grey eyes. 'We did our best to find the necessary papers but they've gone for good. Even in this country many archives have been damaged or destroyed and documents lost. However, Jack did name her in his will as his wife, and left her shares in the company, so it could be that any protest you make would be deemed inappropriate in the circumstances. You have no more proof that she is lying than Miss Brenda has to prove she's telling the truth.'

Melissa felt as if she'd been slapped in the face. How dare this fellow say such things to her? 'You're sounding as bad as Hugh. Are you seriously claiming you prefer to believe this charlatan rather than me, despite having worked for our family for years? Quite outrageous! My husband would most certainly have something to say about that attitude.'

Giving a mincing little smile, he quickly apologised. 'We can try looking into the issue again, if you wish, milady, but can offer no guarantees.'

Glancing up at the wall clock, as if she really hadn't time for all this nonsense, she pulled on her gloves. 'There's no need for that. I appreciate you've done whatever is necessary. Just make it clear to my brother, whom she's now attempting to seduce, that without such proof she can be given no rights or shares in the family business, or take any part of our inheritance.' Now she forced crocodile tears to form in her eyes, and pulling a handkerchief from her bag delicately dabbed at them. 'You should be aware that she has also attempted to offer favours to my husband.'

'Goodness!' The family solicitor looked quite shocked by this news. 'Are you sure about that?'

Melissa gave a melodramatic little sigh, blinking hard to make the tears slide down her cheeks. 'I heard her talking to him out on the landing one night, opened the door and saw how she'd wrapped herself into his arms. There is no doubt about it, she is a harlot of the worst quarter.'

Not for a moment would Melissa admit that it was actually her husband she'd seen clenching the girl in his arms, kissing and fondling her while the chit firmly resisted, and thumped him off. But then it wasn't the first time she'd seen Gregory paw a girl, particularly when drunk, as he'd been on that occasion. She'd just turned eighteen when she married him, naively believing he worshipped and adored her, when in actual reality he was probably only after her money and status. She'd done everything she could to excite and please him, as she had the other night when she suspected he'd paid that chit a visit, but to no avail. He was a real man-about-town, a philanderer of the worst degree. So why should she not use everything in her power to rid herself of this madam? Melissa decided she would do whatever was necessary, no matter what the risk.

*

Brenda cycled to the factory quite early each morning, arriving before the rest of the staff clocked in so that she could start to get things ready for them. Her goal was to improve conditions for the women workers, and she felt pleased to have resolved various problems. She'd arranged for them to have a ten-minute break morning and afternoon, with tea and biscuits provided, plus an hour for dinner. Access to water was now available in the utility room next to the kitchen where the washing up was done; a stock room had been set up downstairs, much closer to the bakery, and a trolley purchased to transport the heavy bags of flour.

In addition, Hugh was in the process of making plans for creating a new kitchen, even if it meant taking out a small loan in order to pay for it.

An increase in the profits of the business was now even more essential. Whether they would achieve that was very much dependent upon the success of the processes she'd put in place. All equipment and ingredients required had to be available when and where needed. In addition to the eggs, milk and fruit that Prue provided, they required various types of sugar, treacle, cocoa powder, raising agents and fat, which weren't necessarily used for biscuits. These had to be ordered and delivered at the right time. Other jobs too had to be completed on time and within budget. Brenda knew it would not be an easy task and sales of cakes and puddings must continue to increase, as she really had no wish to land Hugh into deeper difficulties. Dare she hope that all of this would work?

The air was growing cooler as summer drew to a close, and this morning, as she crossed the factory yard back to the bakery, having spoken to the coal delivery man, she saw the Daimler car draw up and Hugh climb out.

He instantly came over to her. 'Ah, Brenda, I am told the new schedule is working very well.'

'Really? Oh, I'm so pleased to hear that.'

'The union representative has informed me that the workers are immensely pleased with what you have achieved. The fact that you were prepared to listen to their problems and change the system to suit them, also worked a treat. Sadly, no one has ever asked them their opinions before. Certainly, my father never thought to do so, being entirely obsessed with his own theories and principles. I feel a little guilty for not asking them either.'

'But then, you have had problems of your own.'

'As do we all after this dratted war. But yours were much worse than mine.'

'Maybe that's why I felt more sympathy for everyone,' she said with a smile.

'Good point, but I am learning. Haven't seen you for a while, Brenda, not even back at the Hall. I dare say because you've been very busy getting everything organised. How are you?'

Meeting his gaze, her heart clenched with longing. Brenda had found herself deliberately avoiding him, worried about the emotions he stirred within her, and whether they were quite appropriate. She strove now to remain businesslike. 'I'm fine, thank you. The question is, are we making the necessary profits?'

'Ah, let me show you the sales figures.' And taking her arm he led her into the factory, tipping his trilby hat and saying good morning to everyone they passed along the way, seeming much more cheerful than usual. Once she'd examined the figures, Brenda could understand why.

'So the business really *is* doing better?'

'Indeed we are, thanks to your efforts and care towards everyone. You're a very brave and determined lady, and have picked up the tricks of the trade amazingly quickly. You've also brightened me up too by giving me a purpose to move forward.'

'That's good. I'm delighted to hear it. I do like to keep busy and really enjoy new challenges.'

His expression softened as he smiled at her. 'I'm beginning to see what it was about you that captured my brother's heart, because I rather think you're now capturing mine.'

Brenda gazed up into his sparkling eyes in stunned disbelief. Would that be the right thing? she asked herself.

Seeming to read her mind, he gathered her hands in his to gently rub them with his thumbs. 'That's not a crime. We are not blood-related. Such a relationship might have been forbidden in the past, but not any more. I live in hope that you might come to feel the same. But if you aren't yet ready to move on, then please find it in your heart to forgive me. I did apologise for my inappropriate attitude towards you in the past, so we can at least be good friends, can't we?'

'Of course,' Brenda gently murmured, feeling a flush of desire conflict with a small spurt of uncertainty. What kind of relationship was he suggesting? Did he still think she was prepared to spread her favours? Could this be the start of true love between them, or were they simply sharing their sense of loneliness and loss for Jack? What a muddle she felt herself in.

*

Prue and Dino were happily running the farm as well as supplying Brenda with fruit, milk, eggs and flour. Unfortunately they were suffering a few problems of their own. Whenever they walked together through Trowbridge village with their lovely child, they found people would stand watching them in grim silence, their anti-Italian sentiment most evident. It made Prue shiver to her toes to still see the disapproval and indifference in their eyes. 'I'm quite sure they gossip about us behind our backs.'

'Don't worry about it,' Dino said, tucking her arm into his as they pushed the pram along. 'Such is war. We have been very fortunate to find each other. This is my home now and I like these people, so smile and say hello.'

Giving a little giggle she did just that, although received no response.

'According to my mother, some Italian youngsters who were evacuated during the war for their own safety, avoided attending school, as teachers constantly ridiculed them.'

'Goodness, that's appalling!' Prue gazed at her beloved baby, aware of the pain it would cause her if darling Flora were ever to suffer such harassment. And to lose her child as had happened to poor Brenda, would be unbearable.

'Some Italian young men deserted the army after being ridiculed or attacked. My mother hid a conscript in our home for a while as MPs were searching for him. Yet he wasn't a criminal or anti-British. Admittedly, the attitude towards Germans is worse, but we Italians are still seen as unwelcome aliens by many, our loyalty towards Britain not always taken seriously. Even those who were against Mussolini have been interned.'

'How can the government consider that to be fair?'

'It's what happens in war. Most people consider intern- ment to be necessary. Don't worry, my darling, this animos- ity will pass, although it might take a while, even though the war is at last over. And sadly some internees and PoWs are still being held, particularly Germans. We have been most fortunate.'

'We have indeed, and I'm sure things will get better,' she said, hugging his arm close.

They continued with their shopping, thankful whenever anyone chose to smile at them, or say hello, although plenty still crossed the road to avoid them. When they called in at the local grocer to order a slab of butter, Mr Higginson stated he had none available.

'But you generally do have some for regular customers,' Prue responded.

'Not today, sorry,' he frostily remarked.

And noticing how he cast a scathing glance at Dino, she gave a sad shake of her head. 'Very well, then we'll take our custom elsewhere,' she declared, and swiftly marched out.

'You shouldn't have done that,' Dino said, as he hurried to catch up with her. 'One of your hasty decisions you might come to regret. They are a good business.'

'Drat the stupid fellow! Why would I continue to be a customer when he was so rude and refused to supply us? He'd no right to be so dismissive of you. But not to worry, darling, we'll cope with this resistance, however frightful and unfair it might be.' And they happily walked home together arm in arm.

*

A few days later Prue received a letter filled with hate. It gave no name and made vile accusations against her marriage. '*It was stupid and dangerous of you to marry the enemy. Italians are not to be trusted. Can we even trust you?*' She received one the next day too, and another a few days later. The number of these dreadful letters increased over the following weeks, all anonymous, the handwriting of each different but the language and comments becoming worse and worse.

Dino found her quietly weeping one morning as she read the latest piece of hate mail. Taking it from her, he quietly read it.

'It's not the first,' Prue admitted, and finally revealed the huge bag of vile letters she'd received.

A sad expression cloaked his face as he quickly scanned them, then tossed every letter into the fire. 'Don't read these ever again, as they're only saying nasty things. Most hurtful.'

'I did get one that seemed to be on our side. It says, "*You can't choose who you fall in love with, so I hope you'll be happy*", which was good to hear.'

'And we are happy, darling. I love you with all my heart, so it doesn't matter a jot what other people think.'

'Oh, I love you too. But it's so sad that some people's attitude towards you is so negative and wrong. It makes me angry, particularly since I've known many of these villagers all my life. I wonder, should we invite them round to celebrate our marriage and new life on the farm? We could hold a little party, which would give them the opportunity to really get to know you. Do you think that might work?'

Giving a wry smile, Dino made no comment.

Twenty-Seven

Prue sent off dozens of invitations to all friends and neighbours to join them in celebration of their marriage and the new future they were building together at the farm. She then spent ages planning the party, in particular the food, but felt she was getting nowhere. 'I don't think I know what I'm doing. Can you help?' she asked Brenda.

'Of course. Just let me know what you'd like to eat and we'll provide it. No problem.'

'Oh, thank you so much, but I think you should make the necessary choices. I'm a gardener, not very good at party planning and even worse at baking. What do people like to eat at parties these days, and what sort of food is available? I really wouldn't know.'

Brenda laughed. 'We'll keep it simple: small ham sandwiches, cheese straws, chicken patties, biscuits, of course, and I'll make you a lovely cake.'

'That would be wonderful.'

'It will be good for our business too. Let's hope you get a good turnout.'

The glance Prue exchanged with her in response to this remark was one filled with doubt, revealing her fear that nobody would come to welcome her new husband. 'Next question. What do we wear?'

They spent a happy hour trying on clothes, which helped to take Prue's mind off her worries. This celebration had been her idea, so she must do her best to make sure it worked. In the days following, whenever she came across a neighbour or friend while out shopping, she would remind them of the party. 'Do hope to see you there,' she would say with smile. But when the day arrived she felt jittery with nerves. Would anyone at all turn up?

'I'm sure it will be fine,' Dino assured her, giving her a kiss as she fussed with her hair for the umpteenth time. 'People do love a party. Joe and his wife are definitely coming.'

Old Joe did in fact arrive first, quickly followed by Hugh and Melissa, who was making one of her regular visits. She looked as glamorous as ever in a swirling gown of pale-pink silk with an off-the-shoulder neckline.

'Has anyone else arrived yet?' Hugh whispered to Brenda in the kitchen, as she set the sandwiches out on a tray.

She shook her head. 'Not that I know of. I do hope people come. I think Prue feels quite lost without her old friends.'

'Marrying Dino was her choice. I did warn her there could be problems.'

'Fortunately there are none between the two of them,' she firmly responded, 'which is all that really matters.'

'Folk are still a bit prejudiced,' Mrs Harding said with

a sniff as she busily set the cake on to a stand, topping it with a tiny posy of silk flowers. 'Yet, why would they when he's such a lovely young man?'

'Even I now appreciate that,' Hugh acknowledged, and with a wry smile he left the kitchen to go back into the sitting room. The door bell rang at that moment, and everyone fell silent. 'Shall I go?' he asked his sister.

Prue shook her head and cheerfully smiled. 'No, this is my party, I'll go.' She walked to the door only to be stopped by Dino.

'Let me, darling.'

Stepping back, she gave him a smile and a nod, watching with pride as he looked so handsome in his smart grey suit. He pulled open the door to find a darkly clothed man standing on the step. Prue cried out in horror as Dino was instantly swamped with muddy water tossed from a bucket. She at once ran for a towel, while Hugh rushed out after the perpetrator. Unfortunately he'd quickly escaped. 'Drat the fellow,' he snapped, and stormed back into the cottage to slam the door shut.

'I shouldn't have bothered buying myself a new suit,' Dino said, giving a little chuckle as Prue attempted to rub off the messy mud and pat him dry.

As he dashed off to his room to change, the doorbell rang a second time and they all jerked back, half-fearing the same thing could happen again. Hugh opened the door to find a crowd of friends and neighbours gathered there.

'Hello, hope we aren't late?' one lady said.

'Really looking forward to celebrating your wedding,' said another.

Prue gazed upon them in disbelief. 'Oh, how wonderful to see you all. Of course you aren't late. Do come in.' She dashed to hug each of them in turn as the room quickly filled with people, her heart exploding with relief and happiness.

'I told you everything would be fine,' Dino murmured, returning to her side with a big grin on his handsome face. 'Now let's enjoy ourselves.'

*

The evening proved to be a great success. Brenda felt so pleased for Prue that it was going well, and happily carried trays and plates around for people to snack from.

'You're an absolute treasure,' Hugh whispered, coming to join her on the back porch where she was taking a short break.

Gazing up at the star-filled sky and feeling her heart glow almost as brightly, she smiled. 'Only too pleased to help, and so thrilled that things are going right for them at last.'

'I hope they will for you too eventually,' he told her, then pulling her into his arms, softly kissed her.

How content she felt in his arms, as if she truly belonged there. Brenda arched her neck enticingly as he smoothed his lips over her bare throat, then down to the swell of her breast beneath her blouse, giving a little gasp of pleasure. What was happening between them? She did feel an increasing attraction towards Hugh, but would that mean abandoning her love for Jack?

'I think I may be misbehaving a little,' he said, and releasing his hold, gave an apologetic little smile. 'I'm going to fetch you a glass of wine. You deserve it after all your hard work and I need one to calm myself down. Stay right here, I'll be back in a moment.'

'I see you are winning him round,' a cold voice stated, seconds after he disappeared through the door.

Spinning round to face Melissa's caustic gaze as she approached from the garden, Brenda stifled a sigh. 'Hugh does now believe in me, so what's wrong with that? And we're good friends, nothing more.'

Sauntering into the porch, a glass of champagne in her hand, Melissa gave a snort of disbelief. 'You've been planning this from the moment you first got a job here all those years ago, determined this would be the best way for you to get out of the gutter. And since you've lost Jack, why would you not try to snap up Hugh instead?'

Brenda felt an all-too-familiar sense of inferiority echoing within her, and valiantly attempted to banish it. She was in no way responsible for what had happened to herself as a child. Everything this woman accused her of was entirely false. But then, Melissa had a grandiose sense of her own importance and a strong desire to feel superior. 'I've no wish to snap up any man right now. I'm quite enjoying the peace and a new sense of freedom and independence.'

'As well as trying to seduce my darling Gregory. You

even encouraged him to pay you a visit, now you are living at the Hall.'

Shock reverberated through Brenda. 'I did no such thing! *He* attempted to kiss *me*. I expect he was a bit drunk and didn't realise who I was, although as a married man, he shouldn't be doing that to any woman. I slapped him off. He also attempted to visit my room and I threatened him with a poker. If he comes near me again, I swear I'll report him to the police for harassment and assault.'

Melissa's lips curled into a sceptical glower of disbelief. 'He is obviously convinced a whore like you would welcome his attention, as you'd no doubt flirted with him.'

'I most definitely had not!'

'And now you want to get your greedy little mitts on our business.'

'No, I'm just involved in the work, doing what Jack would expect of me,' Brenda said, finding it difficult to come up with the right words to defend herself. Perhaps this entire enterprise had been a bad mistake. She really was growing tired of this haughty madam.

'It is such a pity you managed to escape from France,' Melissa caustically remarked. 'A real shame you weren't on that bridge when it blew up. That would have spared us all the trouble of having your filthy hands attempting to get hold of our cash. We really don't want you here.'

Brenda gave a puzzled frown. 'How do you know about that bomb? I've never spoken of it.'

Half turning away, Melissa gave a careless shrug of

her bare shoulders. 'I expect Mama mentioned it in one of her letters.'

'If so, then that would have been after I was arrested and Camille and Adèle had left Paris, so you would then know their new address.'

Melissa's cheeks flushed crimson. She took a sip of champagne, pausing for some seconds before she responded. 'I must be wrong about that. Probably it was Mary Dobson, the solicitor's secretary, who told me.'

'Why would she know? I haven't mentioned it to her either, or the solicitor. It didn't seem relevant to what I was asking of them, and far too painful to discuss.' Brenda's eyes narrowed with suspicion as she glared at her sister-in-law. How much more did she know that she wasn't telling?

Hugh came to join them just then, carrying a glass of wine for Brenda and one for himself. 'Melissa, do you need yours topping up?' he asked with a grin.

'No thank you. I can do that for myself.'

Brenda watched as she strode back indoors, chin held high and her silver-blonde hair swaying in the evening breeze, convinced there was something she wasn't telling her. What a difficult woman she was. It crossed Brenda's mind to speak to Hugh about what his sister had just said, but as he took her hand in his, she instantly changed her mind. She may not be guilty of scheming to make this relationship happen but really had no wish to destroy whatever was developing between them. In any case, surely the best way to deal with Melissa's snobby attitude was to ignore it.

*

The next morning, being a Sunday, Prue was taking a much-needed rest with her husband. So it was Brenda who let the hens out of their coop, welcoming a day off from baking. Young Ross came scampering over. 'Ain't Nobody Here But Us Chickens,' he sang, watching them scratch about for food.

Laughing as he carried on singing, Brenda joined in. 'Hobble, hobble hobble hobble with your chin.'

Ross burst into a fit of giggles. 'I've fetched the basket, Bren. Do we collect the eggs now?'

'You can if you like, while I give the coop a little clean.'

'Why are some eggs white and others brown?' he asked, as he carefully picked them out of the nesting boxes. 'Is it because of what kind of hens they are?'

'Clever boy, yes it is. Some of these hens are mixed breed and lay white eggs, while the Rhode Island Reds lay brown. But they all taste delicious.'

'I asked Mama if we could keep hens, but she said no. So did Dad. Yet some of my friends do.'

'That's because eggs have been rationed for so long, keeping your own flock in the back garden is the only way to get more than the one egg a week allowed. Even poultry food is rationed, but you can give hens a bit of mash and vegetable scraps as well, as long as you don't have too many to feed.'

He listened with close attention to her explanation, then began to count the hens. On reaching ten and perhaps unsure of what numbers came after that, he looked around at the large flock poking and scratching in the grass and the dusty holes they made. 'Why are you allowed to have so many, then?'

'We are fortunate because we have a farm, although I still use powdered egg for my baking. Does your mummy?' Brenda cheerfully asked, so enjoying the conversation with this bright little boy.

Ross shook his head and gave another little giggle. 'Mama doesn't cook.'

'Oh, of course not, I forgot. Well, she's probably right not to keep hens, as you live in the centre of London. They do need a garden and have to be well fed and properly looked after or they won't lay well,' she added.

'I shall have a garden when I grow up,' he solemnly informed her.

'*Ross*, where are you, boy?'

He froze, tightening his mouth in agony when he heard his mother's voice and the clatter of her heels crossing the farmyard. Pushing the basket into Brenda's hands, he turned and dashed off, running as fast as his little legs could carry him to hide behind the hedge.

'Have you been exploiting my son yet again?' Melissa snapped, standing before the hen coop with clenched fists upon her hips.

Brenda paused in her cleaning to gaze at her, eyes wide with innocence. 'No idea what you're talking about. As you can see, Ross isn't here.'

'He damn well was, I heard him singing. Where is he?'

'I've no idea,' Brenda said, and turned back to her

sweeping and cleaning, not wishing to get involved with this mother-and-son issue. But then she heard a little cry.

'*Ouch!*' The small boy came tumbling out of the hawthorn hedge rubbing his arms and legs, obviously having been pricked by the thorns on the branches.

'Come here this minute,' Melissa roared.

Brenda stepped quickly forward. 'Please don't tell him off, or shout. He's done nothing wrong. He's just having fun.'

'Don't you dare keep interfering with my child. You'd no right to teach him to cycle on that filthy old bike, or to have him help with these hens. Leave him alone.' The moment he reached her, Melissa swung him round and smacked his bottom. He let out a yell, but ignoring his cries she smacked him again.

'That's enough!' Brenda said.

'Mind your own business,' and sweeping him up, his wriggling body tucked under her arm like he was a naughty puppy, she marched away.

*

'I can't believe what a dreadful bully that woman is. How can she justify being so harsh towards that child?' Brenda fumed when she joined Mrs Harding for a cup of tea and a slice of cake later that afternoon. The housekeeper was appalled to hear what had taken place.

'So that's why she's shut the poor lad up in his room for most of the day. He didn't even get any lunch. That's no way to treat a little one.'

'Goodness, he must be so hungry.'

'Nay, I took him up some leftover ham sandwiches while she were enjoying her own fine lunch,' Mrs Harding admitted with a smile. 'He looked so bored, but very grateful. He'll be fine.'

Later that evening, on her way to Jack's room, which now felt like her own private little world, Brenda sneaked in to see if Ross really was all right. She took him a small piece of cake and a cup of milk for his supper, but found him fast asleep. Gazing down upon him in wistful envy, she thought what a lovely little boy he was. Life would have been such fun if her own son was still with her. In her head she saw him as a baby, with soft blue eyes and tiny fingers and toes, and he was always in her heart. How she ached to find him again, to see how he had grown. Setting the cake and cup on the bedside table, it was then she noticed a small cuddly toy monkey tucked up beside the child.

Twenty-Eight

It was as if a light bulb had exploded in her head, filling her with joy. This was her son! She wanted to scream and shout: *I've found him, I've found him at last*! Brenda remembered buying this cuddly toy back in Paris just days before he was born. She loved it because it was so unusual, a beautiful silver grey, and rather French. Not at all like the simple teddy bears that British children generally had. No wonder she'd felt an attraction to this little boy from the moment they first met, and an even closer bond had developed between them since. All these years she'd been searching for him, and he'd been back home with his family, safe and well the entire time.

Brenda longed to wrap him in her arms but, restraining her desire to touch him, she bent to look at the toy more closely. The child suddenly woke to gaze up at her with his soft brown eyes.

'Hello,' she whispered. 'Is this your favourite toy?'

He gave a little nod. 'Minki is my friend. Mama doesn't like him and keeps throwing him away, but I always rescue him.' And grasping hold of the monkey, he hugged him close.

'Take good care of him, sweetie. Never lose a friend.'

Or a son, she bleakly reminded herself. And as his eyes closed and he fell back to sleep, she quietly slipped out, her heart pounding with excitement.

It wasn't until Brenda was lying alone in the big double bed in her late husband's room that grief dissolved the burst of joy she felt, and she buried her face in the pillow to muffle the sound of her sobs. How could she ever hope to win him back? In his young mind Melissa was his mother. Remembering the stories Emma had related in her many letters, she knew this could be virtually impossible to achieve, even if she took the matter to court.

Overwhelmed by emotion, Brenda spent a sleepless night, feeling utterly stunned and betrayed. She could scarcely believe that despite accusing her of being a fraudster and a charlatan, it was Melissa herself who had lied, as she must know who this child really was. Could that be why she was always so caustic towards her? Although how she'd got hold of him in the first place was a mystery still to be resolved. Nor did the pair of them appear to be particularly close. Melissa was constantly smacking and bullying the poor child, which could be because she hated to see him spending time with his real mother. Brenda felt quite unable to get her head around how to deal with this issue.

Had the entire family been aware of who he was all along, and was that the reason no one had welcomed her, not even Hugh? Had they all been determined to evict her from the house in order to keep secret the fact they'd stolen her son? If that was the case, what a cruel and heartless lot they were. Yet Hugh seemed to have softened towards her lately. Was that a genuine emotion, or was he attempting to disguise this wicked plot? Perhaps he just felt the need of a few favours and fancied having her in his bed. How could she trust any member of this family, save for dear Prue?

And what would be his reaction were she to tell him what she'd just discovered? He was the kind of man who always demanded proof, so how could she hope to simply use a cuddly toy in order to prove her case? Quite impossible.

It came to Brenda in that moment that she could be entirely wrong. This toy monkey might well be available in England too, and just a coincidence. She decided it would be wiser to keep quiet on the subject until she'd found some way to investigate it more thoroughly.

As dawn broke, a pink sheet of light flooded the background of hills. Propped against her pillows, Brenda again wrote to Emma, telling her dear friend what she'd found and asking for advice. She then quickly dressed and cycled to the bakery as she had a great deal of work to do, dropping the letter in the post box on the way. She lived in hope that Emma could help.

*

Despite seeing Hugh on and off during the course of the day, Brenda steadfastly held her tongue, saying nothing.

'Sales of cakes are getting better and better,' he told her with a satisfied smile. 'Well done! The new plan is working brilliantly and profits are improving daily. I'm so pleased you won me round to the idea, but then, you are a very tempting lady.' And kissing her on the cheek, he strolled off whistling.

How she longed to run after him and tell him what she'd discovered. Just the feel of his warm smile set her heart tingling with happiness, but she managed to hold herself in check. You still have very little proof, she sternly reminded herself.

On returning to Trowbridge Hall late in the afternoon, Brenda spotted Nanny Holborn walking in the garden and went over to chat with her. 'Hello. How unusual to see you without the children. Where are they?' she asked with a friendly smile as she fell into step beside her.

The stocky, solemn-faced woman gave her a weary glance. 'Whenever separated from her husband, either because he's abroad or too busy in London to spend much time with her, Mrs Fenton soon becomes bored. She tends to fill her time with social functions, meals out with friends, shopping and beauty treatment, leaving the children entirely in my care. Today, however, she has taken them to the circus, which arrived in the village a few days ago. Apparently she used to love the show as a child, and thought her own children might enjoy it too.'

'How lovely, although according to Hugh, Jack did not enjoy such visits. He hated seeing lions and elephants confined. I have some sympathy with that. I can remember being taken to the circus once as a child by the nuns, and was terrified of the clowns.'

'Oh, I didn't care for them either,' Nanny Holborn agreed with a smile. 'Fortunately I was not invited to join them on this occasion. But let's hope these little ones do enjoy it.'

'Have you worked for the family long?'

She shook her head. 'Only a few years.'

'Just in time to help with her latest birth, I suppose?' Brenda blithely remarked, feeling her heart start to pound in her chest.

'No, the baby was a few months old by the time I was appointed.'

'Really, so who was the nanny before you?'

'A delightful young woman I happened to know, who found herself sacked after some disagreement or other with Mrs Fenton.'

'Oh dear, did you find out what that was about?'

'She didn't say and I never asked. None of my business. But then, Mrs Fenton is not an easy woman to work for,' she added, giving a droll little slant to her dark brown eyes.

'I don't suppose she is,' Brenda agreed, her mind racing as she struggled to decide how to get the necessary information. 'Actually, I have a friend in need of a nanny. Would you mind telling me this young woman's name and where she lives?' It was a complete lie, of course, and would Nanny Holborn even possess such information?

She was looking a little doubtful. 'It's likely she'll have found another job by now. But you never know, she could well be in need of employment in this difficult post-war world. She's called Nancy Seymour and lives in Hackney, London,' she said, and happily gave the address.

'Thank you,' Brenda said with a smile, even though Manchester would have been so much more convenient, as she could then have met the woman face to face. But she would write to her, without delay. 'I'm most grateful.'

The family car drew up in the drive at that moment and Nanny Holborn looked at it in stunned disbelief. 'Goodness, back already? They've only been gone an hour.'

The little girls bounced out of the back seat, all three of them weeping. Then Ross appeared, dragged screaming out of the car by his furious mother. He began to stamp his feet, fully engrossed in a tantrum.

'Stop this racket, you naughty boy,' Melissa shouted, giving him a rough shake.

'This is all *his* fault. The stupid boy ruined our afternoon when he started screaming and crying,' Claire yelled, sounding as angry as her mother, while her twin sisters sobbed.

'Don't like them animals!' he yelled, falling flat on his back to beat his heels on the gravelled drive.

'Oh dear,' Nanny murmured to Brenda. 'Not a happy bunny. Looks like he didn't much care for the circus either. I'd best go and help,' and she dashed off, calmly calling out to him as she ran. 'There, there, don't cry, dear. Come with me and I'll put you down for a little nap.'

'Do indeed,' his mother snapped. 'And keep him confined to his bed until I say he can get up. I'll take the girls for a picnic instead. Please speak to Mrs Harding and get us a hamper of food.' And flinging the child into Nanny's arms, Melissa stalked off, her three daughters running along beside her. How Brenda longed to gather the little boy into her own arms and rescue him from this dreadful bitch of a woman.

*

It took Brenda longer than usual to work out what to say in this vital letter to a complete stranger, struggling over how frank she should be. In the end, after tossing away several failed attempts, she blatantly told the truth. If she needed this young woman to be open and honest with her, then she must be the same. It was most definitely time to speak of the traumas and loss she'd suffered to anyone who asked. Finally satisfied with what she'd written, she sent up a silent prayer of hope as she dropped the letter in the post box while taking Kit out on his evening walk.

'You could have told me you were going for a walk,' Hugh said, coming to meet her as she walked back across the lawn. 'Then we could have enjoyed it together.'

'Sorry, it didn't cross my mind.' Perhaps there was a slight expression of distrust in her eyes as she avoided his gaze, which caused him to frown.

'So, relaxing together no longer appeals? You prefer the dog's company to mine, is that it?' he quietly asked, rubbing Kit's ears as the collie happily wagged his body.

Something inside of her seemed to crack with pain. Was her life falling apart yet again? 'That's not at all what I meant. Actually, I'm not in a good frame of mind right now. I've got a bit of a problem to deal with.'

Taking her arm in his, Hugh gently led her to the bench

in the summer house. There was a chill breeze in the air and dusk was falling, but she made no protest, his presence feeling so warm and comforting. Kit trotted after them and, turning round and round a few times, settled himself in a corner. 'Tell me what the problem is. Maybe I can help.'

Drawing in a breath and valiantly keeping a tight hold on the information she still must keep private until she'd found the proof she needed, Brenda opted for a different problem. 'As you are fully aware, Melissa is most bombastic towards me. Even the fact that I taught Ross how to cycle did not go down well. She keeps accusing me of interfering in her family. And she still refuses to accept the truth about my relationship with Jack, seeing me as inferior, a harlot interested only in stealing money off her and her children, which is entirely untrue.'

'I'm afraid that's how she is. Argument over status is an obsession with my dear sister, as if she needs to prove her own value in some way.'

'Even worse, last evening at the party she accused me of seducing her husband, which is entirely untrue. He did make an attempt to kiss me once, but I managed to slap him off.' She decided not to mention how he had slipped into her room the other night, in case Hugh took that as a reason to again dismiss her from the house.

'Good lord, but then Gregory is a bit of a womaniser.'

'I pretty well implied as much, absolutely denying it was my fault. And as I explained, nor did I stay at that brothel. I am *not* a whore, yet she refuses to believe that too.'

'Would you like me to have a word with her on the subject?' he quietly asked.

Brenda shook her head. 'No, I've decided to ignore the fact she's snobby towards me. And if she has any domestic problems, they are nothing to do with me either.'

'I think they do have issues in their marriage. They spend very little time together. That is probably why she's so uptight at the moment, even worse than usual.'

'Yet despite having problems of her own, she has not a shred of compassion for any of the traumas I've been through.'

'I doubt she's interested in hearing them,' he wryly remarked.

'She's fully aware that I'm desperate to find my son.' This comment set her heart racing, as Brenda longed to reveal what she'd discovered. 'Do you think Melissa knows more than she's admitting?'

Hugh's brows puckered into a frown. 'What do you mean? How could she know more?'

'I-I've no idea,' Brenda stammered, thinking she'd perhaps taken one step too close to the main issue before she had the information she needed about that little monkey. Questions, in fact, she might never find the answers to. Coming to a hasty decision, she drew herself away from him in order to hold her emotions in check. 'I perhaps reacted badly to Gregory's drunken behaviour because of something that happened to me while I was interned. I think it's time you heard about that.'

'Tell me,' he quietly said.

Brenda paused for some moments to rally her strength before continuing. 'While in the camp at Besançon, I was assaulted one evening by a German guard.'

'He attacked you? Oh, that's dreadful!

'He raped me.'

He stared at her in shock. 'You poor love.'

Tears flooded her eyes as she met his sympathetic gaze. 'I tried to push him off, but failed. He was far too strong and aggressive. And his mates were standing by watching and laughing. Fortunately, I did manage to run away before they decided to join in.'

'Thank God for that. What you must have suffered at that camp.'

She gave a caustic little laugh. 'You don't know the half of it, and apart from my friend Emma, who was also interned, I've never told this to anyone. I find it quite difficult to talk about. We were also strip-searched in Biarritz after we'd crossed the Pyrenees to make our way home through Spain, which fortunately involved nothing more serious than some unpleasant fumbling. Please don't mention any of this, particularly not to Melissa. Such information would only convince her that she's right in her low opinion of me.'

'Your secret is safe with me, darling,' he murmured, slipping his arm around her to hold her close and give her a soft kiss. 'I believe in you absolutely.'

'Thank you.' The use of this endearment resonated deep into the heart of her. Did he genuinely mean this, or was

Always in My Heart 317

this his way of helping to keep Tommy's presence in the family a secret?

'May I suggest that you stop fretting about my sister. Melissa's life too is in something of a turmoil right now, which is why she keeps coming back home,' he explained with a sigh. 'I think she dreamed of enjoying a rich social life in London with her bureaucrat of a husband, but sadly it hasn't quite worked out that way. He does seem rather neglectful and bombastic. But I will speak to him, and make sure he doesn't ever bother you again. I can't bear the thought of any other man kissing you, particularly after what you've just told me,' he said, gently stroking her cheek.

Was this the moment to reveal what she'd discovered? Brenda wondered. Or was she so desperate to find her son that she imagined any child with a cuddly toy similar to the one she bought, could be Tommy? Feeling completely confused and vulnerable, she said no more.

Twenty-Nine

'I believe you've been harassing Brenda, or perhaps fondling and attempting to seduce her is a more accurate description, which you should not be doing.' Hugh confronted his brother-in-law with what he deemed to be appropriate calmness. Thanks to Brenda, he'd learned to control his temper. He no longer suffered from knots in his stomach, headaches or sleepless nights. He was not only overcoming his own problems but their relationship too was improving, growing closer by the day. She'd even re-ignited his interest in the business so that Hugh felt he was leading a much happier and more satisfying life. Surely all of that meant he had the right to protect her? He certainly had no wish for dear Brenda to be put in any more danger. Hadn't she suffered enough already?

Gregory laughed. 'She's a single woman known for spreading her charms wherever she fancies, so why would I not tease and flirt with her?'

Hugh's expression tightened to one of grim determination, even though his irritation remained in check. 'She is my late brother's widow and deserves to be treated with proper respect. May I also point out that my sister would be deeply hurt and offended were she to hear of your philandering.'

'Then don't tell her,' he chuckled. 'Not that the state of my marriage is any of your business. You know damn well Melissa is a difficult woman, not the perfect wife at all.'

'And you're an egotistical bully,' Hugh calmly retorted. 'I agree, the state of your marriage is not my concern, but do not ever touch Brenda again. Nor any other young lady in this house. You have no right to do that.'

'So you imagine you can control my personal life as well as our finances?' he snorted.

'What are you talking about? I have no say over those.'

'Then why have you stopped paying Melissa her allowance?'

Hugh sighed. 'That came from my father, not me. Now that he is no longer with us and we've had to face a huge payment of death duties, not forgetting the effect of the war, we do not have the necessary funds to provide allowances any longer. Nor does Prue receive one, but she's quite happy to do her bit on the farm to earn herself a wage that way. Brenda is also helping with the business. As Melissa is your wife, she is now your responsibility, not mine.'

'So what about her inheritance?'

'As you are fully aware, Papa did leave us all a percentage. Sadly, once the probate was dealt with and death duties settled, there was no money left. Which is why we are all working hard to rebuild the business as well as improve the farm. We may one day receive something of the inheritance he promised us, but it could take years to achieve.'

'Is that because of your damned incompetence?'

Hugh pressed his lips together, feeling almost amused by this reaction. 'Such is war and reality.'

'So convincing me she was a woman of substance had been a complete lie,' Gregory snapped.

'Don't be ridiculous! How could Melissa have known what life was going to bring when war broke out, and our father grew old and even more cranky? Now, returning to the point of this discussion, I say again: Keep well away from Brenda. Understand?'

'With pleasure. I shall return to London at once.'

'Excellent!'

*

Melissa marched into Hugh's office with tears filling her grey-green eyes. 'How dare you order my husband to leave when you know we are rarely able to spend much time together?'

Lifting his attention from the accounts he was working on to stare at her in dismay, he quickly stifled a sigh. 'I did no such thing. That was his choice.' How could he even begin to explain to his sister the true nature of their disagreement? That could damage her marriage even more, and make life yet more difficult for poor Brenda. 'We were discussing the difficulties over the inheritance and he was not pleased with the sorry state we are currently in, blaming it on me, not the reality of war or the behaviour of our father.' Hugh decided not to mention her husband's accusation that she'd lied to him, which implied he'd married Melissa only for her money. 'He then announced he would be returning to London. That decision had nothing at all to do with me.'

'Gregory told me you argued over that little tart, and you chose to ignore the fact she was attempting to seduce him.'

'I do not believe that for one moment,' he said, entirely unmoved by the tears running down her cheeks, fully aware of his sister's ability to turn them on whenever she felt them to be appropriate.

Melissa tilted her chin, her mouth quivering with emotion. 'Why will you not help me to protect my marriage?'

Getting up from his seat behind the desk, he went to put his arms about her. 'I'm so sorry you have these problems, but I don't see how I can help.'

She pushed him away. 'What a naïve idiot you're turning into. You allowed that little whore to stay in Jack's old room, and she invited my husband to join her. And being something of a Lothario, he couldn't resist accepting. But then she's been flirting with him for some time. I *know* he spent part of the night with her, as he came very late to our bed, and looked filled with guilt. He wouldn't even look me in the eye, let alone touch me. It's *her* you should be banishing from our home, not Gregory.'

Feeling stunned by this, Hugh struggled to find the right response. Had that really happened, or was Gregory the instigator, just as he'd been that time over Christmas? Brenda had made no mention of being approached by him again, let alone that he'd come to her room. 'Is this what he told you?'

'It is.'

'Have you checked it with Brenda?'

Bursting into fresh tears, she shook her head. 'Why would I risk hearing what they got up to? Please get her out of here this minute, or my life will turn into even more of a nightmare. Yours too, once she has helped herself to the family money.'

Putting his arms about her, Hugh led her to the door. 'Go and take a rest. I'll do what I can to help, and if the opportunity presents itself I will ask Brenda what happened, and why.'

Closing the door as she dutifully departed, he wondered if he truly had any wish to do that. Who was he supposed to trust, his difficult snobbish sister or this young woman who had unexpectedly entered their lives?

*

Wrens and tree pipits woke Brenda at dawn with a cascade of trilling calls. Smiling, she slipped out of bed to step to the window and watch them spiralling in a bright blue sky blushed with pink. What a beautiful sight it was. September was upon them and the wild roses were no longer in bloom, but heather was beginning to cloud the hills in glorious purple, which she loved. She quickly dressed, as today she intended to have a go at making Yorkshire fruit teabread, and Goosnargh cakes, which could prove popular with customers. She had other options in mind and as it was a Saturday and the factory was closed, Mrs Harding had agreed she could experiment in the kitchen here. Baking would at least keep her mind off her problems.

Deciding to take breakfast later as it was barely six o'clock, Brenda gathered all the necessary ingredients together, then sifted the flour into the large yellow baking bowl. She added baking powder, cinnamon, nutmeg, a spoonful of marmalade and a little brown sugar, then a beaten egg and melted butter to mix into a soft dough. The fruit had been soaked overnight in tea and draining this off, she added those last.

While the cake was baking she was just starting to make a bit of courting cake, which was like a chewy rich biscuit, when Ross came scampering in, still clad in his pyjamas. As always, Brenda's heart melted at sight of him. Even more so now.

'Ooh, you're baking, can I help?'

'Of course. You'll need to wash your hands then put on an apron. Is that a problem for you?'

He eagerly shook his head and ran to do as he was told, having first stroked Tiddles the cat who was curled up in his bed by the range. Brenda helped the little boy to tie the apron around his small waist, carefully tucking it up, as it was far too big, then perched him upon a stool.

'I will roll and cut this dough into small rounds with this tart cutter, and you can spread each one with jam,' she said, slowly demonstrating how that should be done. Brenda watched with pleasure as he carefully followed her instructions, his little tongue poking out the side of his mouth as he concentrated. 'Now I shall cut a heart-shaped hole in each second round, which you can put on top. That's perfect, well done,' she said.

They worked together until all were done, by which time the little boy had jam all around his mouth, being unable to resist tasting it. Chuckling, Brenda told him to stay put while she put the tray into the oven and removed the Yorkshire teabread, to set it on a rack to cool.

'Can we make some gingerbread men? I love them,' he excitedly asked.

'What a good idea. Let's see, we need treacle, ginger and a touch of cinnamon to go with the butter, sugar and flour. Oh, and a little salt and bicarbonate of soda. Then we mix it all together.' Brenda started the job then handed over the wooden spoon to let him take a turn at the mixing, which he did with a big grin on his face. 'Now you roll out this piece, and I'll do this one,' she said, handing him a ball of dough and a small rolling pin.

She fetched Mrs Harding's pink gingerbread-man cutter and showed him how to press it on to the rolled-out dough. Ross carried out this task too with great precision. They took no time at all to bake, while Brenda found some currants and candied peel. Ross was happily forming eyes and noses on the faces of the gingerbread men with this fruit when Melissa marched in.

'So this is where you are, child. What the hell is going on here?'

Brenda's heart sank. Was this narcissistic bully about to create problems yet again? Noticing how Ross had jerked at the sound of his alleged mother's harsh tone of absolute authority, she calmly started to chop up a few small cherries for him to use as lips, then offered Melissa a bland smile. 'He's doing really well at this baking.'

'He's not a damn servant. You are!' she snorted, sounding utterly derisive. 'And as a boy he has no reason to learn to cook. Look at his face, it's filthy, covered in stuff he should not be eating at this time of day. He isn't even dressed yet.'

'It's not quite eight in the morning,' Brenda said, glancing up at the kitchen clock.

Striding over to the table, Melissa pulled the boy off the stool, marched him over to the sink and began to scrub his face and hands. Ross at once began to cry and protest. But when she smacked his leg, he gave a scream and ran out the door to bump straight into Nanny Holborn. The dear lady quickly gathered him up in her arms.

'I'll take him for his bath,' she said, looking flustered and a little guilty over the fact she'd been quite unaware that he'd risen so early and had come down to the kitchen.

'And this time keep a proper eye on him!' Melissa yelled as Nanny Holborn hurried off upstairs with the sobbing child in her arms.

Brenda felt anger spark within her. How dare this dreadful woman treat the child so appallingly? She was constantly putting him down and humiliating him for no good reason. 'Why do you keep shouting at him? Ross has done nothing naughty. He was just enjoying making some gingerbread men for his afternoon tea. What's wrong with that?'

'How many times do I have to tell you that you have no right to interfere in my family in any way? And this kitchen is a dangerous place for him to be in.'

'Nonsense, he was perfectly safe. I would not let him go anywhere near the oven. He was just having fun. Why can you never allow him to do that?'

'With you, a harlot? Never. Leave my child alone. I'm well aware that you've even lured my husband into your bed.'

Brenda blinked with shock. 'I did no such thing. He is the one pursuing me, as I made clear before.'

'Now you're after my son too.'

Brenda paused to take a breath. 'I think it's time we sat down and talked.'

*

Refusing to be seated, or accept the cup of coffee offered her, Melissa stood tapping her fingers on firmly folded arms, her expression rigid with disdain. Brenda faced the woman with a feeling of tightness in her belly and a tremor in her heart. The moment seemed to have come to challenge Melissa on this matter, if only to defend her son. But she couldn't quite resolve the dilemma of how much more she dare mention. It was probably best not to say a word about what she'd discovered until she'd found the necessary proof.

'You should be ashamed of the way you treat this little lad. You keep on smacking him and shutting him up in his room just because he loves playing and is keen to learn new things. You're far too overbearing and controlling, a real bully. Doesn't it ever occur to you that this could be very upsetting and damaging for him? He could lose all faith in himself as well as the ability to make friends and form decent relationships. With this sort of treatment he too is likely to grow up to be a bully. Isn't that exactly what happened to you and Hugh, although thankfully not to dear Jack and Prue?'

'Don't talk nonsense, and mind your own damn business.'

'Actually, I think this is my business. I made an interesting discovery one night when I took a little supper up to him.' Brenda felt emotions churn within her as these words popped unbidden out of her mouth. What had she done? Hadn't she vowed to say nothing?

'What right had you to do that?'

'Because you'd left him hungry for much of the day. It was then that I saw a small cuddly monkey tucked up beside him, his best friend, which apparently you keep tossing away.'

Melissa's cheeks flushed crimson as she glowered at Brenda. 'That monkey is a scrubby mess and should indeed be thrown away. What has that to do with you?'

Should she tell the truth, or keep silent? Confusion clouded Brenda's head as she struggled to decide. 'He loves it, so why would any loving mother do that? Maybe because you aren't his mother.' All those memories of caring for children in the OSE now flared up in her mind, and the resounding courage that had grown within her through those difficult years blazed afresh. Or else her heart had taken over her brain.

Melissa's face turned ash pale as silence fell between them. 'What the hell are you suggesting?' she finally murmured in cold, stern tones.

Whatever the reason, Brenda felt all too aware that she'd dropped herself into this mess. So why not go the whole way, even if she was shaking inside? 'That you stole my son. You may claim the boy to be yours, but he's not.'

'He most definitely is,' Melissa snarled.

Panic was making her heart pound as Brenda struggled to find the right words to prove her case. 'I recognised the monkey instantly. I bought it to celebrate his birth, days before he was born.'

'What nonsense you talk. It's just a toy.'

'Quite a rare one, so I don't believe it to be a coincidence. I think it's most definitely the one I bought.'

Melissa gave a caustic little laugh. 'You have no proof of that. Having wheedled your way into our home and business, you're now attempting to steal *my* son? You're a vicious little thief.'

Brenda watched in horror as Melissa marched into the hall and snatched up the phone. The moment it was answered she quickly announced who she was before bursting into a flood of crocodile tears. 'Oh, PC Matthews, please come quickly. There is a woman here at Trowbridge Hall who is attempting to steal my child.'

*

PC Matthews stood before them in the drawing room with pencil and notebook in hand, a grim expression upon his face. 'Name, please,' he said, licking the pencil as he glared at Brenda.

Giving a deep sigh, Brenda told him, quietly adding, 'I'm Jack's widow, and perfectly innocent of this charge.'

'What's going on here?' Hugh asked, walking in upon them.

Before Brenda had the chance to give her side of the story, Melissa flung herself into her brother's arms. 'This tart of a woman is trying to steal Ross.'

He blinked in surprise as he looked over at Brenda. 'What is she talking about? That surely cannot be true.'

'Of course it isn't,' she answered, feeling a wave of relief as Hugh came to put his arms about her. 'I would do no such thing.'

'Quite,' he said, glaring at his sister. 'Why would she?'

PC Matthews gave a cough. 'I am the one asking questions, sir, if you don't mind. 'Miss Stuart, have you abducted Mrs Fenton's child?'

Finding her courage in the comfort of Hugh's arms, she firmly responded, '*Mrs* Stuart. No, of course I haven't. But he isn't *her* child, he's *mine*.'

'Good lord, what are you saying?'

Meeting his sympathetic gaze, Brenda felt her panic start to subside. 'How she got her hands on him I've no idea, but I know in my bones that he is most definitely my son, and…'

'How can you know that?'

'Because he has a toy which…'

Melissa instantly interrupted, 'Don't believe a word this madam is saying,' she cried, crocodile tears starting to roll down her cheeks. 'This harlot is lying yet again, determined to get her greedy hands on the family inheritance by any means possible. She is a most dreadful woman and should be arrested. That is the reason I called you, PC Matthews, in case she runs off with my child.'

The police constable cleared his throat. 'Are you saying that the boy is safe?'

'He is upstairs with his nanny, yes.'

Tucking his pencil and notebook back into his top pocket, he gave a little sigh. 'Then I cannot charge this young lady with abduction, or anything, in fact. Should there be a dispute over custody, the court is the only means of resolving the matter. I can do nothing. Good day to you,' and with a polite bow he turned to leave.

'I'll see you out,' Hugh politely said, opening the door to lead him through the hall.

The moment they left, Melissa glared at Brenda, twisting her mouth into a cynical grimace. 'Be assured you'll never get your hands on him while I live and breathe. He's *mine*!'

Thirty

In the days following, the atmosphere in Trowbridge Hall became quite chilling. Hugh had gone away for a few days, claiming he had an important meeting to attend, or was he simply avoiding Brenda? He hadn't said another word on the matter, promising they'd talk when he returned. It felt as if it had become a taboo subject. Nor did Brenda see any sign of Melissa, the children or Nanny Holborn. Finding herself ignored by the entire family, she went to speak to Prue. Seeing the doubt in her friend's eyes as she explained about the monkey, filled her with fear and trembling. Brenda began to wonder if she'd made a terrible mistake.

'Flora has a teddy, of which there are any number the same,' Prue gently pointed out. 'There could well be dozens of those monkeys too.'

'I haven't seen any, not here in England. And in my heart I know that Ross is my son.'

Prue stifled a sad sigh as she put her arms around Brenda's quivering shoulders to give her a comforting hug. 'I can fully understand your anguish, and how you might imagine such a thing to be possible. I hardly dare to think how I would react were I to lose little Flora, but I'm afraid that toy is more likely to be a coincidence.'

'I am aware that without proof I'll get nowhere,' Brenda admitted. She'd latched on to this toy as a possible solution without logic or proper thought, let alone the evidence she really needed. Was she failing to see things sensibly, due to all the traumas she'd suffered? Brenda felt the need suddenly to withdraw from life, to hide herself away and nurse the pain plummeting within her.

'If I can help in any way, just let me know,' Prue promised as Brenda made hasty excuses and left. As she hurried away she experienced emotions that frightened and overwhelmed her. Was she going mad? Would these feelings of fear, anger, guilt and grief ever go away? How she longed for a quiet, happy life of peace, one over which she had some control.

Over the next few days she found herself withdrawing more and more from the family, occasionally eating in the kitchen with Mrs Harding and Carter, otherwise in the peace and quiet of her room. Then one evening, when she returned after a long day's work, it was to find her old brown suitcase packed and set at the foot of her bed, with a note attached. 'LEAVE NOW', it stated in bold print.

Is that what she should do? Clearly she was no longer welcome here, not even by Hugh, who perhaps held the same doubts as Prue. She was beginning to feel that they could be right and she had made a terrible mistake. She could go and stay with Cathie in Castlefield, or find another flat to rent. Then she could seek advice from the family solicitor about PC Matthews' suggestion to take the matter to court. Although, even if she did find proof, she held little hope of ever winning her son back, particularly when she remembered all that Emma had told her about such cases.

Brenda's eyes flooded with tears as she contemplated spending the rest of her life without him. Too dreadful to imagine. The vision of him cuddled in her arms with Minki the monkey filled her with pain yet again. She really must strive to stay strong and never give up. Wasn't that what Emma constantly urged her to do? But it may be wise for her to leave Trowbridge Hall to avoid further dispute, which could completely destroy what little was left of her courage. Brenda went downstairs to ask Mr Carter if he would drive her to the station. Giving a slight frown, the butler looked out of the kitchen window at the rain filling the darkening sky.

'I doubt that would be sensible at this time of an evening.'

'And you haven't eaten any supper yet, chuck,' Mrs Harding reminded her, scurrying over while exchanging a worried glance with Carter. 'We know you have some problem with the family, which is nowt to do wi' us, but tha needs to sit down and eat summat, to keep thee strength up. Carter can take you to the station in the morning, if tha still wants to leave.' And taking Brenda's coat and suitcase from her, eased her into a chair at the kitchen table and placed a plate of roast beef and Yorkshire pudding before her. 'Now eat up every scrap. Oh, and a letter arrived for thee today.'

Her heart skipped a beat as she stared at the envelope

Mrs Harding placed before her. Could this be the answer she was seeking?

*

Brenda lay curled up in bed that night reading the letter from Nancy Seymour, the young nanny. She was amazed to discover that following the telegram the family had received announcing Camille's death, Adèle had written to Melissa to inform her that she was now in charge of Jack's son. Why had it been addressed to Melissa? Brenda wondered. Then she remembered Prue saying she would have no wish to even read such dreadful news. It was true that people lived in fear of telegrams, and would sometimes take days to pluck up the courage to open them. Or else Melissa had deliberately kept it from the rest of the family because it held information about baby Tommy. She may have been the only person who responded to the telegram, and gave Adèle her London address. Opening the letter again, Brenda continued to read what Nancy had to say:

'*That lovely lady, Adèle, brought the baby to London, believing that as Camille was now dead, it would be safer for him to be in England with his family. We met her at Victoria Station. She put him into my arms and I fell in love with the little one at first sight. She told us that you, his poor mother, had been interned in some camp or other but she'd no idea where, or if you would survive. I'm so pleased to hear that you did. She was on her way to join her late husband's family in America in order to stay safe herself, having been helped to escape France by the US Consulate. The thing is, Mr Fenton was annoyed with his wife for producing three daughters and no son. And as he'd been abroad for some time, she took it into her head to pass the boy off as her own. I believe she saw this child as the answer to all the problems in her marriage. I don't think she told anyone about Adèle's letter or the arrival of this baby.'*

'So I was right,' Brenda muttered to herself. And despite being desperate for a son, it was the nanny who'd instantly taken him into her arms, not Melissa. So she viewed him only as a means of saving her failing marriage. How cruel and selfish of her. Wiping the tears from her eyes, Brenda punched up the pillows to prop herself against them with new determination, and carried on reading:

'I pointed out to Mrs Fenton that the child's mother could well survive and come looking for him. She kept saying you were probably already dead, and even if you did survive would never find him as France was in such turmoil. And what a lovely surprise it would be for her husband to find he at last had the son he so badly wanted. We argued furiously over her decision. I insisted it was perfectly legal for her to foster the boy but surely entirely illegal to claim him as her own. As a result, I was instantly dismissed. That was disappointing in a way, as he was a lovely baby and

*I adored him. Yet it was a great relief that I would
not be charged for being involved in such a crime. I
do hope he is well and happy. I'm afraid I don't have
Adèle's address. Oh, and please don't use my name
or reveal what I've just told you. She's a nasty piece
of work and would be sure to come looking for me
and create fresh havoc. No doubt get me sacked from
my current job too.'*

Brenda quietly wept as she read the letter over and over
again. What a selfish brute of a woman Melissa was. What
on earth possessed her to imagine she had the right to steal
a child when there was no proof that she, his mother, was
dead?

What to do next was the question. Clearly this young
nanny was very fearful of her former employer, which
Brenda could well understand. She felt obliged to keep her
name secret, as the poor girl had poignantly requested. Nor
was she any nearer to finding Adèle. Sadly, this meant that
gathering the necessary evidence the court would demand,
remained a problem. Brenda still had no proof other than
that little monkey. Should she challenge Melissa again
on the subject, or just keep quiet for now and deal with it
later in court?

*

Brenda was standing in the hall the next morning waiting for Carter to bring the car round when Hugh arrived.
Tossing his trilby hat aside, he came quickly over to give

her a hug and a peck on each cheek. 'Ah, there you are, darling. How are you?' Noticing the suitcase by her feet, he frowned in puzzlement. 'Goodness, where are you off to?'

'Back to Manchester,' Brenda coolly responded, anguish in her heart. 'I can't stay where I'm not wanted.'

There was a slight pause before he answered, a sad bleakness in his eyes as he met her troubled gaze. 'You are wanted, my love. Not only by me but also at the factory. You're a hard worker and a real entrepreneur.'

Could she believe him? Brenda felt a strong desire to fall into his arms and ask if that was the only reason he needed her, but managed to hold herself firmly in check. It was vital for her to remain clearheaded and not be ruled by emotion. 'All those ladies are now fully trained, so I'm sure they can manage perfectly well without me.'

'I very much doubt it. You are our star representative when it comes to gaining sales, as well as brilliant at organising the staff's work routine. Has this decision anything to do with that incident with Gregory?'

She frowned. 'If you mean his attempt to kiss me, I made sure to avoid him after that.'

'Yet according to Melissa, you invited him to your room,' he quietly remarked.

Brenda gasped. 'How dare she suggest such a thing? You surely don't believe her?'

He appeared to relax as he smiled at her. 'Not really. She does tend to dramatise things to suit herself. So what did happen?'

Brenda briefly described how he'd slipped in but she'd

managed to see him off with a poker. 'The next day I got Joe to fix a bolt on the door.'

'Well done. That makes much more sense. Then why leave?'

Just then Melissa emerged out of the dining room, arms folded in her usual arrogant stance. 'Why should she not? It's such a relief to hear that she's going at last.'

Carefully choosing her words to avoid revealing the young nanny's name, Brenda met the other woman's triumphant gaze with an outward show of calmness she was far from feeling within. 'Was it to please your husband that you stole my son, because you'd only given him daughters? Is that the reason you decided to claim him as your own?'

Melissa flinched as if she'd been slapped in the face, then turning to Hugh said, 'This harlot is absolutely insane. Get her out of here.'

'Don't keep calling her by that dreadful name. In any case, Brenda is making an interesting point. I've been making a few enquiries myself these last few days, with the solicitor and at the Public Record Office, but found no evidence of Ross's birth. Now why is that? Tell us the truth, Melissa. Are Brenda's suspicions about Gregory's demands correct, or not? He certainly is a dictatorial sort of man.'

In the taut silence that followed Brenda felt a warm glow of gratitude that Hugh was not only still supporting her, but had done some research on her behalf.

'I've told you a thousand times that she is a liar and a cheat, a tart of the worst order. You know damn well that Ross is *my* son! Hasn't he lived with us all his life?'

'Or else he was brought to England when he was just a baby,' Brenda said. 'Was that with Adèle or the OSE?' How she wished she could confront her with the true facts she'd learned, but felt a responsibility to keep that young nanny safe.

Arrogantly ignoring her, Melissa continued to address her brother in fury. 'I haven't the first idea what she is talking about. Ross does not belong to this greedy little whore who is simply eager to get her hands on anything she can, in order to drag herself out of the gutter.'

Hugh flapped his hands in an attempt to calm his sister down. 'I appreciate you have problems, Melissa, but do try to cool that temper of yours. Constantly losing it achieves nothing, something I've learned these last few months, thanks to Brenda. And I really have no wish for her to leave,' he said, slipping his arm around Brenda's waist. 'Like it or not, Melissa, she is a part of our family and playing a vital role in the growth of the business. Besides which, there is absolutely no proof that she's a liar and a cheat. Nor did she invite your husband into her bed. He made that decision and she beat him off, being the brave woman she is.'

'Drat you! What an idiot you are to believe every damn thing she says,' Melissa roared, and strode off upstairs still steaming with temper.

Shaking his head in despair, Hugh gently led Brenda into the dining room. 'What caused you to ask that question about Gregory? Was it because of what he did to you or something more that you know?'

She gazed up at him, her eyes filled with tears as she quivered with emotion. 'I suspect he could be behind Melissa's decision to take the baby. I do have some evidence but am not free to share it.'

'What sort of evidence?'

'I'm afraid I'm not at liberty to say. But I do intend to take this matter to court, should I be fortunate enough to find further proof.'

'I'm sorry I dashed off without properly explaining where I was going. But I was anxious to do what I could to help prove your case.'

'I'm so grateful for that. But if you found none, who do you believe?'

'I believe you, darling, but am worrying over how the matter can be resolved. It won't be easy. This toy monkey is not very convincing on its own. But please don't go. We need you. *I* need you, my love. You have become an important part of my life.'

Brenda's heart pulsated with joy. Wrapping his arms about her, he was moving close enough to kiss her when suddenly a child's scream rang out. Jerking apart, they rushed out into the hall to see Melissa come tearing downstairs with the monkey in her hand, and the little boy chasing after her.

'I want him! I want him! He's my *friend*!' he yelled.

'Oh, my goodness, don't tell me she's again robbed the child of his favourite toy.' Brenda stepped out to snatch the toy from her. 'Don't you dare throw his little "friend" away. You have no right to destroy it. It belongs to Ross, not you.'

'This child is *mine*, and as his mother I can do what I damn well please. Mind your own bloody business,' Melissa snapped.

Hugh wagged a finger at her. 'Don't use such dreadful language. Didn't I advise you to remain calm?'

'Oh shut up!' she barked, and turning to Brenda, slapped her across the face. 'Give that bit of rubbish back to me this minute!'

'Never!' Aware of the little boy standing on the stairs, his small face a picture of anguish as he wept, Brenda lifted the cuddly toy higher to avoid Melissa's grasping hands. It was then that her fingers suddenly felt something crackle and, pulling it down again, she examined the monkey more closely. Brenda noticed a line of tiny, neat stitches across its back, and beneath this was a small bump over the monkey's bottom. Going to the drawer in the hall table, she pulled out a small pair of scissors generally used to open parcels, and began to snip at the stitches.

'What the hell are you doing?' Melissa screamed, and the little boy again began to cry.

'Don't fret, Ross. He's quite safe. I won't hurt him.'

Hugh watched in wide-eyed astonishment as Brenda opened up what appeared to be a pocket in the back of the stuffed monkey and from it drew out a small brown envelope.

Her heart burst with joy as she pulled from it two sheets of paper, which, when she opened them up, turned out to be her marriage certificate and her son's birth certificate. Below these in the envelope she found her wedding ring.

Hugh met her thrilled gaze with love and admiration in his eyes, before pulling her close in his arms to give her a soft kiss of compassion.

'So the proof was here all the time? How amazing!' he said. 'You definitely *are* Jack's widow, and Ross *is* your son.'

It was then they heard the front door slam and, looking around, realised that Melissa had gone, carrying the child in her arms.

Brenda and Hugh stood frozen in shock for a moment. Then seeing the three little girls come rushing down the stairs to chase after their mother, they both leapt into action, if sadly far too late. By the time they'd run down the front steps, Melissa was already roaring away in her Humber car at great speed, the little boy sitting in the back and her weeping daughters standing in the drive in horrified dismay.

'Oh no, where is she going?' Brenda felt utterly distraught. Just when she'd at last found the evidence she needed to prove Ross was her son, he'd vanished yet again.

Thirty-One

Hugh held her close, attempting to console her. 'Don't worry, darling, we'll marshal everyone to help look for them right away.'

Carter, Mrs Harding and old Joe quickly gathered in the hall, anxious to take instructions on what could be done. Nanny Holborn rushed to gather the girls in her arms, sharing a glance with Brenda filled with sympathy and curiosity as she led them back upstairs.

'I'll tell you all about what happened later,' Brenda told her. 'Do take good care of these little ones, Nanny, and assure them we'll find their mother.'

And hopefully her son too.

Prue and Dino also arrived, having been alerted by Carter. 'We're happy to help with the search too. We can use the farm van,' Dino said as Prue handed baby Flora into the care of Nanny Holborn.

'I need to ring Gregory first,' Hugh said and went off to do that, returning moments later to tell them he'd explained to the man that his wife and son had gone missing. 'I also said there was a problem regarding his son, which couldn't be discussed on the phone. Astonishingly, he said he was too busy to come north immediately, but would get here as soon as he could.'

'What a selfish man he is,' Prue stated. 'Doesn't he give a jot about them?'

'I'd drop everything and give my life to save my wife and child,' Dino said, grim-faced.

'So would I, were I to be fortunate enough to have a family,' Hugh agreed, glancing across at Brenda. She felt her heart melt as their gaze locked. He then went on to instruct them about which direction each of them should take. 'Are we ready? Then off we go. I'm sure Melissa can't have gone far. She'll be parked up, sulking some place. I suggest you stay here, Brenda, in case they return.'

Watching them all dash off either on wheels or on foot, Brenda really had no wish to stay put. He was her son, and felt she really must help find him. Hadn't she been searching for years? She could still barely allow herself to recall the anguish she'd suffered. And here in her hands was at last the evidence she'd been seeking for so long: her certificates and wedding ring. Wouldn't Jack expect her to remain strong and do her best to find little Tommy? Running to her room to lock these precious items in the desk, Brenda dashed back down again, collected her bicycle and set off up the drive.

*

'Too fast! Too fast!' cried the little boy as he slid about on the back seat. 'Where are you taking me, Mama? Are we going home to London?'

His words reverberated in her head as Melissa slowed the car down a little, realising she had no idea where she was going. She'd been so desperate to escape that slut of a girl who was threatening to entirely destroy her life, she perhaps hadn't thought things through properly. Thank goodness Gregory had chosen to go back to London by train, leaving the car with her. But having left her darling daughters behind, she couldn't possibly go home without them.

Even worse, the last thing she needed was to be charged with the abduction of that chit's son. She could well find herself sent to jail as a result, even though she'd done what seemed to be a good idea at the time.

Adèle had revealed that having been arrested and interned in some concentration camp, Jack's wife may well not survive, as so many other parents had not. Nor did the woman have any notion of where she was being held, or for how long. So why, as Jack's sister, should she not have taken the child, particularly bearing in mind her marriage problems? The chance to get her hands on a baby boy had felt far too good an opportunity for Melissa to miss.

How could she begin to explain to anyone how controlling her husband was, demanding she produce a son, despite spending months far from her side either in some foreign country, or no doubt in his latest mistress's bed. Melissa had believed that this boy could save their marriage by bringing them close again. Sadly, that didn't happen. Not only did Gregory fail to build any meaningful relationship with the child, but had left her bed for good.

'I no longer need to trouble you,' he'd coolly informed her, moving into his dressing room. 'You've done your duty at last and provided me with a son and heir. Now we can happily live separate lives.'

This reaction had been the last thing Melissa had expected or hoped for; a total disaster. It appeared she'd achieved nothing by acquiring this boy. It had also made acting as his mother exceedingly difficult. As he wasn't her child why would she love or care a toss about him? But nothing on earth would persuade Melissa to admit to what she'd done and risk being imprisoned. Far too terrifying a prospect! And certainly not for the benefit of that greedy little harlot, even if she really was Jack's widow. The prospect of Gregory learning the truth about this child was equally alarming. He would be sure to walk out on her, and how could she possibly survive financially without him?

'Mama, I want to wee!' Ross cried.

'Oh for goodness' sake, don't you dare wet your trousers, or ruin the seat of my car. I'll stop in a minute.'

Finding they were in a narrow lane surrounded by trees, Melissa wondered which part of the woodland they were in. She'd paid little attention to where they were heading as she'd driven away in total panic and fury. Now, looking around it came to her exactly. Wasn't this the lane that led to the shack where she and Hugh used to play when they were small? If so, she could hide the boy in there while she went back to collect the girls. That seemed like a good idea. She couldn't take the risk of that madam getting her hands on him and turning her life into even more of a nightmare. No doubt everyone would be out looking for her, so she'd shut him up safe, then quickly nip back to the Hall to fetch her daughters, and Nanny Holborn, of course. She really couldn't manage without that lady. After that, she would escape back to London and make sure Gregory learned nothing of this accusation. And if it ever did come to court, she'd fight that chit tooth and nail.

'Mama, I'm peeing in my pants!' he screamed.

'Oh, you stupid boy,' said Melissa, and quickly drew the car to a halt.

*

Autumn was upon them, rust-brown leaves coating the path as Brenda cycled along at a fast pace. The branch of an ash tree arched above her, almost knocking her off the bike. As she approached the woodlands she asked herself where she should begin her search.

How could she have been so stupid as to lose her son again when it had taken all these years to find him? Not that it was her fault, and Melissa's reaction reminded her of the experiences she and Emma had faced when dealing with rescuers of Jewish children while working for OSE. She remembered each and every one of the children they'd managed to help escape during the war, including dear Kurt and Walter, and the anguish when all efforts had failed. Some foster parents were honest and caring, while others were definitely not to be trusted, as they'd learned to their cost. Even though the war was now over, there were still issues when attempting to repatriate these lost children to their true parents, as Emma had explained. Nor did the reason always concern love. Sometimes it was simply prejudice against religion, or else abuse of the poor child, and some of them were treated like slaves.

Did Melissa love him after all, despite her temper, which was probably directed more at Brenda than the little boy? She very much doubted it. Melissa had other, more pressing reasons for keeping him, so would she hide him away as some foster parents did, for whatever reason? If so, then where might that be? Hopefully not too far away, or anywhere too dangerous.

It was then that Brenda recalled once seeing a shack, although she couldn't quite remember where. She set off to search, as it would surely be the ideal place to hide a child. Hadn't Jewish children been hidden in cowsheds, cellars, attics and other odd places.

Abandoning her bicycle, she made her way into the woodlands, following the cairns she and Jack had placed there years ago. She reached a dry stone wall that split this part of the woodland in two, one path leading up over a hill, the other to the right into the lower depths of the woods. Brenda struggled to decide which direction to take, as she'd done when lost that time Kit had led her home. Today, she did not have the collie to help her, but still opted to walk deeper into the woodlands. A young oak stood sentinel before her, tall and sturdy, bringing back a memory of Jack leaning against it with her in his arms. What a happy life they could have had together were it not for the war.

Spotting another cairn, Brenda placed a stone upon it, out of habit and in memory of him, then made her way through a clump of hart's-tongue ferns, their shiny green fronds brushing against her legs as she hurried along. Eventually she emerged on to a path. It grew ever wider, finally leading to a wide-open expanse of grass with more lanes leading off it in different directions. These were no doubt used by the foresters' horse and carts when they were doing the coppicing. And in the centre stood a small timber building.

'Ah, there it is,' she muttered to herself in relief.

Glancing about at ash trees and sycamores rustling in the breeze, it came to her that she must take note of which path she'd come down, otherwise she could get lost yet again. Hadn't Jack warned her not to come too far into the woods on her own, which seemed to be what she'd done, if for good reason. And this was surely the most likely place for that arrogant woman to hide the child. Keeping to the edge of the trees, Brenda made her way slowly round towards the shack.

Reaching the door, she found it was locked, and called out. 'Ross, are you in there?' She could hardly breathe, the tension in her so strong. Was he safe? Ferns and cow parsley were growing all around the shack and she began to push her way through them, searching for a window or another entrance, when she heard the sound of an engine behind her.

Glancing back over her shoulder, Brenda thought it might be Dino or old Joe driving the new tractor, and they'd be able to help her break in. To her horror, she saw it was Melissa's car heading towards her at great speed, the roar of the engine increasing by the second, and the contemptuous image of her face sneering through the windscreen was utterly chilling. Spinning on her heels in shock Brenda ran back towards the woods for cover, only to find herself moments later flying through the air.

Thirty-Two

Brenda woke to find herself lying in bed, a throb of pain pulsating through her left hip and leg. Blinking in the dim light from the lamp on her bedside table, she tried to recall what had happened, and why she was there. Had she fallen while helping Prue with the hens or digging the garden? Or did she have a crash on her bicycle? She couldn't remember, her mind a complete blank.

'Ah, thank the lord, you're awake at last,' said a soft voice at her elbow, and she turned to gaze up into Hugh's beloved grey eyes. 'How are you? Where are you hurting most, darling?'

It came to her in that moment. The terrifying image of a car driving towards her flashed into her mind, as all the traumas she'd suffered through the war years would do, often erupting into a nightmare. She'd find herself crying, or screaming at some invisible person in her head to get off her, which would at least wake her up. This time the image of the car approached in slow motion, not at its true speed, which made it all the more terrifying. Brenda could see Melissa smiling in triumph as she peered at her through the windscreen, looking very much as if she'd deliberately set out to kill her. An icy chill swamped Brenda when she recalled how she'd been desperately trying to rescue Ross from the shack. Then she'd had to run for her life, only to find herself hit by the wing of the car. She well remembered the sound of that bang before darkness descended.

'Have I broken my leg, or worse, my spine?' she asked Hugh, beginning to shake a little with shock.

He stroked her hair and gently kissed her cheek, the sad expression on his face quite heartrending. 'Thankfully, I think it was just a glancing blow, but the doctor's on his way. We won't know the full extent of your injuries until then. Stay calm and don't move, my darling. I'm sure you'll be fine.'

She didn't feel in the least bit fine. The pain was increasing by the second, as if a fire had been lit within her, flaring through her hips and limbs. Gritting her teeth together, Brenda strived to do as he said and make no attempt to move, much as she longed to check that she still could feel her feet. She felt wracked with pain, just as she had that time when the bridge had been bombed and she'd been close enough to be smothered in rubble. She'd been knocked unconscious then too, but fortunately had lived to tell the tale with no serious injuries, as hopefully she would now. 'Where was I, and how did you find me?'

'Fortunately, we all heard the sound of the crash and reached the spot within minutes of each other. You were unconscious and, as the rain began to fall, we managed to carefully lift you into the Daimler.'

'Where is Ross? Was he in the shack? Is he well?'

The doctor walked in before he had time to answer, and leaping to his feet Hugh went to stand with him by the window while he explained what had happened. They spoke so quietly that Brenda couldn't hear a word they said. Then as the doctor came over to inspect her, Hugh quietly left. She watched him go with anguish in her heart, as he still hadn't answered her question. Did that mean they hadn't found the child? Prue slipped in to sit beside her and hold her hand while the doctor began his examination.

'Did you find Ross?' Brenda asked Prue, then winced with pain as the doctor probed her legs and hips, rolling her gently over to examine her spine. When she was again lying straight he put a thermometer in her mouth, perhaps to silence her.

'Nothing looks deformed or too swollen,' he assured her. 'And there's no sign of any broken or splintered bones. Just strained muscles.' He lifted and bent her legs to make sure they were working properly.

'We found him safe and well,' Prue whispered, gently squeezing her hand. 'And he's very worried about you.'

Tears sprang to Brenda's eyes, more with relief than from the increasing pain the doctor's examination was inflicting upon her. Finally he stepped back to check the thermometer, and giving it a little shake, he smiled at her. 'I think you have avoided any serious injury, although suffered massive bruising. You've been most fortunate.'

'Thank you.'

'You need to stay put and rest for a day or two. I'm going to give you something to ease the pain and help you sleep.'

Brenda took the pill he gave her, washing it down with the glass of water Prue poured. Then handing the packet over to her friend, the doctor proceeded to give careful instructions on how many and how often these pills should be taken.

'I'll pop back tomorrow to see how you are doing, my dear,' he said, and with a gentle smile departed.

*

Dawn light was filtering through the bedroom window when Brenda woke again, having enjoyed a sleep without a single flicker of a nightmare. This time she found the small toy monkey lying by her side on the pillow. Smiling, she pulled it into her arms just as the door quietly opened.

'Is Minki giving you a cuddle?' Ross whispered.

'He's such a kind fellow, as are you, to share him with me.'

Climbing on to the bed to sit beside her, he stroked the cuddly toy. 'Aunty Prue said you weren't well, Bren, so I thought you might need a friend to keep you company.'

Brenda felt her heart pumping with happiness. Just seeing him safe and well filled her with joy and relief, as well as hearing the lovely way he spoke to her. 'Are you all right?'

He nodded, widening his small mouth into a wry smile. 'Mama was in one of her moods and forgot to pick Minki up. I didn't want to go home to London without him, so I told her I wanted to wee. She stopped the car and I jumped out and ran off back to the Hall to get him.' Putting his hand over his mouth, he gave a little giggle.

Normally Brenda would have felt guilty for taking the toy off him, but as it had produced the necessary evidence she'd long felt in need of, she simply returned his smile. 'And you found Minki safe and well, as are you, thank goodness.' Turning the monkey over, she examined the empty pocket in its back. Brenda remembered carefully stowing away the certificates and ring in her room, so they were perfectly safe. But as a result of her probing this cuddly toy, it was in need of some attention. 'I'll stitch his back up and give him a little bath. Do you think he would like that?'

Happily nodding, Ross continued with his tale. 'Mama wasn't best pleased and shouted at me to come back this minute. I just ran all the faster. She didn't come after me. Mama doesn't do running.'

Letting out a big yawn, he slid his arm about her waist, put his thumb in his mouth and snuggled under the blankets beside her. Putting her arm around him too, Brenda drew the boy close to stroke his hair, loving the sweet scent of him as she had done when he was a baby. Within moments his breathing had changed and he was fast asleep. How she had longed for this moment for five long years, but knew in her heart that it was only temporary. She would have to accept that Tommy, or Ross as he was now called, might never be hers.

*

Brenda was confined to her bed for several days, the doctor visiting a couple more times. As she slowly recovered, she was allowed to sit in the easy chair by the window, and he gave her a few exercises to do to help ease the pain. Gradually the pain in her limbs eased and she felt able to move them about more freely. Ross continued to call in to see her each and every day. He would often bring a book, which she'd happily read to him, his favourite being *Tootle*. This was the story of a baby train who was told to stay on the rails but kept escaping to play in the meadows. He eventually learned that this was entirely the wrong thing to do and settled down to help and teach others. Very much as she had done in life. The little boy loved it, almost learning the words off by heart, as he kept asking her to read it to him over and over again. Oh, it felt so wonderful to spend time with him.

There was no sign of Melissa.

'I assume she's avoiding me,' she said to Hugh on one of his regular visits. 'That wouldn't surprise me, as she wasn't driving at speed for no purpose. I believe she deliberately aimed the car at me. I could see it in her eyes. She wanted to be rid of me any way she could.'

His expression clouded with sadness. 'I realise she did set out to hurt you, darling, and I do wish we'd found some way to stop her. I feel so guilty that we went off in the wrong direction.'

'It wasn't your fault. You did your best to calm her down but she'd completely lost it. I'm afraid Melissa's temper seems completely out of control. Her rage is beyond redemption. So what happened to her?'

He sat in silence for some moments stroking her hand

before meeting her enquiring gaze. 'We haven't told Ross this yet, but when my sister drove the car towards you at great speed, she didn't manage to break in time and crashed into the shack.'

Brenda stared at him in shock, a mix of emotions ricocheting through her. Melissa was his sister, so if something terrible had happened to her he would be devastated. But finding the necessary words to express sympathy wasn't easy. 'Are you saying that she was killed?'

'Thankfully not, but she is in hospital, quite badly injured. Broken ribs and neck injuries. A total mess.'

Putting her arms about him, Brenda gave him a comforting hug. 'I'm so sorry. Oh, what a stupid woman she is. She behaved so badly. If only she'd been honest with me from the start.'

'I do so agree. I did on more than one occasion attempt to dampen her temper and persuade her to accept that you were telling the truth, but got absolutely nowhere. I asked her to be more friendly with you, but I'm afraid she was swamped in a self-obsessed neurosis.'

'And perhaps the demands made upon her by her husband. I realise you did everything you could to help, and I accept that Melissa will not give Ross up easily, if at all. I may have to learn to live without my son.' Her throat constricted at the thought.

'I do hope not. Marry me, darling,' he said, kissing her softly. 'Should the worst happen, remember that you're young enough to have more children, and I really don't want to lose you. I love you so much.'

'Oh, I love you too, Hugh.' Her heart burst with happiness and, wrapping her arms about his neck, Brenda gladly responded to his kisses with increasing passion.

'Is that a yes?' he asked with a smile as they finally broke apart.

'It is indeed.'

*

A week later a letter was delivered by the post boy on his bicycle. It was from Emma. Brenda read it in amazement.

'Dear Brenda,

Thanks to the OSE I have at last found Adèle Rouanet. She is so thrilled to hear that you are alive and well. And now that the war is over, most anxious to see you and little Tommy again. She hopes he settled in all right with his Aunt Melissa. From what she has said to me it seems your suspicions are absolutely correct. We're both on our way to see you. Will be arriving just as soon as we can get the necessary transport, me from France and Adèle from America. We intend to meet up in London, then head north by train. See you soon.

All my love, Emma.'

Brenda could hardly believe what she was reading. Here at last was confirmation that her accusation against Melissa had been entirely correct. But would this be enough for her sister-in-law to return the boy to her, his true mother? Why would she agree to do that when her husband so badly wanted a son of his own, rather like an heir to the throne? Melissa's motivation for stealing the baby had been entirely wrong, although Brenda couldn't help feeling a nudge of sympathy for her, considering that brute of a husband's demands upon her, not to mention his infidelity and their failing marriage.

Yet she'd shown little love for the boy.

Brenda thought of the friendship that had developed between herself and Ross, which felt wonderful. Did this letter mean she could go to court and claim custody? And would it work if she did? He looked upon her as Bren, a friend, not a mother. Why would he wish to give up his family of wealthy parents, and those three lovely girls he thought of as his sisters? Wiping the tears from her eyes, a mixture of anxiety, hope and pain echoed within her, as it had done so many times in the past. Brenda read the letter one more time and sent up a silent prayer that she would somehow find the courage to cope with whatever life threw at her.

A week later Gregory arrived.

Thirty-Three

Hugh chose not to tell Gregory anything at this stage, other than the fact his wife had suffered from a dreadful accident. He drove him straight to the hospital.

'What on earth were you thinking of to drive so fast?' he asked, as he stood by her bed. 'You've smashed our car to bits, you stupid woman. It's a complete write-off.'

Melissa, sitting up in bed clad in a classy bed jacket with a pad around her neck and dark shadows beneath her eyes, cast her brother an anxious glance, appealing for his support. Hugh gave a little shake of the head and quickly left, realising the conversation between them could be difficult, judging by the expression of anger upon Gregory's face; not to mention his lack of compassion at the sight of his wife.

Drawing a breath into her pain-wracked lungs, Melissa gave him a pitying little smile. 'Aren't you going to ask me how I am, or are you more interested in your precious motor car than me, your wife? I'm in a dreadful state.'

Gregory began to pace about the room in barely constrained fury. 'The doctor has already told me about your injuries. I accept that you must be in something of a mess, but he says you're on the mend and will be home soon. I just can't believe you would be so stupid as to drive into that shack. *Why didn't you watch where you were going and slow down*?'

Refusing to meet the savage fury in his glaring dark eyes, Melissa did not respond. Had she succeeded in ridding herself of that chit of a girl, then she might have found a way around this problem, but the little madam apparently survived with fewer injuries than she herself was suffering from. Melissa felt as if she was caught in a trap. Whatever explanation she gave for rushing off in the car with the boy could lead to accusations of criminal intent. The police too had visited to ask her similar questions. Melissa had let her eyes close and remained silent, pretending she was slipping back into unconsciousness. The nurses had kindly shooed them away. Gregory, however, would be less considerate.

'I really don't remember,' she murmured, putting her hand over her eyes as she sank back into the pillow. 'I never meant to smash the car. It was an accident.'

'Hugh tells me you were engaged in a family row and drove off in a huff.'

'Sorry, it's gone completely out of my brain as I feel so ill.' Terror now ricocheted through her. Would Hugh tell him the whole story? Could she urge her brother to keep quiet and say nothing? She feared he would not listen, being totally captivated by that girl. 'Do *not* believe a word he says!' Melissa again pretended to slip back into sleep, and with a snort of revulsion, her husband swiftly departed.

*

It was later that afternoon when they arrived back at Trowbridge Hall that Gregory demanded Hugh tell him exactly what the row had been about and the reason Melissa had stormed off in the car. 'Why would she drive off in such a bad state of mind it resulted in an accident? What the hell was this row all about? Money?'

'I think you'd better sit down. It isn't going to be easy to explain.'

Taking him into the drawing room and pouring them each a glass of whisky, Hugh sat opposite, his mind in complete turmoil over how and where to begin. Should he challenge Gregory about how he'd harassed Brenda, and whether he really did slip into her bedroom uninvited? But they'd had this argument before, so better to come straight to the point about what had happened to cause this crash. 'The fact of the matter is, Gregory, we have discovered that Ross is not your son. Nor is he Melissa's.'

Gregory stared at him in stunned disbelief. 'What did you say?'

Hugh took a welcome sip of the whisky then told the entire story, finishing with how Brenda had discovered a pocket in the back of the toy monkey. 'It contained her marriage certificate, wedding ring and…'

'That doesn't prove a damn thing,' Gregory interrupted with a snort. 'She could have put those in herself.'

Hugh stifled a sigh. 'She also found her son Tommy's birth certificate, which proved that this was the stuffed toy monkey she'd bought for him just days before he was born.'

Gregory was silent for some moments. 'It still doesn't

prove this Tommy and Ross are one and the same child. She could have made that up too, or forged that damn certificate.'

'Do you have one for him?'

His brother-in-law's face went blank. 'I've no idea, as I was living abroad at the time dealing with more important foreign issues,' he snapped.

'Quite. Perhaps you should have checked. I have made enquiries and failed to find one.'

'I don't believe a word of this.'

'I do appreciate that it must be difficult, even quite heartrending to hear that you no longer have a son. The fact is, we do have further proof. A letter came from Brenda's friend Emma, with whom she was incarcerated in France. The pair of them were arrested simply for being British. Emma is still working with OSE to repatriate children to their parents and has managed to find Camille's cousin, Adèle Rouanet. That good lady brought the baby over to London when Mama died, handing the child over to his Aunt Melissa, in order to keep him safe. It would seem that your demand for your wife to provide you with a son gave her the idea to steal him, and pretend that he was hers.'

Now the silence went on for much longer, Hugh feeling quite unable to find the right words to explain what happened next. How could he say that his sister had set out to kill dear Brenda?

'So having been accused of this, Melissa then drove off with Ross in an effort to save him? I can fully understand that.'

Hugh nodded. 'Sadly, when she found Brenda searching for the boy in the woods, she drove directly at her, perhaps because she'd lost control of the car out of fury. Brenda was hit by the wing and sent flying. She is entitled to bring charges against Melissa, but has promised not to, thanks to the fact she was not too badly injured. She's a very brave lady. And as you know, Melissa was not so lucky, since she crashed the car into the shack.'

Gregory glowered, then jumping to his feet, stormed out.

*

Melissa arrived home a few days later. Mrs Harding helped her upstairs and settled her into bed where she could recover in peace and comfort. 'There you are, Mrs Fenton. Would you like a cup of tea?' the housekeeper asked, drawing the curtains a little to keep out the bright sunshine so she could rest.

'Oh thank you, that would be wonderful,' Melissa said. 'And a slice of cake, too, would be lovely. The food in the hospital was quite awful.'

'You can bring it when I say you can,' Gregory barked, hustling Mrs Harding out the door.

'Goodness, having suffered this dreadful accident, surely I'm entitled to some love and care,' Melissa sulkily grumbled.

'Stop pretending it was an accident. You deliberately drove at that woman you claim to be a whore. Hugh has told me the entire story. Did it never cross your stupid mind that the lie you've been living all these years, and the fact this boy is no relation to either of us, could have a lot to do with why we never got on? I can now understand the reason why I have never felt particularly close to the child. He's not mine. You stole him.'

Melissa stared at her husband in anguish. 'Hugh told you that? It's not true, just another lie from that chit of a girl.'

'Really! Is that the reason you deliberately attempted to run her down, even though she had proof that Adèle handed the boy over to you at Victoria Station when he was just a baby?'

Now her face turned white with shock. 'How would they know that?'

Giving a sneer of disgust, he told her briefly about the letter from Emma.

'I did it for you,' she cried. 'I believed that if I finally managed to provide you with a son, our marriage could be saved.'

'Highly unlikely. And since we hadn't slept together for some time, I did wonder if he was the result of an affair you'd had while I was away.'

'You are the one who has affairs. Probably because you never really loved me in the first place, just wanted to get your filthy hands on my money,' she roared.

He laughed. 'That could well be the case, although you did look quite attractive and elegant in those days. But there's unlikely to be any inheritance, so I see no reason for me to go on pretending I feel any love for you, when I clearly don't. Besides, I do in fact have a son, with my mistress Caroline. So I definitely no longer need this one, or you,' he sternly informed her. 'I shall now return to London and move in permanently with her.'

Letting out a scream of fury, Melissa flung the pillow at him, then leaped from the bed to hammer her clenched fists against his chest. 'You cannot do this to me! Don't you *dare* leave! You are my husband.'

'Not for much longer,' he said, pushing her away. 'I intend to arrange for a divorce. Stop your grumbling and be grateful for the fact that this alleged whore has agreed not to bring charges against you. At least you will escape prison.' And ignoring her further cries of fury, he strode to the door to find Hugh, Brenda and Prue standing out on the landing, looking extremely anxious. 'You can have him,' he said to Brenda. 'That child is no longer of any interest to me. Nor is your sister, Hugh. You can keep her too.'

Then he strode off down the stairs, calling for Carter to take him to the station. And without even asking to see his daughters, he left.

*

'Now what?' Brenda asked that night over supper, horrified by what had happened. 'Does this mean I can now claim my son, or will Melissa hang on to him like grim death, having lost her husband? What do you think?' she asked Prue and Hugh. They both looked at her, their faces a picture of sympathy as they glanced at each other then shook their heads in bewilderment.

'We'll speak to her and work something out,' Hugh said, squeezing her hand in comfort.

'I don't think you should speak of this to young Ross,' Dino said. 'Not yet, anyway. It could upset the little one greatly to discover that the man he believes to be his father has just tossed him aside and abandoned him.'

'Oh, you're quite right,' Brenda agreed. 'That would be so painful for him. I remember feeling much the same when I first learned that's what my mother had done. Abandoning me in the orphanage.'

Prue nodded, a sad smile on her face. 'What happens next is too difficult to imagine. Let's wait and see what Melissa decides to do.'

'I very much doubt she'll relinquish him,' Brenda quietly remarked. 'I expect he is still lost to me.'

'Don't give up hope,' Hugh said, giving her a warm hug. 'Prue and I will speak to her tomorrow.'

When they went to see her early the next morning, Brenda hovered in the background, not wishing to become involved in this family discussion, although deeply anxious to hear Melissa's reaction.

'Don't say a word about any of this to my darling daughters,' she snapped.

'Of course not,' Hugh agreed. 'That's something you'll have to deal with in your own time.'

'Maybe I will, maybe I won't! I still have the right to do exactly what I think best, and once I'm fit enough we will return to London. Even though, thanks to that madam, my marriage is over.'

'The reason for that disaster lies with you and your

husband, not with Brenda,' Hugh firmly reminded her. 'So what about Ross?'

Melissa curled her mouth in distaste. 'He's a little brat who never does a thing I tell him. Not at all like my lovely daughters. I never was interested in having a son except to please my husband, which clearly didn't work. That harlot is welcome to him,' she said.

Brenda gave a little gasp, hardly able to believe what she'd just heard.

Prue looked equally surprised. 'Are you sure? Have you thought this through properly, Melissa? You won't be able to change your mind once you leave. And eventually, at some appropriate moment, Ross will need to be told the truth, as will the girls.'

'Not right away,' she snapped. 'Let me deal with this dratted divorce first.'

Brenda stepped forward. 'I will never say that you stole him. I'll explain that you were acting as his foster mother, looking after him until I returned home, as has happened with thousands of other children. That will be much easier for him to cope with.'

Melissa met her gentle stare with a glint of relief in her eyes, perhaps because she still lived in fear of prison. When she left later that day, taking her daughters with her back to London, she did not even say goodbye to the little boy.

Thirty-Four

Seeing the car draw up, Brenda ran pell-mell out the door to gather Adèle in her arms. 'Oh, it's so wonderful to see you!' she cried, with tears in her eyes. The dear lady looked a little older and rounder than in those earlier days in Paris, now dressed in a smart suit in her favourite green colour, with a fox-fur stole about her neck and a neat little hat upon her bobbed hair. 'I've been searching for you so long.'

'Me too. I've spent years looking for you, dear. Thank God you survived. And how is little Tommy, or Ross, as I believe he is now called, bless him?'

'He's fine, but hasn't yet been told the full story of who he really is.'

Her dark eyes behind gold-rimmed spectacles glimmered with sympathy. 'I can well understand that. But I'm sure he will accept everything, given time, and once he's learned more about his brave father.'

Emma appeared at her side, her lovely face alight with happiness at the sight of her dear friend, and there were more hugs and tears. 'What a joy it is to see you both again,' Brenda cried. 'Mrs Harding is providing us with tea and cakes, and you can meet Hugh. Then I'll introduce you to Prue and the rest of the family.'

'Will that include his Aunt Melissa?' Emma whispered, as the three of them walked arm in arm into the house.

'Thankfully, she has left,' Brenda said with a gentle shake of her head, and began to tell her story. 'Ah, here is Hugh.'

He was waiting in the drawing room and warmly welcomed them, helping Mrs Harding serve the delicious sandwiches, cakes and biscuits she'd prepared. They happily chatted for hours. Emma and Brenda recalled some of the fun times they'd spent at the camp, taking part in shows and poetry reading sessions, firmly blocking out all the troubling incidents and the resulting anguish. Emma went on to speak of the years she'd spent helping the children in the OSE, revealing that she'd met a delightful young Frenchman who worked as a teacher.

'We soon became quite attached, and have recently married,' she told them with a smile.

'Oh, how wonderful!' Brenda cried with joy in her heart. 'I'm so glad to hear that. You deserve to find happiness, Emma, after all you've done for other people, especially those precious children.'

'I shall be giving birth to one of my own soon,' Emma said, patting her stomach, and congratulating her in delight Brenda gave her another hug.

Adèle then began to speak of Camille, and how brave she'd been as her health had slowly deteriorated. 'She never stopped thinking of you, darling girl, or trying to find you. She wrote to everyone, asking where you were.'

'Sadly, without success,' Brenda said.

'I'm afraid so, which was the reason she came up with the idea for me to bring Tommy home once she had passed on. She also carefully stitched the proof of your marriage and his birth into the toy monkey, knowing she never did get around to telling Sir Randolph about it, and wanting to be sure that he knew. She was a smart and canny lady, and wonderfully kind and thoughtful. My best friend.'

Hugh smiled. 'She was a wonderful mother too. Thank you for being there for her. I'm sure she welcomed your companionship and care in those last months of her life.'

'It was my privilege to help. She will live forever in my heart.'

'Mine too,' Brenda agreed, and there was a pause as the three of them brought Camille into their minds once more, and raised their tea cups in her memory.

'I have some news about Jack too,' Adèle said.

'What sort of news?' Brenda asked.

'He is to be honoured with the French Resistance Medal for bravery.'

Her face lit up. 'Really?'

Hugh beamed. 'That's wonderful, and well deserved.'

'It is indeed,' Adèle agreed. 'It is given in order to recognise remarkable acts of courage that have helped to maintain the strength of the French against their enemy.'

'Do tell us what he did?' Emma said. 'I'd love to hear more about him.'

'So would I,' Hugh said.

'I don't know everything he did, as much of it was

kept secret, but Jack was very much involved in acts of sabotage,' Brenda explained. 'He was keen to make things as difficult as possible for the enemy. The Resistance would divert freight trains to the wrong location, cause derailments by damaging the switches, and cut telephone lines so that German communications were halted.'

Adèle nodded. 'Which no doubt put the enemy in greater danger if they received no warning of bombing raids about to be carried out by the Royal Air Force. Later, the Resistance worked closely with the British, passing on messages they'd intercepted. And they'd attack, kidnap or even kill German officers whenever they could.'

'Jack was also involved in blowing up bridges and derailing trains, which is what he was doing when he was killed,' Brenda softly told them. 'He was a brave man, and I'm so proud of him.'

'As am I,' Hugh said, his grey eyes glinting through a cloud of tears as he smiled at her.

'The last thing Camille, your dear mother did before she departed this world, was to write to various military officers and Members of Parliament telling them what her son had done for France, being half French himself. And how she felt his courage deserved to be honoured,' Adèle explained. 'I forwarded those letters as soon as the war was over. And fortunately, they agreed. The ceremony is to take place on Saturday, which is another reason why I came.'

'Oh, my goodness, that's amazing!' Brenda said, grasping Hugh's hand in joy. 'I can hardly believe it. What an honour that will be.'

*

Brenda found Ross cycling around the farmyard as he so loved to do, roaring to himself as if he was flying a plane.

'Would you like an ice cream?' she called, and with a beaming smile he braked, propped the bike against a tree and came running over. Following the departure of Melissa and the girls, he'd asked only once where they were. Brenda had told him that they'd returned home to London but he'd been allowed to stay on here to continue to enjoy a little holiday. Looking into his eyes when she'd said that, Brenda knew he suspected there was more she wasn't telling.

They sat together in the summer house enjoying a dish of ice cream, Brenda turning over possible solutions in her head. Having talked things through with Hugh, and not wanting the little boy to feel lost and abandoned, they'd decided the time had come for the two of them to talk. Hugh had promised to join them later, but deciding how much to say still felt like a problem not easy to resolve. 'Ross, how would you feel about going to the school in Trowbridge village?'

'I go to school in London,' he said, blinking up at her with a puzzled expression on his face.

He was a bright little boy who attended a private kindergarten close to his home in the city. But if that had to be changed, wouldn't he wish to know why? 'I know, love, but I wondered if you would mind going to the one in the village while you're staying here.'

There was a slight pause while he thought about this for a moment. 'How long will I be here, d'you reckon?'

Brenda drew in a quiet breath as she smiled at him. 'It could be quite a while. Is that a problem for you?'

He gave her a big grin as he shook his head. 'Nope. Like it here. Like the hens. Like the garden, and my bike. Can I make new friends at this school?'

'You can indeed. Would you like that too?'

He briskly nodded.

'Actually, there's something I think you should know.' Taking a quick swallow, Brenda clasped her hands on her lap to stay calm, hoping that might help to stop her heart beating too fast. 'Melissa is actually your aunt, not your mother. She's acted as a sort of foster mother to you, if you can understand that, and was perhaps a little wary of telling you the truth.' Brenda had no wish to tell him the truth either, not in its entirety.

He was staring at her now in open-eyed amazement. 'Why would she not do that?' he asked.

'During the war your real mother was stuck in France, arrested just for being British.'

'Like your friend Emma?'

'Yes. So no one knew whether she would survive and come home again, which thankfully she has done.'

He was looking at her now with wonder in his gaze. 'Does that mean you are my mum, Bren?'

Astounded by this, she almost jerked. 'Yes, I am.'

Her heart pounded more slowly now as he stared at her. Would this be the moment he'd start crying for Melissa or his dear sisters? Would he fall into one of his tantrums and stamp off? Seconds flicked by that felt like long moments, if not hours. Then reaching up to wrap his arms about her neck, he tucked his head against her shoulder. 'I'm so glad. Love you.'

'Oh, darling, I love you too,' and putting her arms about him, Brenda gave him a cuddle.

'Have I got a new Dad too?' he asked, and she gently told Ross about brave Jack. He sat cuddled beside her with his thumb in his mouth, listening carefully to every word she said. Hugh had come to join them by this time, and he added to the story by talking about his brother when he was a young boy, as lively as Ross.

'He loved the hens and didn't care for the circus either, wanting all the animals to be free to roam. I remember him once asking the circus ticket man for his money back because he hated to see them so confined, and when he was refused, Jack gave him a real telling off.'

Ross began to giggle and asked for more stories, which Hugh gladly shared: how Jack loved to play cricket and swim in the river, make bonfires and keep rabbits. 'We were sorry to see him leave when he went to look after our mother in France.'

'Which was where we got married and happily lived,' Brenda said. 'Then when the war started, he joined the French Resistance Movement.'

'Gosh, was he a hero?' Ross asked, his brown eyes bright with admiration.

'He was indeed. Now he's about to receive an award for

his bravery, so we're all off to the ceremony on Saturday in London. And as he is no longer with us and you are his son, it will be presented to you.'

The little boy beamed with pride.

*

The ceremony, which took place at the French Embassy, was attended by the entire family: Hugh and Brenda, Prue and Dino. And, of course, Adèle and Emma, neither of whom would have missed it for the world. Emma was accompanied by her handsome French husband, with whom she was clearly very close. Melissa and Gregory were, thankfully, not present, being locked in their personal war of divorce and finance. When Jack Stuart's name was called, Ross proudly stepped forward to collect his father's medal.

'What a brave little boy he is,' Hugh whispered to Brenda as they watched him chat to the French Ambassador.

'He definitely takes after his father,' she said with a smile. 'Who will live forever in our hearts.'

'He will indeed, as will Ross, who is very much a part of our family now. And you too, my darling. You are the love of my life,' he said, giving her a kiss.

That night, at the hotel where they were staying, Brenda tucked Ross up in bed, together with Minki the monkey, then happily settled into Hugh's arms on the sofa in the lounge as they began to plan their wedding and future together.

HQ
One Place. Many Stories

The home of bold, innovative
and empowering publishing.

Follow us online

 @HQStories

 @HQStories

f HQStories

 HQ Stories

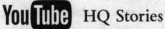 HQMusic2016

40 years of marriage
8 golden charms
One man's journey of discovery

On the anniversary of his wife's death, 69 year-old
Arthur Pepper finally musters the courage to
go through her possessions, and happens upon
a charm bracelet that he has never seen before.

What follows is a surprising adventure that takes
Arthur from London to Paris and India in an epic
quest to find out the truth about his wife's secret
life before they met, a journey that leads him
to find healing, self-discovery, and love in
the most unexpected of places.

One Place. Many Stories

M445_TCCOAP_Rev